The Melody of the Mulberries

Endorsements

"An unreservedly recommended work for school libraries"
– James Cox Midwest Reviews, 2020

"Exceptionally well-written and entertaining work of historical romance." – Northwest Book Review, 2020

"Amazing and creative writer! Another Masterpiece! Well done. I am blown away by the author's gift to create such a story…"

–Diane Andrews,
Pastor & Founder/Director R&R Retreats

"Tonya Blessing has captured the industrial times of the Appalachian culture and has brought to light that all races have a 'Charlie' as well as a 'Charley' in their midst. Racial tensions concerning color of skin were very eloquently presented and fulfilled the mission of drawing together instead of tearing apart. I enjoyed editing this book and look forward to seeing more books from Tonya Jewel Blessing. Indeed, this book is a *blessing*. The Melody of the Mulberries is a story of redemption, forgiveness, and love…for family, friends, and enemies. The characters are alive and vibrant, characters that will cause readers to look inside and see where their hearts are in the whole scheme of life."

–Beatrice Bruno, Editor, Author – Speaker,
US Army Veteran, Pearl of Great Price

"I loved *The Melody of the Mulberries*. Characters developed quickly. I remember some of the folk lore sayings at the beginning of each chapter, which I heard as a child. I easily picked up the continuing story from the prior, *Whispering of the Willows*. I don't want someone to purchase the book and feel like she can't read it before reading book one in the Big Creek series.

The whimsical illustrations along with the beautiful stories that interrelated all the characters had me mesmerized and I did not want to put this book down! As a matter of fact, I read it in two days.

"Tonya Jewel Blessing's Appalachian people and countryside made me feel I was there with them. Her examples of racism were believable and reminded me of how different parts of the country deal with bigotry. The moral lessons in the story were real and made me think about my own relationships. The sibling relationships between Emerald, Ernst. and Coral as adults were realistic, refreshing, and made me feel happy for them. They showed love and support of each other during difficult times and remind us of how important talking directly is when facing differing opinions. This book demonstrated that God created everyone with the capacity to love and forgive each other. I highly recommend reading this wonderful story."

– Polly Dougherty, B.S. Business Management, Ministry Leader in Divorce
Recovery and Grief Counseling, Teacher and Facilitator for Women's Groups

"What a joy and pleasure to read a novel that not only faces darkness and evil head-on but also gives a clear picture of what it looks like to forgive and find peace in the presence of Jesus. Tonya Blessing tells a compelling story using delightful colloquialisms from 1920s Appalachia, drawing the reader into the life of the characters who struggle as we all do to know God's will. Reading this story made me wish I lived in this world where time moves slowly and easily, and people are genuinely pleased to see one another. The Melody of the Mulberries delivers on so many levels and is a must-read for anyone grappling with this frenzied, sometimes unforgiving world."

– Charmayne Hafen, Author of The Land of Twilight
and Indebted; The Berkshire Dragon

My heart is so amazed! Tonya Blessing is an excellent and imaginative writer! Intriguing. Historical. Fun. Heartwarming. Encouraging. Healing. Hopeful. Inspiring. God-Honoring. I so love the way Appalachian folklore entwines with the hymns throughout the entire book--such a beautiful job! The Melody of the Mulberries plays off the first book... a great continuance. I love the way the traditions, beliefs, smells, tastes, sounds, and life of Appalachia kept hooking my interest--not predictable at all!

–Nicole Fitzpatrick, Educator, Pastor,
    Missionary in Mexico.

Reviews

Traveling back in time to life in the 1920's Appalachian Mountains, the author brings folklore, facts, and biblical teachings to life instructing us in such a way that we can sit right down at the dinner table with these characters. A very enjoyable read!

– Stacie, Colorado

"I enjoyed peeking into 1920's life amidst Appalachian family dynamics mixed in with longstanding traditions, superstitions, and faith. Like its prequel, The Whispering of the Willows, this book grabbed my attention from chapter one until the final page. The author has a way of engaging the reader and bringing her characters to life; I felt as if I really knew them. I will be reading this book again!"

–Tracy, Ohio

"Tonya does a fantastic job of weaving together history and culture in Appalachia during the 1920's. An entertaining and educational story."

–Kathy, Ohio

The Melody of the Mulberries

Tonya Jewel Blessing

Library of Congress Control Number:2019910154
Publisher's Cataloging-In-Publication Data
(Prepared by The Donohue Group, Inc.)

Names: Blessing, Tonya Jewel, author. | Sequel to (work): Blessing, Tonya Jewel.
    Whispering of the willows.
Title: The melody of the mulberries / Tonya Jewel Blessing.
Description: Littleton, Colorado: Capture Books, [2019] | Series: Big Creek series ; book
    2 | Includes bibliographical references.
Identifiers: ISBN 9781732753686 (hardcover) | ISBN 9781951084004 (paperback) |
    ISBN 9781951084011 (ebook)
Subjects: LCSH: Man-woman relationships--Appalachian Region--History--20th
    century--Fiction. | Interracial dating--Appalachian Region--History--20th century--
    Fiction. | Siblings--Appalachian Region--History--20th century--Fiction. |
    Spiritualism--Appalachian Region--History--20th century--Fiction. | LCGFT:
    Historical fiction. | Romance fiction. | FICTION / Christian / Romance / Historical. |
    FICTION / Romance / Multicultural & Interracial. | FICTION / Cultural Heritage.
Classification: LCC PS3602.L47 M45 2019 (print) | LCC PS3602.L47 (ebook) DDC
    813/.6--dc23

The Melody of the Mulberries
By Tonya Jewel Blessing
Capture Books
5658 S. Lowell Blvd. Suite 32-202
Littleton Colorado 80123
Cover Design: Sonia Freitas Sonia@CloebelleArts.com
ISBN-13: 9781732753686 hard cover
ISBN-13: 9781951084004 paperback
ISBN-13: 978-1951084134 (bulk)
ISBN-13: 9781951084011 eBook

To my handsome husband,
an adventuresome world changer and
legend maker.

Preface

The Melody of the Mulberries is Book Two in the Big Creek Series. Both books are set during the late 1920s in the wild and wonderful state of West Virginia. The Appalachian Mountains were untamed in the 1920s and remain so in part today. The wonder of the hills is breathtaking, magnificent, and glorious.

In 1937, my mother, Virginia Ashby, was born in the rural hills of West Virginia. She spent several of her formative years in an area known as Big Creek. I have borrowed my mother's maiden name, several names from her past, and the name Big Creek.

The term "wild wonderful West Virginia" was used as early as 1969 before being adapted in the 1970s as the state slogan.

The morning mist hanging in the lowlands, the dew on the ground, along with the green of spring and the deep red, sparkling gold, and brilliant oranges of fall draw me visually, emotionally, and on some level spiritually to its feral fascination. John Denver recorded in his tribute to West Virginia, "Take me home country roads to the place I belong…" Certainly, there are seasons in my life where I long for the steep, curvy country roads of my youth. This is one deeply satisfying reason for writing about hope with connections to West Virginia, a life held close to my heart.

It is both a pleasure and an honor to share this southern story with you. It is an authentically derived historical romance for young adults and for women of all ages who love Appalachian lore and West Virginia history. It contains some depictions of spiritualism and traditional Christianity during the 1920s in West Virginia. It continues with the inter-racial dealings between two communities, where, some are friends, and some are foes.

Chapter One

If you tell a bad dream before breakfast it will come true.

Appalachian Folk Belief

Charlie and Charley were coming to Big Creek. Charlie was a man. He had a spirit, soul, and body. He grew up in the hills and was sent away because of the harm he did to others.

Coral had invited Charlie back to the holler. He wouldn't be physically present, but, according to Emie, Coral might as well have sat him down at the table to enjoy Sunday dinner with the family.

The other Charley was an evil spirit. He was ancient and from a faraway land but returned to Big Creek when invited. His ways were frightening and mysterious. He was best left alone, but he had also been invited to Appalachia by Mercy, a returning resident of the holler who considered him a friend.

"Rudy, you best get leavin'," Emie declared. "Time's a wastin'."

"Emie, darlin', I've plenty of time." Rudy sighed. *When his bride got this way there was no reasoning,* he thought. "I am timin' my trip up the mountain, so I arrive when Ernest and Charlotte have their learners enjoyin' lunch."

"It won't hurt none to be early. This is urgent. Coral's headin' to

Charleston to meet with that lying, abusing murderer, Charlie. I know he's in prison, but it's like he's living here again. I'm hopin' Ernest can talk sense into our little sister."

Rudy hesitated to say anything. He knew whatever he said would be wrong; yet he found himself unwisely plunging forward. "Your sister ain't so little anymore, darlin'. She's sixteen and wantin' to find her own way."

"Sixteen ain't that old Red, and you've done takin' her side. I knew it!"

"Emie, I ain't takin' anyone's side. I'm headin' up the mountain to talk to Ernest, ain't I? Fighting with Coral ain't helping no one. Remember, Emie, we was married and had a baby when you was fifteen."

"Coral's done reminded me several times," Emie sighed. "I'm just so scared. Something could happen. Charlie's got deceptive ways."

"I talked with Grandpappy. He's got some church business in Charleston, and he's willin' to travel with Coral."

"Rudy, I love your pappy, but he's got them soft manners sometimes. He'll be loving on Charlie instead of telling him about hell."

"Darlin', love is telling someone about hell. Pappy's a pastor; he knows what the Good Book says about hell, and he ain't never been one to mince words."

"You're twisting what I'm sayin'. I know you know what I'm meanin' to say…"

"Truly, Emie, you got me so confused right now, I don't know what you're meanin'," the young husband interrupted. "Your heart's ruling all of you, and you ain't making sense.

Emie sighed loudly.

"I don't want Coral seein' Charlie any more than you do," Rudy thoughtfully continued. "He hurt you and hurt you bad. He even kidnapped our baby. It's my job as your husband and Jewel's daddy to be watching out for you both. But I also know, though Coral's soft-spoken, she's got backbone. If she feels like God is directin' her, she ain't gonna give in. You've talked. I've talked. Aunt Ada and Uncle

Christian have tried convincing her to forget about Charlie and ain't none of it worked. If Ernest can't help, then we best let her go with Grandpappy aidin' her along the way."

"Red, I ain't ready to resign myself." Emie rose from the wooden rocker in the sitting room and went to the kitchen.

A vase of white daffodils with yellow centers sat on the small table in the corner. Several diminutive vine baskets filled with dried herbs and roots were clustered together on the narrow counter, and a jar of sugared honey sat open next to the wood stove. The honey, along with sweet cream butter, had topped the flapjacks Emie had served for breakfast.

"I know, darlin'," Rudy spoke as he took the few steps from the sitting room into the kitchen. His bride was facing the water pump. Her quivering shoulders told him that she was crying. He gently turned her around. Emie's head fit perfectly on Rudy's shoulder next to his heart. He held her for a few minutes and let the tears roll down her cheeks. He knew his embrace brought more comfort than his words.

He started having thoughts of other ways to comfort his wife and began nuzzling Emie's neck. She sighed sweetly and leaned into her husband.

"Rudy, I can hear Jewel stirrin' from her nap."

"I don't hear nothin', darlin', but your heart beatin' next to mine."

Jewel was sleeping on a blanket in the sitting room. Emie stood on her tiptoes and peeked around her husband's shoulder. "She's wrestlin' with her covers." Emie quickly kissed Rudy on the lips and playfully tickled him until he released his embrace. He couldn't help but smile.

Rudy turned to see the four-year-old sit up and rub her eyes. She wasn't a baby or even a toddler anymore. Jewel was getting too old for naps, but Rudy had exhausted the child earlier with a game of chase in the yard. The sunshine, wind, and playtime had brought great pleasure to him and his daughter. He also knew that their time in the sun had given Emie time alone so she could contemplate what to say and do about the dilemma with Coral.

The Appalachian Mountains were named after a Native American village. Indian ancestry ran deep in the hills. Rudy, even with his red hair, fair skin, and freckles, had Cherokee blood. While many Appalachians felt disgraced to be part Cherokee, Rudy was proud of his ancestry. Walking the mountains made him feel like a warrior-provider who at all costs protected those he loved from seen and unseen dangers. He imagined himself a man who hunted the hills for precious meat that fed his family throughout the year.

His father and mother ran a small store in Big Creek, but he had always preferred being outdoors. On occasion, Rudy worked in the store; but, in truth, he felt more alive in the sunshine than in candlelight. Only when Emie was by his side did he enjoy being indoors. The rustling trees, chirping birds, and occasional grunt of a buck showing dominance all brought a smile to his face and a wave of pleasure to his soul.

He knelt to look at the fresh footprints of a mama bear and her two cubs. Female bears often woke from their deep slumber in January or February to give birth, and then fell back asleep with a baby or babies by their side until early spring. Some of the holler boys liked to play poke the bear. Rudy thought it plain foolishness to sneak up on a big ol' bear sleeping the winter away, poke the fury beast, and run. God created bears, even hibernating bears, with an innate sense of danger.

He would have to remember to tell Ernest and Charlotte about the bear tracks. It was best to give a mama bear and her babies a wide berth. *There ain't no tellin' what a female will do to protect her young ones,* Rudy thought. He reflected on Emie's courage and strength in tracking Charlie when he had kidnapped Jewel.

It grieved him to think of Coral visiting Charlie in prison. Pride, selfishness, and indulgence had taken Charlie down a troubled path. Everything and everyone he touched was tainted and tortured by his evil acts. Rudy was thankful for God's healing hand in the lives of those he loved, especially those Charlie had hurt.

As he neared the schoolhouse, he wondered how Charlotte was faring. Emie's eldest brother, Lester, had shared a brief time with his bride, Charlotte, before Charlie murdered him. Charlotte was Lester's widow now. And since she lived near Ernest, the two seemed to be sharing more than just their mutual interest in teaching. This year, the colored children who lived in the hills were thriving due to all the activities the remote schoolhouse provided them. In fact, Ernest and Charlotte were treated like local heroes. They received little in the way of monetary benefits, but the students' parents gave them meat, vegetables, homemade goods, and the fellowship of soul and spirit.

Rudy's parents purchased dyed fabrics, rag rugs, knotted quilts, woven baskets, carvings, and other wares from the remote community in the hills. The wares of the talented craftsmen and women were popular with store customers.

The school was located just outside the wooded area where Rudy was walking. As he pulled back the canopy of leafing and budding trees, he could see the children sitting outside enjoying their lunches. The sun was warm, and the breeze carried the laughter of the learners to Rudy's ears and heart. When he spotted Charlotte and Ernest, he waved. Ernest waved back, yelled his greeting, and bounded toward Rudy. The two men shook hands and briefly embraced, each patting the other's back.

"Have you asked her to marry you yet?" Rudy said with a smile.

"It might be a tad easier if she'd quit callin' me 'brother,'" Ernest replied.

The two had shared this same conversation about Charlotte several times over the past few months.

"I ain't quite clear, but when did the lovebug bite?" Rudy asked, breaking into a broad grin.

"Don't seem right to call love a 'bug bite,' but I'm bitten, and she don't have a clue." Ernest shook his head in confusion. "Lottie went for a walk round about Christmas time. She was visitin' a learner and didn't tell me. When dark came and I couldn't find her. I was beside myself with worry. I started thinkin' about what life would be like without her, and I knew I wanted her to be mine."

"You need to make a move, Brother."

"Not yet. I'm bidin' my time."

"Time's a passin', Ernest. Every moment you wait is a moment she ain't in your arms."

"Don't I know it. She just don't seem to care for me that way. We work with the children durin' the day and often share meals in the evenin', but..."

"But nothin', Ernest. You ain't never gonna know unless you tell her what you're thinkin'; and if you ain't ready to tell, start showin'."

Rudy nodded toward a wild lilac bush. "Pick her some flowers." When Ernest hesitated, Rudy, with a glint in his eye, spoke the challenge, "I dare you."

Ernest gathered the buds and blossoms, and the two men headed toward the school.

Charlotte readily embraced Rudy and smiled warmly at Ernest. When Ernest presented the lavender lilacs, she blushed slightly and softly spoke, "Thank you, Brother."

Rudy couldn't help but notice Ernest's look of frustration. While he felt pity for Emie's brother, he also wanted to laugh. *The ways of love are certainly mysterious,* he thought.

"Rudy, what brings you our way?" Charlotte asked.

"Well," Rudy hesitated.

"Is somethin' wrong with Emie or Jewel?" Ernest quickly questioned.

"No. It's Coral." While Rudy could see the look of concern on both Charlotte and Ernest's faces, he didn't quite know where to start. "God's directin' her to do somethin' odd. Somethin' strange."

"The good Lord's asked a number of folks to do strange things. The Bible's full of such stories," Ernest responded.

"Not like this."

Charlotte took Ernest's hand in her hand. Rudy couldn't help but notice how fragile and small Charlotte's hand looked in comparison to Ernest's large broad hand. *They complement one another,* Rudy thought.

"Brother, let me take the learners inside for schoolin'. You go ahead and talk with Rudy."

When Ernest nodded in response, the lovely young woman rang the school bell which was firmly bolted to one of the porch posts. Rudy knew that the bell rang at the beginning of each school day and after lunch to summon the learners from their time of play. He also knew the bell rang to alert the community of danger. He hoped Coral's idea was like the bell ringing for a time of learning and not a warning that danger was present.

The children could sense that something was amiss and looked to their teachers for assurance. Charlotte smiled. With her loving pats, she guided the learners into the schoolhouse. Ernest told the children to be on their best behavior. He also gently squeezed the shoulders of two older boys. Rudy assumed it was Ernest's way of telling them to mind their manners.

When the students had all entered the schoolhouse, Ernest directed Rudy to a log in the yard, and the two men sat down.

"Rudy, tell me straight out the goin's on."

"Coral wants to visit Charlie in jail."

"What!"

"She's convinced it's God's doin'. She says the Lord spoke to her to go and can't be persuaded otherwise."

It took Ernest a moment to process Rudy words. "What? Has Coral gone crazy? What is she thinkin'?" Ernest pounded his fist on the felled tree.

"We've all tried, Ernest - Emie, Auntie, Uncle, me. We've all told her that it ain't nothin' but craziness. She won't listen. She's quiet but got them stubborn ways. Seems she's made up her mind. Emie sent me to ask for help. She's thinkin' Coral will listen to her brother."

"Rudy, I'm done bewildered. I thought we was rid of Charlie. Now, my sister is wantin' to invite him back into our lives. It don't make sense."

The two men sat in silence for a moment.

"I know this won't bring comfort now, but if Coral can't be moved, Grandpappy's agreed to go with her."

"I need to do some prayin', and I need to talk with Lottie." Ernest declared. "She's still hurtin' over Lester's passin'. I'll try and head down the hill first thing tomorrow mornin'."

"It's hard sometimes to get past the worryin' to start the prayin'. Pappy says that worry should drive us to pray, not away from it. I'm hopin' you find peace in your prayers."

"Me too, Rudy. Can you stay a spell?"

"I'm appreciatin' your hospitality but you got things to ponder on, and Emie will be chompin' at the bit."

The two men turned to small talk. Their chit chat about weather, family, and mutual friends was overshadowed by concern.

When Rudy stood to leave, he remembered the paw prints along the path up the mountain. "By the way, I saw some bear tracks on the trail–a mama and two babies. Best tell the learners to be careful–you and Charlotte, too."

Coral sat in contemplation under a mulberry tree. It was spring, and the fragrant female blossoms promised the mid-summer arrival of first white, then pink, then crimson, and finally deep purple berries. The white berries were hard and tart and enjoyed by the quail, wild turkeys, mockingbirds, and blue jays. The blackish purple berries were soft and sweet–perfect for pies and jams.

When the berries turned white, Coral would thank the good Lord for providing food for the birds. When the berries ripened, she would thank the good Lord for the sweetness savored in her mouth and curse the birds for wanting more than their share.

All of Coral's sisters were named for gems. In her younger years, it bothered her to be different from her six sisters. These days, she enjoyed her uniqueness. She had learned in her McGuffey reader all about the ocean coral that varied in color, just like the mulberries: white, pink, crimson, and deep purple.

Coral knew she was changing. The Good Book said that it was right to no longer think like a child. But at what age did one cease being a child and think like an adult? She wasn't sure.

Coral's contemplation caused her mind to race and her heart to rush. Though her thoughts and feelings were random, they were also connected. She first considered the mulberry leaves that were shaped like hearts. Next, she thought of the last line of Elizabeth Barrett Browning's poem, My Heart and I.

I think, we've fared, my heart and I.

Then, she thought about Joshua who received divine instruction that if he loved the Lord with his whole heart, then he would walk in obedience to God.

The pastor at Big Creek Church recently talked about obedience. During the sermon, Coral felt like Pastor Rex was talking directly to her. The elderly pastor said that obedience meant to "hear under." At first, the words confused Coral. By the end of the message, she understood that obedience was to hear the words of God and to obey those words under the authority and power of God. True obedience wasn't legalism or conformity but faithfulness in hearing and following the Lord's instruction.

The mulberry tree that shaded her from the afternoon sun sang a melody of obedience. It grew, blossomed, and bore fruit in submission to God. All flora and fauna flourished in Big Creek through obedience to the Maker of All Things.

Chapter Two

If you hear a dog howling in the middle of the night, it is a sign of death in the community.

Appalachian Folk Belief

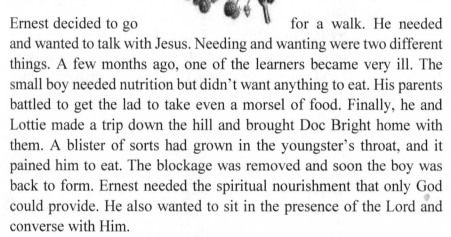

Ernest decided to go for a walk. He needed and wanted to talk with Jesus. Needing and wanting were two different things. A few months ago, one of the learners became very ill. The small boy needed nutrition but didn't want anything to eat. His parents battled to get the lad to take even a morsel of food. Finally, he and Lottie made a trip down the hill and brought Doc Bright home with them. A blister of sorts had grown in the youngster's throat, and it pained him to eat. The blockage was removed and soon the boy was back to form. Ernest needed the spiritual nourishment that only God could provide. He also wanted to sit in the presence of the Lord and converse with Him.

The situation with Coral pressed on his mind and on his heart. His thoughts roared, and his heart was gripped with fear. He knew that only the good Lord could help Coral. He ambled without clear direction and eventually came to rest under a leafing tree. The fresh, moss green leaves and the tender shoots at the base of the tree reminded him about Jesus being the tree of life. Resting against the sturdy trunk, he started to sing.

Far away in the depths of my spirit tonight rolls a melody sweeter than psalm; in celestial-like strains it unceasingly falls o'er my soul like an infinite calm. Peace, peace, wonderful peace, coming down from the Father above! Sweep over my spirit forever, I pray in fathomless billows of love!

The lyrics ministered to Ernest, and he began to pray, "Help me to have peace, wonderful peace." He also prayed for Coral to have wisdom and understanding. When his mind quieted, and his frustrations subsided, he began to feel pain in his hand. "Lord, forgive me. I'm like Moses hittin' at things that don't need hit, allowin' anger to take over my common sense and fill my mind and heart."

He wasn't prone to anger and couldn't remember a time when he had struck somethin' or someone out of frustration.

He loved Coral. He loved all his sisters, but that was no excuse for leaning on his own strength instead of looking to God. Ernest sat in contemplation for some time. He sensed God's grace and enjoyed experiencing the Lord's fathomless billows of love. As the afternoon drew to a close and the sun shifted in the sky, he felt the warmth of both the sun and the Son in the heavenlies and knew it was time to talk with Lottie.

He found her behind the schoolhouse target practicing with her bow and arrow.

Until recently, he had admired her skill. Lately, however, targets, bows, and arrows reminded him how Lottie and Lester had met. He didn't begrudge his brother the time he had shared with the lovely Charlotte; he simply wished that with Lester gone that Lottie would look his way.

He smiled when he witnessed Lottie hitting the squirrel shaped target time and time again. Ernest thoroughly enjoyed Lottie's fried squirrel. He had made the target as a joke last summer after they had reached a mutual understanding that it was his job to clean and cut the critters and her job to roll the pieces in flour and fry them in lard or bacon grease. Ernest wasn't sure if it was the spices she added or just the thought of her hands preparing the meat that made the meal so delicious.

"Gettin' ready to squirrel hunt?" he asked. When Lottie jumped, Ernest felt bad for startling her, but before he could apologize, she spoke.

"I was gettin' worried, Brother."

"Ain't no cause for worry. I was talkin' with the Lord."

"Knowin' you, I figured as much. Is He talkin' back?"

Ernest smiled. "Are you gonna hunt us up some squirrel?"

"I was thinkin' on it."

"Maybe we can go together, but I'm wantin' to talk first." Ernest paused and then turned to look Lottie directly in the face. "Charlotte…"

"This is serious if you're callin' me by my given name."

"It's serious, and I ain't wantin' to hurt you." He saw fear in her eyes and took her hands. "I know you loved and still love Lester, and I don't want to pain you by callin' up your grief."

Lottie gently squeezed his hands. "Ernest, please say what's needin' said."

"Coral has a notion to visit Charlie in jail. She says God's directin' her and can't be convinced otherwise." When he saw Lottie's tears, he released her hands and drew her into his embrace. Her hair smelled of flowers, and her skin was warm from the sunshine. There was also chalk dust on one of her cheeks. He spoke softly in her ear, "I'm sorry to pain you. I ain't wantin' you to grieve no more."

"It's not grief that's makin' me cry, Ernest." The breath of her words tickled his neck. "I've grieved till there's no grief left. It's been over four years since Lester died. I'll never be forgettin' him, but life has to move forward. I know I need to forgive Charlie, and I've been prayin' for God's help. If it's safe, maybe Coral's visitin' him is what we all need."

Ernest, stunned, was speechless. His back stiffened. His hands dropped to his sides.

"Now I've hurt you," Lottie spoke.

Taking a deep breath, Ernest answered. "I'm just needin' time. I wasn't thinkin' about you responding in such a way. Guess it ain't good to have a talk in your head before the actual talk."

As he started to walk away, Lottie called to him. "I'm askin' the Lord to speak back to you, Ernest. Maybe He'll say the same things as He's been sayin' to me, 'It's time. It's time to be movin' on.'"

He heard Lottie's words but didn't respond.

He rounded the corner of the wooden schoolhouse and sat on the porch steps. He was relieved that Lottie was ready to move beyond her grief and start living again. He had hoped, dreamed, and prayed for as much. He was also glad that Charlotte was trying a find a way to forgive Charlie. He was baffled, however, that she might consider Coral to be part of that plan. Coral was only sixteen. Even with Pastor Rex helping her, it just didn't seem right. He put his head down, placed his hands over his face, and began to sing once again.

Peace, peace, wonderful peace, coming down from the Father above! Sweep over my spirit forever, I pray in fathomless billows of love!

Hymn after hymn came to mind. The words were muffled by his hands. He sang for himself and the Lord alone. Some words were in worship to God; and other words were a cry for help in understanding divine purpose and plan.

As the late afternoon cooled, so did Ernest's emotions. He knew it was time to make peace with Lottie. Just as he stood to his feet, a rustling in the school yard distracted him. Next to the log where he and Rudy had been sitting earlier, he spotted a meandering black bear and her two cubs. The female was larger than most. Ernest estimated her weight to be 300 pounds or more. She was blue-black. The cubs, which were busy wrestling, were cinnamon-colored.

Ernest stopped breathing when the mama put her nose in the air and sniffed and snorted. The bear slapped the ground with her large, clawed paw and shook her head. Black bears were usually shy. Typically, when seeing a human, they grunted and bluffed aggression; but with cubs close-by, Ernest was troubled. He knew not to run and to remain submissive in his posture.

His heart seemed to quit beating when he heard Lottie enter the back door of the schoolhouse. He could hear her brisk steps on the worn wooden floor. The mama bear began a slow approach and started to growl. He yelled a warning to Lottie. Within seconds the front door opened to the porch where he was standing. She had her bow and arrow in hand and was preparing to shoot.

"Where do I aim?"

"Upper chest. But wait," Ernest cautioned. "She's movin' slow. I think she's bluffin'."

The bear turned tail and headed back to her cubs. Eruptive gas escaped from her backside which signaled her cubs that it was time to move on.

When the odor reached Charlotte, she began to gag. "What is that?"

Ernest couldn't help but laugh. "Bear fog."

When Charlotte joined in his laughter, it seemed natural and right to place his arm around her. She lowered her brow and snuggled next to him.

"Where were you headed, Lottie?"

"Tryin' to find you."

"Were you lookin' only for me or was someone else on your mind?"

"Only you, Ernest." She smiled and then added, "Lest I saw me some squirrels."

Early the following morning, Ernest and Charlotte shared breakfast.

Charlotte lived in a small cabin behind the schoolhouse. Ernest lived in a rough-hewn-log room that had been added onto the school building. The two often shared dinner, but sharing breakfast was something new. Before dawn, Lottie had quietly knocked on his door inviting him to join her. He was pleased by her invitation. She was a wonderful cook; more importantly, he was anxious to see her before heading down the mountain to talk with Coral.

The morning was cool, and there was a mist in the air. Lottie made everything special, and their time together was no different. Her cabin was warm and inviting, decorated with treasures she'd found outdoors and modest gifts from her students.

A large glass bowl sat on a pine table in her parlor. The bowl was filled with whatnots dear to Lottie's heart: a marble, a dried sprig of lavender, three songbird feathers, a uniquely shaped rock, a broken pencil, and a wooden carving of a small arrow. The nicked, scarred table added to the charm of the room.

A fire burned in the wood stove. Home-style buttered biscuits, sausage gravy, fried eggs, and freshly made applesauce teased Ernest's senses. All his senses were heightened. Lottie was a beauty, and he couldn't take his eyes off her. Her cheeks were flushed from cooking over the fire. He longed to hold her. It was all he could do not to take her into his arms.

"You've outdone yourself."

"Thank you, Ernest. It's always a joy sharin' a meal with you."

He smiled. "Lottie, I want you to be extra careful while I'm gone. You know I don't like leavin' you."

"I'll be just fine, Brother."

Ernest winced inside. "I'll try and be back this evenin'; and if not, first thing tomorrow mornin'. If the older boys get too wild, send 'um on home." He then added with a gentle voice, "And, don't be calling me 'brother,' Lottie. I ain't thinkin' of you like that."

Ernest reached across the table and took her hand. "I've had feelings for you for quite some time. I've been slow in sharing my thoughts, but I don't want to head down the mountain without asking you to consider spendin' time with me."

Lottie placed her other hand over Ernest's hand, and he responded in return. With their hands sandwiched together, she quietly spoke. "We spend plenty of time together. I'm thinkin' you want to change the terms of us bein' with each other."

"Your thinkin' is right." Ernest released her hands and stood. "I best get goin'. I'm no longer content to just look at you, Lottie." He touched her hair, kissed her cheek and drew her close. "I don't wanna leave with there being a problem between us. I'm prayin' on what you said about Coral."

"I know you are." Lottie paused and then smiled. "And, I'll be working on not callin' you 'brother.'"

Charlotte walked with him past the schoolhouse and the clearing that had looked inviting to the bears yesterday. She stood at the trail head. Ernest could sense her watching as he headed down the hill.

The morning was chilly, but he was warmed by the breakfast he'd shared, the touch of Lottie's hand, and the feel of her embrace. He had wanted to kiss her properly but didn't. *Kissin' ain't something to take casual like,* he thought. *I surely do want her lips touchin' mine but only when the time is right.*

As he traveled the curved, narrow path, his thoughts didn't stray far from the idea of kissing. During the cold season, Ernest had instructed the learners about germs. During his time of preparation for a lesson, he read that King Henry VI of England had once banned kissing. The King was worried about the spread of disease yet died of a contagious disease himself. Ernest wasn't concerned about catching germs from Lottie. He was more concerned that he would enjoy kissing her too much.

Chapter Three

If you whistle before breakfast, you will cry before dusk.

Appalachian Folk Belief

"Emie darlin', please　　　　　　　　quit pacing the floor. See Jewel? She thinks you're lookin' plumb crazy."

Emie placed her hands on her hips. "Red, how did you know? I do like a good plum. Not a crazy likin' but a likin' none-the-less."

"Darlin', we both know, I ain't talkin' about P-L-U-M. I'm talkin' about P-L-U-M-B!"

"Rudy, just in case you've forgotten your learnin', P-L-U-M-B means 'completely'."

"I ain't forgotten my learnin'," Rudy replied. "And by the way, you are actin' completely crazy."

Emie sighed. "You're right, Red. I just can't wait for Ernest to get here. I tried talking with Coral again yesterday and got nowhere. That girl is stubborn as a mule."

Ernest wanted to chuckle but restrained himself. Just like Coral, Emie had a stubborn streak a mile wide. He knew that a mule got its physical ability from the horse and its intelligence from the donkey. He wasn't sure, however, that mules were actually stubborn. With Amos and Andy, his friend's mules, their stubbornness was more an act of self-preservation from four ornery boys.

"Emie, remember the story in the Bible about Balaam's donkey?"

She nodded her head in response, "That donkey was a mean one. She ran away, crushed her master's foot, and lay in the road."

"Darlin', I am wantin' you to know that I didn't call the donkey a she, you did."

"Rudy, we're talkin' about Coral; of course, the donkey has to be a she. Pay attention. You're aggravatin' me."

"Emie, we're in a mess, and we're aggravatin' each other." Rudy blew a puff of air from his lips. "Alright then, Balaam's "she" donkey was protectin' him. Balaam was wantin' to curse God's people, and the donkey was protectin' him from an angry angel."

"Rudy, what's all of this having to do with Coral?"

"I ain't wantin' to make you mad, darlin', but what if Coral's wantin' to protect us and herself."

Rudy couldn't help but notice the odd look on Emie's face. Her mouth was puckered slightly, and her eyebrows were drawn together. *She's angry for sure,* he thought. *A storm is brewin' like the coffee pot when the dark liquid overflows and stinks and stains.*

"If she's wantin' to protect, then she shouldn't be goin' to Charleston! Protectin'is stayin' away, not playin' with a hive of bees."

"Emie, there's sweetness that comes from a beehive."

"You are twistin' my words again. When you twist my words, you twist my insides."

"Darlin', what happens if God is really askin' Coral to visit Charlie? Maybe, He's askin' to keep us from growin' the bitter root that rises up and causes trouble."

"It's hard to hear what you're sayin', Red."

"I know it is."

Ernest arrived just in time to see Coral and Emie arguing in the yard. Coral's hands were balled in fists and settled close to her body. Emphasizing her frustration, Emie's hands were waving in the air.

In Ernest's mind, angry with each other or not, his sisters were both delightful. Their blond heads reflected the sunlight, their long, golden locks ruffling in the spring-time breeze. They both had fair skin and burned easily in the sun. Emie had more sun kisses than Coral, but since Rudy found her freckles fetching, Ernest knew Emie didn't mind the freckles.

"Now, girlies, am I gonna have to stand between the two of ya?"

Coral and Emie ceased their arguing and ran in unison toward their brother. Ernest stretched his arms and gathered the two of them in a big bear hug. He then proceeded to tell them all about his recent encountered with the mama bear and her cubs. Always a spell-binding storyteller, Ernest had his sisters gasping in fear, cheering for Charlotte, sighing with relief, and belly laughing over bear fog.

When the story finished and the laughter subsided, Emie looked toward Ernest. "Now, Brother, how are things goin' with charmin' Charlotte?"

"Why, what do you mean, Sister?"

"You know exactly what I mean. Have you declared your lovin' ways?"

"Now, Emie, how would I declare them ways?"

"With a smooch."

"Now, Emie, you know better than that; I don't drink hooch."

"SMOOCH!"

"Sister, I don't have a pooch. I ain't rightly sure what you're talkin' about."

"SMOOCH!"

Ernest looked at Coral who was laughing loudly. It did his heart good to see her outward expression of joy. She was generally so quiet and reserved.

"Now, sisters, whether it's smooch, hooch, or pooch, I ain't sure, but this I know–a gentleman doesn't kiss and tell."

Emie rolled her eyes and shook her head.

Ernest grinned in response and motioned toward Auntie Ada's front porch. "Let's have a sit."

Once they were settled, silence rested on the trio. Ernest knew his sisters were nervous. He was nervous as well and unsure how to begin their conversation. "Well, Coral, I hear you're wantin' to go to prison."

Coral kept her eyes down and softly answered. "I'm only goin' for a visit, Ernest, and I ain't sure that 'wantin' to go' is completely accurate."

"I know that Emie's heard the story, so she won't be interruptin'." Ernest could feel Emie's glare. "But since I've only heard the gist of it, would you mind sharin' some details?"

"For quite some time, I've been prayin' for Charlie," Coral began. "Now, I know some would say that he's gettin' his just deserts; but if I was to get my just deserts, I wouldn't be goin' to heaven. He's a bad man, but I ain't so good. Ain't none of us good without Jesus."

When Emie started to say something, Ernest held his hand up. "Now, Sister, just be listenin', please. Let Coral tell me the story."

The younger sister continued, "Me and Emie's been wrestlin'. Just like them cubs you described. Only we ain't playin'. We're not seein' eye to eye. Brother, no one is lookin' at things like I'm seein' 'em. I ain't tryin' to be cantankerous. I'm just wantin' to do what God's askin'."

"Coral, how do you know that it's God directin' you and not your own heart? You got a soft heart and more than enough compassion for the hurtin'."

"Brother, I would never do this on my own. I ain't never traveled to Charleston. I'm scared of Charlie. He's a cold-blooded killer and a rapist," she paused, "yet, there's somethin' drawin' me to him. I can't explain it. I've talked to God. I've even cried some and asked the Lord to send someone else. Yet, it's eatin' me up inside. I gotta go. I just know it."

Ernest took Coral's hand. "Now, Baby Girl…"

"Brother, I ain't a baby no more."

"I'm knowin' that. It's just an expression. I'm your elder brother and feel like it's my job to watch over you."

"I love you, and I'm grateful. I know you think sixteen is a might young for what I've got in mind, but Ernest, you know in this holler a girl grows up fast. She's gotta take the good and the bad and build a life. I've finished my schoolin'. I've got a good mind and common sense. I ain't foolish. I wouldn't be goin' unless God was askin'."

"I love you, too, Coral. Now, if you're willin', let's bring the family together and have us a time of prayer. I'm wantin' us to find peace."

Emie scooted next to Coral and placed her arm around her sister.

"I'm willin'. But if God still says I have to go, I have to go."

"I understand, Sister."

It was hard for Ernest to understand the change in Coral. She was a tad stubborn at times, but never bold or outlandish. He'd once seen a picture of a quetzal in his reader at school. The large bird with the golden-green and scarlet plumage was like the q in queue. The creature's captivating beauty set it apart. It stood alone with the smaller less colorful birds paling in comparison. Coral had always been like the pale birds, like the silent letters in queue—u-e-u-e. She was content to let others take the lead and to remain quietly in the background.

It was queer to see Coral depart from her quaint, quiet ways, now that she had grown into a beautiful young woman. Ernest reminded himself to watch her more carefully.

Ernest opened the family meeting in prayer asking for God's guidance. Auntie Ada stood toward the back of the small room with Uncle Christian's arm around her shoulders. She was crying.

Aunt Ada was a love aunt who was related by heart and not by blood. A godly woman, Ernest knew that Aunt Ada's heart wasn't moved by his soliloquy of prayer but her concern for Coral. Emie sat in a worn rocker with her arms crossed over her chest. She looked exasperated and infuriated. Rudy was standing behind his wife with his hands resting on her shoulders. Ernest could see Rudy's hands moving in and out like the old man in the hills who played the squeeze box at church on Sundays. Coral was wringing her hands–a telltale sign for members of the Ashby family that one was anxious. When Ernest looked closer at the younger sister, her azure eyes looked resolute, and her full, pale-pink lips were drawn together and pursed.

It had been decided early on not to include the twins, the Ashby family's oldest siblings, in the family prayer meeting. Emie had told him that the older sisters tended toward bossiness which shouldn't be tolerated at a prayer service. Ernest understood about bossiness and busyness among the twins but didn't agree that unpleasant character traits should exclude someone from prayer. He felt just the opposite. If someone had unseemly attributes, then all-the-more prayer was needed. He knew, however, that there were enough opinions and confusion regarding Coral, and that it was probably best not to add to the many voices already vying to express their views.

Only Jewel seemed at peace. The young child was sitting at Emie's feet, playing with a doll made out of sack cloth. The face was painted on the cloth and the hair made from yellow yarn. The doll wasn't fancy in her faded fabric clothes. The thrown-and-sewn-together baby didn't seem to bother Jewel in the least. She was holding the figure tightly and whispering sweet nothings into her non-existent ear. Ernest was reminded of how Jesus told His disciples that the Kingdom of God was comprised of those who had childlike faith and innocence.

Except for Jewel, everyone was looking at him with expectation. He wasn't sure what to say. If he gave Coral his blessing, Emie would be devastated and the group disappointed. If he sided with Emie, Coral would probably still head to Charleston but along the way feel abandoned by her family. *Lord, help us,* he silently prayed. Ernest instantly felt reassured. *It's not about what Coral wants or Emie wants; it's about what Jesus wants.* Just as Ernest was ready to give voice, Aunt Ada requested the family sing a hymn. Rudy suggested *Tis So Sweet to Trust in Jesus.*

Tis so sweet to trust in Jesus. Just to take Him at His Word. Just to rest upon His promise. Just to know, "Thus saith the Lord!" Jesus, Jesus, how I trust Him! How I've proved Him o'er and o'er. Jesus, Jesus, precious Jesus! Oh, for grace to trust Him more!

Like the arrangement of the four Gospels presenting the same story, the voices blended in perfect harmony. Ernest knew that God wanted his family in harmony about Coral's possible travel to Charleston.

When Ernest looked around the dainty parlor, the expressions of worship were different but in harmony. Emie's arms were no longer crossed but raised in praise. Rudy's hands, like the hands on a clock, were tapping on the back of the chair keeping time. Auntie had overflowing tears because of God's goodness, and Coral's lips were no longer pursed but moving in vocal adoration for her Savior.

When the song finished, Ernest addressed those he loved. "I remember Mrs. Randolph talkin' about the hymn we was just singin'. On a fine spring day, a man, his wife, and their daughter decided to have a picnic by the sea. Just as they were spreadin' their blanket and wantin' to eat, they heard a cry for help. The daddy raced to save a young boy from drownin' only to drown himself. The wife and daughter, without the father providin', became poor. They had nothin'. When they ran out of food, the mama assumed they'd die from starvation. Instead, neighbors helped by leavin' food on the stoop. One night after tuckin' her daughter in bed, the woman wrote them words we sang." Ernest paused and looked at Coral. "I ain't rightly sure what the song and story have to do with you visitin' Charlie, but I'm thinkin' there's a connection."

Coral who was usually so soft spoken that it strained others to hear her, spoke loudly and clearly. "Charlie's the boy drownin'. He's cryin' for help whether he knows it or not, and I'm wantin' to help save him. I'm wantin' to tell him about Jesus' love. I'm thinkin' I'll be just fine. I ain't plannin' on goin' under to help Charlie. But, if somethin' happens and things don't go just right, I know my family will be taken care of. The mama and daughter could have been angry and bitter over their struggles, but they trusted in God just like we need to do."

An agreement was reached that night. Coral would travel by train with Pastor Rex to Charleston. Rudy's grandpappy would make the arrangements for Coral to see Charlie and accompany her to the prison. She wouldn't be left alone with Charlie, not for a minute. Her family would stay behind in flesh but travel with her in spirit as they prayed and believed with Coral for Charlie's salvation. Ernest knew that everyone was struggling in his or her own way, but each was trying to take God at His Word and rest on His promises.

Chapter Four

To cure a sty, stand at a crossroad and recite
"Sty, sty leave my eye,
take the next one passing by."

Appalachian Folk Belief

There were only a few weeks of school left for the year, and Ernest was anxious to get back to his students. He also was looking forward to seeing Charlotte. Even during his family's struggles, his thoughts were never far from Lottie. She was beautiful in flesh and in spirit. She was energetic and fun, full of laughter and mischief, yet thoughtful and serious about the needs of others. She was caring and kind. She had always been kind to Ernest. Now he hoped that her kindness and caring would expand and grow into romantic love.

Ernest's brother, Lester, had made Lottie's acquaintance while racing cars for moonshiners. A part of a performing troupe promoting the racing events and presenting mystifying feats before the races themselves, Charlotte had earned her stage name, "Lottie Legend," from her reputation as an expert marksman. Ernest smirked to recall that she'd once shot an apple off Lester's head. She was an Annie Oakley of sorts with a bow and arrow. When Charlotte and Lester approached a circuit riding preacher, he'd done their rites.

Ernest felt both pride and jealousy thinking of his deceased brother. He knew that he and Charlotte would each continue to grieve at times for the loss of Lester. He hoped, however, that together they might lament their loss and live their lives.

As he headed up the mountain, Ernest remembered as a young boy how surprised he had been to learn about Phoebe Anne Moses, better known as Annie Oakley. At the time, he simply couldn't believe that a woman had the skills to be a sharpshooter. Now, he knew better. Lottie was a better shot with her bow than any man he knew. Mrs. Randolph, his schoolteacher, told him how Annie even wrote to President McKinley about wanting to organize a group of fifty women to fight in the Spanish American War. Ernest wasn't sure if President McKinley acted wisely or foolishly in never responding to Annie's request.

When Ernest heard rustling up ahead, he worried about another encounter with mama bear and her babies. He slowed his pace and looked to and fro toward the wooded area where the noise originated. He gazed intently to the right of the dirt path beneath his feet. Nothing in his wildest imaginings prepared him for the bronze-colored face he saw among the greenery. He felt his heart make a thud, then skip a beat.

"Ernest, why, you look like you're seein' a ghost."

"I ain't believin' what I'm seein'. Miss Mercy, I thought you was gone for good."

"Not for good. I was missin' my family…and you," She added.

He didn't know how to answer. Mercy was his first and only love until Charlotte. He'd assumed that their blossomed limbs of love and roots of commitment would be entangled throughout life's journey, but he'd been wrong. Mercy rejected Ernest based on his skin color; he being white, and she, black. When Mercy left, he'd felt as if she'd pulled up the root of his life.

With his heart broken and bruised, he'd found solace in the higher hills. At first, his students and Lottie only caught glimpses of the true Ernest. As time wore on, his heart began to heal, and his personality emerged once again. Like a butterfly escaping a cocoon, he'd found freedom by spreading his wings of life and hope against the hard walls of his heart.

Ernest finally spoke. "You've been gone a pretty long time."

"Too long."

When Mercy stepped out from among the trees, there was no need to ask what she had been up to. Her swollen belly told him all he needed to know. There was another man in her life. His heart skipped another beat and then continued its regular rhythm. He wondered if his fleeting ache for Mercy was a betrayal to Charlotte.

"Congratulations, Mercy."

"I ain't sure that congratulations is in order."

Ernest was puzzled.

"I ain't married. That's why I've come home."

Looking closer, Ernest couldn't help but notice Mercy's tattered clothes. Her skin was pale. Her hair had lost its sheen, and her eyes no longer reflected innocence. His heart gripped. "What happened to you, Mercy?"

"Life, love, loss," she answered. "Well, maybe not love. More like longin' to fill an empty place."

Ernest saw the tears in her eyes.

"We were friends once, Ernest. Do you remember?"

"I haven't forgotten. We were friends. Then more than friends, and then you left. You left because my skin was light and yours was dark."

"I'm sorry, so sorry," she sobbed.

Moved with compassion, Ernest embraced her. With her head against his chest, she wept. Her tears stained his shirt and strained his soul that had been less complicated and true only a moment ago. He closed his eyes and felt her pain. He sensed that she might be needing a reminder of the Lord's goodness and whispered above her head about the story of God's great redemptive love.

Ernest felt a watershed of sorrow. He felt certain love, familiar– the protecting, defending love from the heart of the Father, and an activated concern to cover the weakness of this friend whom he felt tied to. But when he searched deep within, he didn't find the romantic love he'd treasured previously for Mercy. Only the memories of how he had hoped and yearned for her for so long remained.

Maybe it was the shock of the condition in which she had returned to him. Maybe it was the ebb and flow of life. Maybe his heart had finally accepted what the law said about mixed race marriage. But mostly it was about recovering bit by bit from her shocking rejection.

When Mercy's sobs quieted, he ceased praying and opened his eyes. In the distance, he saw Charlotte watching. Her head dipped down. Waves of red hair covered her face. Ernest knew that Charlotte had witnessed his expression of comfort toward Mercy. Her ruby-colored tresses were a wall of protection. She was trying to comfort herself. He felt a stab of pain. His beloved was wounded, and he had inflicted the blow.

A mulberry tree resided next to the worn path where Charlotte stood. Some mulberry trees could first be male, then female, and then change back again. It was a mystery. The differences between the male flowers and female flowers were hard to discern. The tree's gender blending reminded Ernest of marriage where a man and a woman became one. Mulberry trees could even begin the season as one sex and change to the other. He dreamed of marrying Charlotte, of blending their lives together and creating something as unique and intriguing as the ripening berries on the mulberry tree.

He gently moved Mercy aside. When he looked back toward the path, Charlotte was gone.

"Charlotte," Ernest began. "You're thinkin' you saw somethin' you didn't see."

"My vision is just fine, Brother. Doc Bright took a look at my eyes when he was examinin' the learners last fall."

He reached for Lottie's hand, but she stepped back. It also hadn't gone unnoticed that she was referring to him as "brother" again.

Ernest didn't understand women. He didn't understand how they thought, how they acted. He had sisters and Lottie in his life, all of whom he loved and cared for deeply. Yet, he sometimes felt the height of the walls they erected were insurmountable. He was clueless.

Baffled, Ernest tried to explain. "I was offerin' comfort –nothin' else. Mercy's had a terrible, bad time of it. She told me her story. She's come home to her family."

"She's come home to you, Ernest."

He closed his eyes momentarily and sighed. "There's only room in my heart for you, Charlotte. I'm feelin' pity for Mercy."

"Pity has a way of turnin' to love."

"Please let me tell you her goin's-on."

Lottie nodded.

"She met a no-good white feller. He sweet talked her with words of love and marriage. She said at first that he'd brought remembrance of me." When Charlotte's eyebrows lifted, he knew he had said the wrong thing. "He must have reminded her of who I used to be, not who I am now."

"Hmmm."

"Before makin' judgments, please let me finish."

"I'm listen', Ernest. But you don't understand the ways of women. I know you got them sisters, but only a woman understands the wiles of another woman."

Ernest didn't bother correcting Charlotte. "Wiles" indicated deception and ulterior motives. He didn't think Mercy was out to manipulate anyone. She was hurting and had come home to heal.

"Mercy found herself pregnant. She didn't know the man was married. Knowin' she needed help, she left for the holler."

"Why was she waitin' for you along the trail?"

"I ain't rightly sure."

"She asked and knew you was headin' home from Big Creek. She was layin' claim, Ernest."

Exasperated, Ernest answered. "I don't exactly know what 'layin' claim' means, Charlotte."

The woman who stood before him was different than the woman he left yesterday. *Where was her sweetness? Her gentle nature? She was like that surly brown bear slappin' the ground and clawing the air. The mama bear had been protecting those she loved. Was the lovely Lottie protecting someone she loved? Was she jealous of Mercy? Was Charlotte worried that he would choose Mercy for his gal?*

Maybe he didn't understand women, but he had a little bit of understanding about jealousy. He was the younger brother after all, and Lester had been his daddy's favorite.

"Now, Sister, not that I'm thinkin' of you like a sister, but since you're callin' me 'brother' again, I'm thinkin' I should do likewise. Jealousy is an ugly thing…"

Charlotte looked like she had been stung by a bee. Ernest knew he had messed things up even more. She hurriedly turned and walked away leaving him gasping for air.

He was restless. His earlier conversation, if you could call the words that he and Lottie exchanged a conversation, left him feeling at a loss. Sleep wouldn't come. His mind was racing. He was dreaming and scheming about how to get back in Charlotte's good graces. He had tried to pray and sing hymns, but the matters of his heart wouldn't quiet. It was like they were alive and clamoring for attention.

The Bible said to take captive one's thoughts. Ernest knew that the answers and guidance he sought wouldn't come from his emotions, but from time spent with the Lord. Emotions by themselves made for an unhealthy seed bed, the fruit of which would bring more confusion.

He needed understanding and the wisdom to know what to do. He fumbled in the dark, lit the oil lamp next to his bed, and opened his Bible. The brown leather cover was worn, and a few of the pages were torn. In-order-to keep his mind from racing and his emotions at bay, he read aloud from Scripture.

The Proverb he read spoke to his soul, and an element of clarity came. Charlotte was right about one thing. Mercy had waited for him. She somehow knew where he would be and hid herself until just the right moment. But why? She could have just as easily visited with him at the schoolhouse or sent a message through one of her brothers.

When his eyes finally grew heavy, he turned the wick down, extinguishing the flame, and laid his head on the down pillow. He felt a prick at the base of his neck and fumbled in the dark until he located and removed the quill poking from the cotton fabric. As a child, he had slept without a pillow and had been grateful if there was a blanket to warm him. The pillow he enjoyed was a gift from Lottie. He had witnessed her butcher the goose, scald the hen, and pluck the feathers. He had welcomed the feast she prepared and enjoyed the luxurious pillow she had offered him several days later. Charlotte brought treasures to his life. The biggest treasure was the gift of herself. Hopefully, the prick in their relationship would be as easily remedied as removing the out-of-place feather quill.

Ernest was looking for Charlotte the following morning when he heard the school bell ring. Ever the attentive teacher, he should have known that she would be in the classroom preparing for the day. He chided himself for not being beside her and focused on the learners whom he now pictured entering the classroom and taking their seats.

He approached the schoolhouse as Charlotte and the students recited the Pledge of Allegiance. He stopped at the open door and placed his hand on his heart.

I pledge allegiance to the flag of the United States of America and to the Republic for which it stands. One nation, indivisible with liberty and justice for all.

He was proud of the learners. Everyone stood tall, facing the flag, and proudly proclaiming their love of country. Though the original Pledge of Allegiance had been written for countries around the world to use, Ernest was glad that a few years ago the words had been adapted to include the personalization of the United States.

He nodded to Charlotte who smiled coyly. He breathed a slight sigh of relief –at least she smiled. There was a glimmer of promise. He greeted the learners and started the day's recitations. Several minutes later, he was interrupted by Charlotte softly tapping him on the shoulder.

"Adam, Beau, Claude, and Dean are missin'."

It was just like sweet Charlotte to worry about absentee students, Ernest thought. He hoped she was herself again and that whatever had invaded her being yesterday was gone. He was also touched that Charlotte was unmoved that the missing students were related to Mercy.

"Ernest, you best go and see the goin's-on."

"It ain't necessary. They'll be along."

"I don't know. I'm thinkin' somethin' is wrong. Them boys don't generally miss out on learnin'."

"Maybe you're right, Charlotte. If all four of 'um is missin', maybe there's a problem. Would you mind makin' inquiries? I'll stay with the students."

"I'll hurry."

"Take your time and do what's needed."

Ernest placed his arm around Lottie's shoulders and gave her a gentle squeeze. He wondered if his touch was to reassure her about the absent learners or to reassure himself about their relationship. He watched her exit through the front schoolhouse door. For an instant, he worried about the reappearance of the three bears. He walked to the window and saw Charlotte heading toward the boys' home. Thankfully, no bears were in sight.

Before he continued the morning's lessons, he talked with the learners about his encounter with the mama bear and her cubs. The students had their own stories to tell about bears, mountain lions, possums, and imagined creatures who stalked the woodlands.

One of the older boys described the mystical Yahoo and another Dwayyo. Snarly Yow was also mentioned. Ernest did his best to expose the fear filled stories as Indian legends and wild imaginings of the early Appalachian settlers, but the learners couldn't be dissuaded. Thoughts of giant hairy creatures, wolves that walked like humans and had fangs, and snarling monsters who appeared after dark struck fear in the students.

In order to redirect their attention, he thought about telling the story of Goldilocks and the Three Bears but remembered in one of the earlier versions of the fairy tale that Goldilocks was an old woman who ended up impaled on a steeple. He shuddered at the thought.

"Students, start pushin' the tables and chairs to the sides. Stand up. I'm gonna teach you a rollick called the Dancin' Bear."

Ernest explained that dances sometimes mimicked the movements of animals. He used the examples of the turkey trot and the fox trot. Emie had gone through a phase a number of years back where she liked rag time music and the dances that accompanied its syncopated rhythm. She had once demonstrated the Dancing Bear. Ernest remembered some of the movements and spontaneously created the rest.

Chapter Five

A knife placed under the bed during childbirth will
ease the pain of labor.

Appalachian Folk Belief

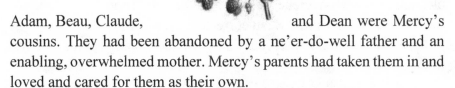

Adam, Beau, Claude,   and Dean were Mercy's
cousins. They had been abandoned by a ne'er-do-well father and an
enabling, overwhelmed mother. Mercy's parents had taken them in and
loved and cared for them as their own.

Charlotte had experienced first-hand the boys' mischievousness.
Ernest said they were naughty, but Charlotte liked to think of them as
creative and energetic. In moments of frustration, she reminded herself
and Ernest that the two older boys were improving. Adam was thirteen,
and Beau was eleven. They were starting to mature and do away with
their more foolish pranks. The foursome wasn't malicious, just overly
rambunctious. She hoped the boys weren't in harm's way yet knew
even seemingly harmless lads could rigorously rouse a ruckus.

Her thoughts wandered as she hurried from the schoolhouse to the
opposite side of the small nameless town where she lived. She had
accompanied Ernest up the hillside three plus years ago to escape the
grief of losing her husband. Grief, however, had followed her like a
shadow. In time, she began to heal and started to enjoy the community
and its residents. One of her favorite fellow citizens was Justice,

Mercy's father and the four missing boys' adoptive father.

She wasn't sure when she started entertaining romantic thoughts of Ernest. She did remember when the sorrow started lifting, and she began feeling pleasure again. Like many things in her life, her ability to feel joy came at the hands and words of Ernest. He had simply quoted a phrase attributed to Charlie Chaplin.

A day without laughter is no day at all.

Being deep in thought allowed the boys to find her before she found them.

"Miss Charlotte, Miss Charlotte," Beau called. "We found us a cussin' bird."

"A bicuspid? Did someone's tooth fall out?" the teacher asked. Ernest had just instructed the learners about the proper names for teeth. He had also taken advantage of the opportunity to discuss teeth cleaning. Personal hygiene was not a priority in the hills.

"No—a cussin' bird," Beau corrected.

"Well, not real bad cussin', just hell and damn," Adam interrupted.

"Daddy said that we ain't supposed to say hell and damn unless we're talkin' about people not goin' to their Maker when they die," added Claude, cutting off his brother.

Charlotte shook her head in confusion. "Boys, I am wantin' to hear from just one of you at time. I don't understand what you're rightly talkin' about."

"I'll do the explainin'," said Dean.

"You can't explain nothin', Dean. You is the littlest. So just shush your mouth."

"You just shush your mouth, Claude. I can to do the explainin'. Plus, Daddy said that we ain't allowed to say, 'shush your mouth.' It ain't plain polite."

"Mercy said 'shush your mouth'," Claude answered in defense.

"Mama said it's because she's actin' the fool. Miss Charlotte, does havin' a baby make you crazy? I once saw a rabid racoon actin' crazy like. Do you think Mercy might have the rabies?" Dean inquired.

Charlotte was tempted to say 'shush your mouth' herself but instead put her hands in the air at chest level with palms forward, signaling the boys to be silent.

"Adam, since he's the biggest, can speak on behalf of you boys," Charlotte said firmly.

Adam looked at the other boys and puffed out his chest a bit. "We was walkin' to school when we heard a voice from there trees. 'By hell, it's a fine day,' it said."

The other boys gasped at Adam's language.

"This has nothin' to do with teeth?" Charlotte clarified.

When everyone started talking at once, the teacher quickly raised her hands again, and the boys quieted. "Adam, please go on."

"No teacher, this has nothin' to do with teeth! We're talkin' about a bird that uses bad words."

Charlotte nodded for Adam to continue.

"At first we thought it might be a person –a tiny person like Zacchaeus. You know the small man who climbed the tree to see Jesus?"

"Yes, Adam, I know whom you're mentionin'."

"Well, it wasn't a person at all; it was a bird. He is still sittin' up there. Quiet like. I think we scared 'um."

"Boys, please keep still. I'm gonna climb up the tree a little and see if I can get me a peek."

"You needin' help, Teacher? I can give you a boost up." Adam asked.

Beau immediately took charge. "She's a big one, Adam. It'll take all of us, Dean included, to lift her up. Maybe I should run and get Daddy to bring the mules to hoist her."

In that moment, Charlotte decided that Ernest was right–the boys were naughty, mighty naughty.

"I ain't big," Charlotte answered sternly. "Large bones run in my family. I'm not like Zacchaeus." She then added through clenched teeth, "And I ain't needin' mules."

The chastised boys didn't utter a sound as she effortlessly pulled herself up from the ground to a low, large branch. Shooting her bow kept her arms toned and strong. She must have showed a piece of her undergarments because Dean was pointing at her legs and nudging Claude. For just a second, she worried about what had been revealed, but quickly reminded herself that Dean was all of seven and that he talked so much, hardly anyone listened to what he had to say.

The supposed talking bird was medium-sized. It had a long tail with green and blue plumage. Its neck was yellow, and its head was red. The bird looked at her, held its head upside down, and then when right-sided, spoke plainly, "Hot damn." Then it added in a husky voice, "Hello, beautiful lady."

What kind of creature is this? Charlotte thought.

The bird pranced back and forth on a branch fluffing its feathers and twisting every which way to preen and model. The under feathers were a lighter color and blended perfectly with the bird's plumage. Charlotte was certain that the feathers would be soft to the touch. The bird's feet were claw-like and an unusual color combination of pink and gray. They curled slightly and gripped the tree limb with each step. The creature's movements captivated Charlotte.

Next, the bird flew from its perch, landed on her shoulder, and started singing.

Every mornin', every evenin', ain't we got fun? Not much money, oh, but honey, ain't we got fun?

"Adam, run and get Mr. Ernest," Charlotte softly spoke. "Boys, find a place to sit real quiet like. I ain't wantin' to scare this creature."

The bird continued its repertoire.

Button up your overcoat when the wind is free. Take good care of yourself, you belong to me. Eat an apple every day, go to bed by three. Wear your flannel underwear when you climb a tree...

She could swear that Dean looked at her when the bird sang about tree climbing and flannel underwear.

Take good care of yourself, you belong to me.

The outrageous looking bird sang bar room song after bar room song. When Charlotte started singing hymns, the bird made background noises but obviously didn't know the lyrics.

"Hey, bubs, how about a cash?"

Charlotte had heard worse things at the moonshiners' races but hoped the boys didn't understand that the bird was talking about her breasts and asking for a kiss. She shushed the bird. Problem was, it shushed her right back.

"How about a gasper? I'm needin' some giggle water."

Ernest better get here soon, Charlotte thought.

"Hey, tomato. Whoopie!"

Perplexity gave way to disgust and then disgust to humor at the obscurity of the situation. She started to giggle yet felt ashamed at finding the vulgarity funny. She didn't want to expose her young charges to such words and thought of shooing the bird away when she saw Ernest running toward her.

About fifteen feet from the tree, Ernest stopped dead in his tracks. Charlotte was sitting on a tree limb with her feet dangling in the air hosting a parrot on her shoulder. He started laughing. He couldn't help it. When the parrot joined in, Ernest laughed even harder.

"Ernest," Charlotte spoke. "This bird is foul."

"All birds are fowl, Charlotte."

"I am talkin' foul, as in foul language."

The bird proceeded to pick at Charlotte's hair.

"I think it's removin' lice," Adam declared. "I've seen our chickens do that."

"I don't have lice," Charlotte quickly returned. "Ernest..."

Ernest approached the tree. "Charlotte, I ain't thinkin' you have lice. I'm thinkin' this parrot likes you."

Lottie sighed. The bird sighed in response.

As they headed back to the schoolhouse, Ernest felt almost jealous of the unusual bird who was enjoying such close proximity to Charlotte. The parrot was playing in Lottie's luscious locks and pecking gently at her dimpled check, almost like love taps.

He tried to bribe the bird with springtime seeds gathered along the path, but each time he approached the creature, it dug its claws into Charlotte's shoulders. In the bird's world—it was love—true love. The boys were enjoying their new-found friend; even Charlotte, though she still deemed the bird a reprobate, laughed a couple of times.

Ernest explained that parrots once lived in the Appalachian hills. As farms developed and the natural bamboo that grew in the wetlands diminished, the talking birds died off.

Ernest knew that parrots could live for up to 50 years. The bad boy who liked his sweet, gentle girl must have been someone's pet —maybe a sailor, a barkeep, a gambler, a moonshiner, or even a thief. Though he found the parrot entertaining, he didn't think that a God-fearing man would use such language. Of course, he had to admit that there were times when he thought such words but, other than during a couple of boyhood fights with Lester, they hadn't escaped his lips.

He ushered the boys ahead and spoke privately with Lottie.

"What are you thinkin'?"

"I'm thinkin' I would like a different best friend, Ernest."

"Anyone in mind?"

"A parrot has made his home or maybe her home on my shoulder, and you're flirtin'. It's shameful."

"Nothin' shameful about flirtin' with a pretty girl. I'm thinkin' the bird's a boy. Girls ain't usually so colorful. You know the good Lord made us men more attractive so the ladies would take a shine."

Lottie smiled. "How's that sayin' go? 'Beauty is in the eye of the beholder?'"

She started to whisper, "Ernest, I've got me some concerns about exposin' the learners to the…" Charlotte tipped her head toward the talking bird.

Ernest laughed again. This time it was a belly laugh. "Lottie, he doesn't understand what you're sayin'. You can speak plain. Parrots only mimic. He would need to hear somethin' over-and-over again in the same settin' to repeat the right words."

"I'm knowin' that, Ernest. It just seems wrong to speak bad about him when he's listening."

Ah, my sweet Lottie, Ernest thought.

It was decided that for the time being, the bird would go home with Charlotte. Ernest had laid some turkey traps not far from the schoolhouse. He thought the cage-like trap would hold the bird until a permanent solution was found, although that probably wasn't necessary, given the bird's attachment to Lottie.

They could always release him into the wild but agreed that since the parrot had obviously been a pet, survival in the outdoors was unlikely.

The boys, of course, wanted the talking bird to live with them. Ernest offered to visit with their daddy but thought that he and Charlotte should work on the parrot's language before giving placement with a Christian family.

Ernest addressed the boys, "We'll be teachin' him poems, verses and hymns. Maybe sayings like 'Bless you,' or 'Good mornin'.'"

"Ernest, I've been workin' on learnin' this bird how to say, 'God loves you,' and he ain't gettin' it right."

"Well, he's no evangelist that's for sure. I'm thinkin' if we can just get him to quit swearin' that we'll be doin' good."

Ernest had stopped by with one of his cage-like turkey traps, but, so far, the parrot seemed happy to perch on top of a pine cabinet in Charlotte's kitchen.

He didn't really like trapping animals, but food was necessary for survival. If a child started looking too thin, he or Charlotte would visit the home and bring a gift of newly harvested or canned meat, homemade bread or sweet treats, and, depending on the season, fresh or put up garden vegetables.

Walnuts were also prevalent in the hills and a good food source. Ernest knew that walnut trees released some type of chemical to keep other plants from growing too close to them. He enjoyed cracking the shells, picking out the meat, and eating the mild yet rich and buttery tasting nuts. God's way of providing for His children was miraculous.

"I heard you did some dancin' today." Charlotte smiled like a small child who had just revealed a secret.

"Who told you such nonsense?"

"A dancin' bear," she laughed.

"Charlotte, I ain't seen no dancin' bears in the hills. Only wild ones lookin' for food. Eatin' everythin' they find before and after hibernatin'."

"Well, I'm thinkin' that even the wild ones can dance a few steps."

"You're probably right, darlin'. It would grieve me to see a bear on a chain jumpin' around makin' money from people gawkin'. Some things just belong in the wild."

"Now, Ernest, the bear I'm talkin' about was certainly wild and had some wild young ones with him," she teasingly taunted.

"Charlotte, I like it when you laugh. In fact, there's a lot I'm likin' about you. Are we doin' alright now?"

"I'm thinkin' we're fine, Ernest. I didn't want to hear your words last night, but I was jealous. Jealous of Mercy and who she used to be to you."

"She's a friend, Charlotte. A hurtin' friend needin' help. You ain't got reason to be jealous." And, as a friend, Ernest's instinct was to track down the self-seeking animal who had done this to her.

Lottie closed her eyes and sighed. There was a look of disbelief arched in one eyebrow.

"My heart's beatin; for you," Ernest declared. "But it's too early to be sharin' all I feel. I think we're needin' time to grow in this newness."

"I'm agreein'."

Ernest drew her into his arms. He kissed the top of her head, then her cheek, and thought to himself, *Take that my feathered friend.* Lastly, he kissed her soft sweet lips.

Chapter Six

All wishes are shooting stars come true.

Appalachian Folk Belief

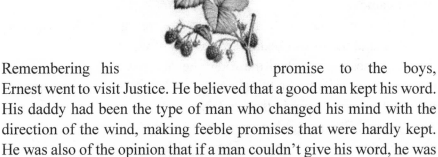

Remembering his 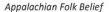 promise to the boys, Ernest went to visit Justice. He believed that a good man kept his word. His daddy had been the type of man who changed his mind with the direction of the wind, making feeble promises that were hardly kept. He was also of the opinion that if a man couldn't give his word, he was weak in spirit. His daddy also was prone to not making commitments. He didn't feel that others were important enough to merit attention over what he might be feeling for the day.

Ernest hoped to talk with Justice without the foursome present. He knew the boys were anxious to take the parrot home as their pet. Ernest wasn't sure how Justice and his wife would feel about living with a reprobate.

Lottie had named the parrot "Bullseye." Ernest said the name was fitting. Lottie's thoughts toward the bird seemed to range from disgust to affection depending on the character's antics. When the parrot became too much, she threatened to shoot him with her bow and arrow, thus the name Bullseye. Ernest could tell, however, that she was also becoming attached to the feathered fellow. The parrot's display of affections for Charlotte had not diminished. He was smitten. He sang, quoted verse, and tried to woo the lovely woman. He also had a thing about Charlotte's earlobes. It was ridiculous that he envied a bird!

No one was in the yard at Justice's home. The emptiness gave Ernest a moment to pause and savor the scents and sights of spring. There were flowers blooming along the front porch. The yellow daffodils, red tulips, and purple hyacinths created a spectacular foreground for the whitewashed clapboard house.

Ernest caught a glimpse of Amos and Andy sowing their oats in the fenced corral. He couldn't help but smile. The two ornery mules had given Ernest a run for his money on more than one occasion. They were cantankerous at best and just like the boys: full of mischief.

A smaller pen contained a sow and piglets, some of which would become fresh meat, bacon, and hams for Justice and his family before winter came.

The home was small and simple yet treasured. The windows sparkled, and the flower beds were cleared of weeds.

As Ernest approached the rough-hewn front door, Mercy called out a greeting. A large budding maple tree hung over the far corner of the porch where she sat in the shadows.

"Ernest, Charley told me you would come."

He felt a moment of panic. The only Charlie he knew was the man who had murdered his brother. *Had Charlie escaped from jail?*

"Charlie who!?"

Mercy seemed to stare right through him, "It's a game, Ernest. Charley answers my questions."

He didn't understand what Mercy was saying.

"Come look."

Mercy was sitting on a worn, wobbly, wooden chair with a small table in front of her. The table had been whitewashed to match the house. On top of the table was a yellowed paper with four squares. Each square had the word yes or no. Two narrow sticks were placed horizontally on the cross lines of the square. The sticks were smooth and well worn. The smaller of the sticks was sitting on top of the slightly larger stick.

Mercy began to explain the game. "Charley is a friend." Pausing she looked but didn't touch the sticks. "Charley, Charley, are you here?" The top stick moved slightly toward the word yes. "Charley, does Ernest love me?"

Ernest quickly and fiercely swept both sticks away and tossed them into the yard. The wind eerily lifted the paper from the table.

"Mercy, what are you doin'? Don't be callin' on evilness for help!"

"Ernest, it's just a game."

"It's not just a game or you wouldn't be hidin' from your daddy and mama."

"I'm a grown woman. I ain't hidin' from nobody."

"Mercy, what are you thinkin'? Who told you about this Charley?"

She didn't answer with words but looked down at her belly.

Ernest put both hands on his forehead and shook his head slightly.

Mercy's voice was barely above a whisper. "He told me that Charley was an old friend. He met him through a coal miner named Joaquin who hailed from a place called Spain. When we was together, we would play Charley Charley. At first, it was just funin'; then Charley started helpin' me. He told me to come back to the holler. That you was pinin' for me and would marry me and make this baby yours."

She stood and firmly grabbed Ernest's arm. "I know it's true. You're wantin' me. You wanted me that day at the church. I was knowin' it. I knew what you was thinkin'. You was workin' things out in your mind."

Guilt and shame washed over Ernest. He remembered the snowy day when he and Mercy, along with a few others, became stranded at Big Creek Church. She had refused his proposal, and in his mind, he had wondered about making her his own regardless. He had planned and plotted on how to seduce Mercy so she would have to marry him.

He pried Mercy's hand from his arm and walked away. As he left the yard, he looked back and saw Mercy frantically searching for the sticks.

Ernest had repented almost immediately of his impure and manipulative thoughts that day. He had even confessed his struggle to Lester. He remembered the relief it brought to confide in his brother. Ernest knew God had forgiven him. Now he knew that Mercy had understood his impure intentions, He was overwhelmed with humiliation and condemnation. Seduction was not the same as love. It was lust. Not only had he wanted Mercy's body, he had also wanted to control her thoughts and actions.

He had never visited the sea but had viewed pictures. The waves beating the shoreline appeared so powerful. Years ago when Ernest was a learner at Big Creek School, Mrs. Randolph showed the class pictures of the Atlantic Ocean. She talked about the crashing waves and had used the lesson to discuss onomatopoeias or words describing sounds.

Bang, bash, crash, clash, groan, growl, howl, pow, rattle, rip, rumble, sizzle, smack, thud, thump, wallop, wham, and yikes all seemed to describe how he felt now.

Ernest knew the ocean tides were determined by the interactions of the sun, moon, and earth. Ultimately God, the creator of all things, governed the deep. If an all-powerful God walked on the bottom of the sea and rode the waves to shore, He could part the waters once again and help Ernest walk on dry ground. As he meditated on God's power, Ernest's sinking feeling began to lift. The waves of emotion calmed, turning to trickles of hope and whispers of peace.

With the need to escape indignity and disgrace dissipating, his thoughts turned toward Mercy. She was playing with the fires of hell and knew better. Ignorance was one thing, but out and out disobedience to God was something else.

Charley Charley was an ancient male spirit. Ernest remembered the Bible story where King Saul became desperate and visited the Witch at Endor. The story relayed how the king went to her to receive direction from the Prophet Samuel who was once the king's advisor but was deceased. The witch summoned an evil spirit pretending to be the prophet.

The story taught that God has lifted his hand from Saul so that the

44

king could no longer hear from the Lord. As King Saul had turned to evil in his desperation for spiritual guidance, so had Mercy turned to evil. Ernest wondered at what point Mercy had decided she couldn't hear from her Maker and made the choice to turn to evil for help and direction.

He needed to leave. He would talk with Justice another time.

Charlotte was hanging clothes on the line. Each time she washed clothes, she thought of Ernest and his concern for her well-being. He devised a system that made scrubbing, wringing, and hanging her clothes easier. The washboard was purchased at Rudy's mama and daddy's store, and the wringer, Ernest's own design, involved pulling her clothes through two wooden boards. The clothesline posts were buried in the ground and stabilized with rocks and dirt.

Her unmentionables were already draped over ladder rungs inside the kitchen. It somehow seemed inappropriate for Ernest or the learners to see her undergarments blowing in the breeze. Her unique drying system involved resting a ladder across the backs of two chairs. The system had previously been effective. Now Bullseye, who liked to peck and nibble, was enjoying hopping from rung to rung. Who knew what he was doing to her ribbon trimmed step-ins?

She looked up from her work and saw Ernest walking toward her. She could tell by his gait that something was wrong. His steps were usually lively. He was also looking downwards. Normally, her beau enjoyed basking his face in the sunlight. She also knew that he took pleasure in cloud drawing; when walking alongside him, Ernest would often look at the puffs of white and help her create pictures from their curling designs. They had once laid on their backs in the sunshine and, drawing with their fingers to the sky, shared their imaginative artwork with one another. Ernest mostly saw animals. She mostly saw flowers and the faces of the holler children. Together, they mostly laughed.

Charlotte started to pray, beseeching God on behalf of her sweetheart.

Looking at Ernest, she felt overcome with the desire to sing. The

45

words and melody played loudly in her head and needed to be expressed. She didn't have the strength of voice and perfect pitch that Ernest displayed. She could, however, carry a simple tune and had often sung silly songs in her Lottie the Legend performances. Rarely, however, did she sing aloud for pleasure or even worship. Mostly, she sang in her heart or hummed softly. She hung the garment she was holding in her hands and lifted her voice.

Lord Jesus, I long to be perfectly whole; I want Thee forever to live in my soul; break down every idol, cast out every foe–Now wash me, and I shall be whiter than snow.

Whiter than snow, yes, whiter than snow. Now wash me, and I shall be whiter than snow. Lord Jesus, let nothing unholy remain, apply Thine own blood and extract every stain; To get this blest cleansing, I all things forego–Now wash me, and I shall be whiter than snow.

As she sang the chorus over-and-over again, the lyrics became a prayer for Ernest.

Whiter than snow, yes, whiter than snow. Now wash me, and I shall be whiter than snow.

Ernest knew that he had a way of sneaking up on people. Except when his students were up to mischief, however, it usually wasn't his intention to startle others. Lottie assumed his quiet ways were due to years of walking and hunting in the woods. She was partially right. He had been hunting practically since the time he could carry a gun or bow. If neither he nor Lester brought game meat home, the family went hungry.

Remembering the sight of his sisters' slightly hollowed faces when times were lean could still bring tears to his eyes. He had also learned at a young age that being overly loud could draw the unwanted attention of his daddy.

As he approached the schoolhouse, he saw Charlotte. She seemed not to notice him. He considered whistling to let her know of his presence but then thought better.

It would do his heart good to let his eyes rest on her for a few moments with his muse unaware. He admired her gracefulness and beauty. She was lovely. Although her long hair was coiled, wisps of her locks had escaped. They were fluttering in the breeze like butterflies.

He wondered what she was up to. With a few clothes on the line and an almost full basket of items ready to hang, Lottie stood inert there. Maybe she was simply enjoying the spring day. He knew that she would eventually sense his gaze and look his way, but in the meantime, he purposed to enjoy the view.

He needed to tell her about Mercy, about the strange evil game, and about Mercy's insistence that he still had romantic feelings for her. No matter the consequences, he didn't want to keep secrets from Charlotte. He didn't want to hurt her. In fact, he wanted to protect her. Yet, the truth had to be told.

In his mind, he understood that he was responsible for speaking plainly and that Lottie was responsible for her reasonings and reactions. He couldn't control her responses. His heart, however, told him something different than his mind. If he used only choice words and told her bits of truth, maybe she would be at peace and not worry.

Ernest saw Charlotte wave to greet him and knew that his time of quietly watching her was over. He lifted his arm, sweeping the air, and headed her way. Charlotte met him between the schoolhouse and her home.

"Heart," she spoke.

It was the first time she had used an endearment. When she opened her arms to Ernest, he stepped into her embrace and drew her close.

"I've been singin' about you," she said very seriously.

Ernest was baffled by the tone of her voice and reluctantly broke their embrace.

Lottie hesitated, "I've been singin' to God."

Whiter than snow, yes, whiter than snow. Now wash me, and I shall be whiter than snow.

"What's happened, Ernest? Why would you be thinkin' that God can't make you clean? You know His teachin's. He washes away all

47

such messes."

Ernest was overwhelmed by God's goodness. He took Charlotte's hand. "We need to find a place to sit. This is gonna take a spell."

From the clothesline, she gathered a lightweight blanket that had quickly dried in the warm May breeze. The couple found a sun filled resting spot and sat down.

Ernest placed his arm around Charlotte's shoulders and thanked her for praying and singing over him. He recounted what happened with Mercy, past and present. Embarrassed, he shared as delicately as possible his shame and the reasons behind it.

"Ernest, you're human. You loved Mercy and had marryin' on your mind."

"Don't be makin' excuses for me. It was more than that. I was wantin' to control her actions to get my way."

"The past is the past. Ain't nothin' you can do to change it. You've talked with God, and He's forgiven you. He loves you and doesn't want you dwellin' on foolishness. We've all got things that need to stay behind us."

Ernest shut his eyes. With lips tucked in together, he nodded yes.

"I ain't worried about what was between you and Mercy. I asked God for help, and He's done give me peace. What I'm worried about is how's she actin' and thinkin' now. She is messin' with bad things. And truth be told, I'm not just worried for her, I'm worried for you. She's manipulatin' and playin' games with your mind. I'm concerned for us, Ernest, and rightly so."

"Lottie darlin' there ain't no need to be worryin' especially about the two of us."

Ernest spoke the words, but he knew that the unresolved issues and the concern about how to help Mercy were like a dark cave. It was impossible to know where the cave would lead and what would be encountered along the way.

It was early evening. The days were getting longer and the nights shorter which suited Ernest just fine. He was glad spring had arrived in the hills. When the days were shorter, the hills seemed gloomy. At these times, Ernest considered perhaps the hills were lonely; lonely for sun and warmth like those who lived in the Appalachians during fierce winters.

He was puttering at the schoolhouse. His students were ready for summer break. As their teacher, he concurred that school dismissal couldn't come soon enough.

If it was up to Ernest, he would spend all his time with Charlotte. Wisdom told him different. The situation with Mercy brought complexity to their relationship. He also remembered the agreement with his gal to take things slowly. He had said the words, but really, he was ready to sweep her off her feet, declare his love, marry her quickly, and begin building a life together.

Of course, in a sense, they were already building a life together. They lived within a stone's throw of each other. They worked together with the learners. They often shared meals, laughed together, talked a blue streak, and enjoyed their surroundings. It wasn't every day that a man found a squirrel hunting companion so pretty. Ernest was, however, looking for more. He wanted tender moments: touching, kissing…

He even liked the way Lottie smelled. Her scent reminded him of the pleasant sweet fragrance of passion flowers. They bloomed in the hills from early spring until late in the fall. Mrs. Randolph once told him that the light purple flowers represented devotion. He felt both passion and devotion for Lottie and believed that she felt the same for him.

He had every intention of marrying the lovely Lottie. Until that time, he was determined to keep his thoughts and feelings in check. He had learned there were particular things a man shouldn't dwell on until the time was right. There were also boundaries that a couple shouldn't cross until they were married.

Ernest's musings were interrupted by Justice's deep voice.

"Ernest, I hope I ain't disturbin'."

The two men shook hands and then soundly patted each other on the back.

"I'm glad you came callin'. I was lookin' for you earlier today. Wantin' to talk about that ornery bird your boys found."

Justice chuckled. "I hear he's the cussin' kind. I ain't rightly heard of a bird that can talk. And truth be told, them boys is takin' too much pleasure in tellin' all the words the bird is knowin'."

"I'm thinkin' he needs to stay with Charlotte for a while. She's workin' on cleanin' him up, but it'll take some time."

"I'll let my boys know. They'll be a mite disappointed, but there's enough goin' on to keep 'um occupied."

When one of Justice's big brown eyes twitched, Ernest knew that his friend had come to talk business–serious business.

"I'm needin' to talk about Mercy, Ernest. She ain't actin' right."

Ernest knew that Justice wasn't aware of Mercy's secret game. He hated to be the one to tell him but knew he didn't have a choice–when evil was kept in the dark and not exposed to the light, it flourished all the more. He knew if he didn't tell Justice, that it was the same as calling evil good, calling light darkness, and calling sweet bitter.

"Justice, she's playin' with fire. Seekin' dark advice. She calls it a game, but it's more than that."

Ernest explained about Mercy's fortune-telling game and the strange behavior he had witnessed earlier in the day.

"She was actin' desperate to find the sticks," he added.

Justice was overwrought, "What am I to do?"

Assuming the question was rhetorical, Ernest didn't answer.

"You know she's convinced that you're gonna marry her and give the baby your name."

"She told me such, but I ain't said nothin' to the like. I want to help, but I ain't knowin' how."

"I'm not wantin' to pressure, but I'm askin' for help," Justice declared. "Her mama and me want to stand by whilst you tell her the truth about your feelin's. She needs to hear it plain. It'll pain her, but it's got to be done."

"What about the game?" Ernest asked. "She won't be right until she gets rid of it."

"I'm thinkin' we'll include that in the truth tellin'."

Chapter Seven

It's bad luck to cut your fingernails on Friday or Sunday.

Appalachian Folk Belief

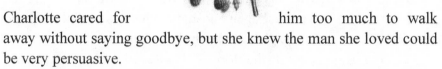

Charlotte cared for him too much to walk away without saying goodbye, but she knew the man she loved could be very persuasive.

He was strong in form and character. When he crossed his arms over his chest and looked at the learners intently, they took notice and did their best. Discipline was not a problem in the classroom. The students weren't frightened of their teacher but respectful. They knew him to be kind, fair, and, when needed, stern.

She wasn't a child, and Ernest didn't intimidate her. There was something about his mannerisms and inner strength that inspired her, like the children, to do and be her best. She liked his name, Ernest. She considered how well it suited him.

Though it had been too soon for them to confess their love for each other, Charlotte reckoned how she felt, and Ernest's gaze and touch told her he felt much the same. She had already loved and lost one of the Ashby brothers and prayed that it wouldn't happen again. Grief came in a variety of forms: the passing of someone loved, the slow process of isolation or alienation, and the separation of one so dear that the heart felt torn in two.

It pained her to leave the hills. After visiting with Justice, she didn't feel like she could stay. A simple greeting between two friends had turned into a conversation that continued to churn in her heart.

Mercy was in a bad way. Apparently, Justice felt Ernest was the key to getting his daughter righted. *A key is a funny thing,* Lottie thought. She had once read a children's book about a magic key stolen by a pirate. The key was said to open hidden treasure chests. Once the key was in his possession, the pirate hung it around his neck. At first, the heavy key was a trophy. He held it and caressed it. With the passing of time, and with the search for hidden treasures proving unsuccessful, the key became a weight that caused his shoulders to slump and his head to stoop.

She hoped that Justice didn't think that her beloved was in possession of a magic key. Magic keys were for children who believed in fantasy.

Her small suitcase was packed. The worn brown, black, and red plaid bag held a Lottie the Legend costume, changes of clothing, and a couple of small trinkets given to her by her charges.

Placing her suitcase on the stoop, she gathered her bow and quiver and blew a kiss to Bullseye. Then, as she closed the door to her home, Bullseye's mimic of her voice saying, *God bless you,* brought a smile to her lips.

She left her load outside the schoolhouse where Ernest was working. She wanted to use words, not visuals, to communicate what needed to be said.

"Darlin', it's good to be seein' you."

She smiled at Ernest's greeting; not a toothy smile, but a whisper of a smile–slight and soft.

"Lottie, are you doin' fine?" His gaze rambled over her. "You ain't lookin' right as rain."

"I ain't thinkin' it's gonna rain today, Ernest."

"I ain't talkin' about rain comin' down from the sky. I'm talkin' about the clouds gathered in your eyes with drops makin' ready to fall."

Ernest took her hand and guided her to the bench at the back of the schoolhouse.

Ernest was a kind and considerate man; his ability to wait was one of the things she treasured most about him. Yet here and now, Charlotte knew that Ernest was anxious to hear her thoughts.

She thought about Saul in the Bible who had grown impatient while waiting for Samuel. Saul took matters into his own hands. His desire to rush the process had created trouble. Then his unwillingness to acknowledge his weakness for taking charge when he wasn't in charge created even more trouble.

There was a time for everything. It showed character and maturity that Ernest could wait until she was ready.

"Ernest," Charlotte began. "I had a sit-down with Justice last night as he was leavin' the schoolhouse."

Ernest released her hand and turned to face her more directly. "Did you and Justice sit down and enjoy a visit, or are you talkin' about sharin' words that have taken a sit down deep in your heart?"

"The latter."

"Charlotte, it wasn't my intention to be keepin' secrets…"

"This is the first I've seen you since yesterday. I ain't here cause I think you're keepin' secrets." She hesitated slightly. She was achin' inside. She dreaded tellin' her best friend and beau about her departure. "I'm leavin', Ernest."

He tried to take it in. Then, Ernest acted on his shock and irritation. "Lottie, are you leavin' me or leavin' the hills? They ain't the same thing."

Lottie knew that Ernest was trying to understand what she had said. Worry and confusion were etched on his face. She closed her eyes and sighed. "I'm just goin' for a spell. Mercy's needin' you."

"You didn't answer my question, darlin'–"

"I'm wantin' to give you a rest to figure things out."

"I ain't needin' a rest. I've figured out plenty. I know it ain't proper to be sayin' it now, but I love you. My dreams for the future are bein' built around you."

Charlotte kissed his check. "I love you, too, Ernest, but I'm still goin'."

Ernest clenched his hands, not because of anger but because of extreme frustration. He hung his head. "I'm wantin' to talk you outa' this…"

"I was knowin' you would, but please listen to my reasonin'."

"I ain't likin' it and I'm wantin' to argue, but I'm listenin'."

She took Ernest's hand and linked their fingers together. As she spoke, her thumb caressed his thumb. His hands were coarse and rough. One of his nails was crooked and torn at the corner. She admired his hands. They represented his hard work.

During a Sunday morning sermon, Pastor Rex explained to the Big Creek congregation that hands represented spiritual work. The right hand was the hand of strength and the left hand the hand of compassion. Lottie thought that Ernest was a wonderful example of firmness and mercy. She often witnessed how powerful yet gentle his works and words were toward the learners, his family, and even her. She was already missing him.

"I'm not leavin' you. I'm leavin' the hills for a time," Lottie explained. "When things are settled with Mercy, you can come fetch me, or I'll come on home. It pains me, but I'm thinkin' that I need to let you be. You're needin' to do what you can for Mercy and her family.

"I know her life is hangin' by a thread, and I can't be distractin' you from matters of heaven. If you're worryin' about what I'm thinkin' and feelin', you might miss what God's askin' of you. I'm wantin' to go to Charleston with Coral. I know Pastor Rex will be with her, but since I know the city some, maybe I can be of help."

Ernest mumbled, "I ain't never heard of a gal leavin' her man for his sister."

"Thank you, Ernest."

"I don't think you should be thankin' me."

Charlotte sighed with relief, "Thank you for lettin' me go and not fightin'. I couldn't bear it if I left and you was angry." She kissed Ernest once again on the check. "A kiss should always be remembered."

"Lottie, you ain't needin' to worry. I won't be forgettin' your kisses.

Her eyes grew big, and, with a mischievous look, she leaned over and kissed Ernest once again on the cheek. "Thank you also for lookin' after Bullseye…"

Ernest spent the remainder of the morning at the schoolhouse. With only a couple of days of school remaining, he packed up books and cleared the walls of pictures and lessons completed by the students. Generally, the learners helped him organize for summer repairs and cleaning, but he wanted to keep busy.

He was already missing Lottie. Her presence soothed and comforted him. She brought peace, among other things, into his world. She was like the tree in Psalm 1. Her roots were deeply planted by streams of water; her life produced fruit that Ernest was privileged to witness and enjoy. Her spiritual tree was bountiful. Others could rest under her branches and find solace. He kept reminding himself that goodbyes shouldn't be painful if you're planning on saying hello again.

It took all his strength to let her go. He didn't like her walking down the mountain by herself. He didn't like her walking out of his life and prayed that their season of separation would pass quickly. They reached an agreement that she would call Rudy's parents' store in Big Creek each week. She would leave a message for him. In turn, he would call to leave a message for her.

He also thought about the mama bear and baby bears who were roaming close by. He quickly mentioned Charlotte's safety to the Lord. He recalled that on a snowy day recorded in the Bible, one of David's mighty men killed a bear with his hands. It was a warm spring day in Big Creek. The snow had disappeared in the holler and was almost gone in the high country. Lottie was a strong woman, the strongest woman he knew. She had internal strength and physical strength. She could bend a bow like no other. He worried for her yet knew that his love had God's power and strength inside of her. He also knew that she was wise and level-headed. If trouble came her way, she would act quickly and with confidence.

Though Lottie could care for herself, Ernest wanted to protect her. He wanted to be her hero. He wondered, however, what could be more heroic than the action of prayer? Through prayer, giants were defeated, enemies were conquered; even bears and lions were taken to task.

He was dreading his visit with Mercy. He hated the thought of hurting her. They had once been close friends—*and more*. It seemed cruel to openly and directly tell her that his feelings had changed. He was also concerned about her game playing and prayed that she would listen to truth and reason.

He reluctantly removed the last of the schoolwork the learners had displayed while chuckling at the limericks they had penned. His students had enjoyed the challenge of working the strict rhyme schemes.

There once was a camel named Gus. Who traveled the desert a mus. His hump was so high. That it reached toward the sky. Creating a stir and a fuss.

As he headed out the door, his thoughts drifted, and, of all things, he began to think about camels: their two sets of eyelashes protecting them from the desert sand, their ability to close their nostrils, and their tendency to spit.

Well, not really spit, Ernest thought. *More like precise vomit directin'.*

Camels can bring up their stomach contents and saliva and then aim the foul spew to distract whatever is threatening them.

Mercy's game was like a spitting camel—repugnant, covering Mercy and others with vomit and bile.

As Ernest entered the yard, he greeted Justice. The springtime grass was splotchy. It was obvious someone had been uprooting the ever-invasive dandelions. The greens probably had been cooked and seasoned heavily with salt.

One spring, Mrs. Randolph had insisted that her learners plant a garden. The fruits of their labor would be donated to Big Creek Church for distribution to those in need. The students had used L.H. Bailey's book on gardening as a guideline for their efforts. Regarding the practice of weeding, the author had instructed, *the man who worries morning and night about the dandelions in the garden will find great relief in loving the dandelions.*

Ernest had to acknowledge the truth of the writer's words. When dandelion greens were cooked properly, they were mighty delicious.

His host was sitting on the front steps of the house. It was unusual for Justice to sit and rest. Generally, his energy knew no bounds. He worked from sunup to sundown and could tire a man half his age.

"If the time's right, I've come to see Mercy."

"She's ailin', Ernest, and won't get out of bed."

Ernest grew concerned, "If she's poorly, should I get Doc Bright?"

"I ain't thinkin' it's her body. I found them Charley sticks and broke 'um into pieces. Mercy took to her bed cryin'. I sent the boys to play and told their mama to go visitin'. Mercy was scarin' 'um all."

Ernest took a deep breath. "Justice, we can't be leavin' her like this. We need to pray and tell the evil to be gone."

"I'm knowin' such, but if she ain't willin' to let go, it'll get worse."

"I'm familiar with what you're sayin', but we can't just let her be."

Justice nodded in agreement. When they walked through the front door, Ernest could hear Mercy calling for Charley. "Charley, Charley I'm needin' you. Are you there? Answer me, Charley…"

Justice directed Ernest to the back bedroom. The covers were thrown to the floor and the curtains were torn. Tangled in her soiled dress, Mercy was lying on the bed. Portions of her hair had been pulled out by the roots, and her eyes were wild.

"Ernest, you've come. I knew you would. Charley told me…"

"We're not talkin' about Charley anymore, Mercy."

Ernest placed his hands on Mercy's head. "Evil spirit we're commandin' you to leave in the name of Jesus."

Mercy cried out. She groaned in a way that almost sounded like a growl. When she started uttering strange words, Ernest boldly told the evil spirit to be quiet.

Ernest stood on one side of the bed and Justice on the other side. They prayed loudly and with authority for Mercy to be freed. At first, nothing happened, but they wouldn't give place to evil and continued their petitions for Mercy.

When Mercy started coughing, Justice wiped the sputum from his daughter's mouth with a handkerchief. The coughing ceased, and Mercy laid her head on the pillow exhausted.

"Mercy, are you free?" her father asked.

She nodded yes and then hid her face in her hands. Ernest and Justice could barely hear her words, "I was just wantin' help. Needin' to know what to do. I was feelin' alone, desperate."

Justice gently removed Mercy's hands from her face. "Daughter, I love you and God loves you. You're needin' to ask His forgiveness and go back to livin' and doin' right. You can't be messin' with evil. It'll overtake you if you invite it."

As Justice led his daughter in a prayer for help, Ernest stood back and witnessed the love of an earthly father and the heavenly Father for this child.

Bullseye was in distress. He wouldn't quit talking.

Ernest understood how the bird felt and it wasn't doing his own heart any good to hear Lottie's voice mimicked. His girl had grown attached to the bird; he didn't share those same feelings. Though the bird could be very entertaining, his constant chatter was wearing. Since parrots could live for 50 plus years, Ernest secretly hoped that Bullseye's years on earth had already been long and happy. It was apparent, they had been extremely interesting.

Ernest's private room was sparse. The cushioned chair next to his bed was often his place of choice to prepare lessons, grade papers, read, and pray. The chair was a cast off. The cushion sagged, the fabric was long-ago faded; yet Ernest felt comfortable there. At least he had until Bullseye took up residence. His mind was already filled with noise about Lottie and Mercy. Now his ears rang with the parrot's obnoxious voice.

Ernest closed the door to his sleeping quarters leaving Bullseye behind and headed to his desk in the schoolhouse. The teacher was proud of the progress his students were making. Most were working at grade level, and those who weren't would receive the needed help throughout the summer months. Just as Ernest began his work, Bullseye began his own work as well.

Hello, hello.

Ernest knew that the words came from Bullseye, yet they sounded so much like Lottie that his heart skipped a beat.

Hello, hello, hello.

With each "hello," the bird's voice raised in pitch.

Something's wrong, Ernest thought. *No one is in the room, so who is the parrot greeting.*

Back in his room, he heard the rattle before he saw the snake. By the number of rattles and body length, the snake looked to be mature. Ernest knew, however, that rattles weren't always an accurate way to judge the age of a snake. Supposedly, each time the snake shed its skin, a new rattle was added. A snake's life wasn't easy, though, and rattles could be lost.

It was commonplace, especially in spring, to see snakes in the hills and sometimes in the primitive houses of the hill inhabitants. Ernest gathered a shovel, corralled the creature, and lifted it from the rough wood hewn floor. At first, he thought to save the pest. After all, snakes are the best killers of other pests: mice, rats, and gophers.

Then he was reminded of the snake in the Garden and its deceptive ways. He thought of Mercy and the deceptive game she had been playing. He thought of Coral facing Charlie's deception. He also thought of sweet Lottie standing by Coral's side fighting snakes unseen. He took the snake outside. Before it could slither away, he used the shovel to remove the head, and then the rattles. He placed the rattles in his pocket and buried the head. Even decapitated, a rattle snake can bite and kill any creature that dares to play with its head. With the shovel, he carried the dismembered snake to the edge of the woods. By night, the snake would be another creature's dinner.

Ernest couldn't help but smile as he headed back to his desk. While he had appreciated that Bullseye's greeting had served as a warning, he chuckled knowing that snakes are essentially deaf. Bullseye had wasted his chiding words on Mr. Rattler.

The granny witches in the holler believed that snakes visited in pairs, and if one snake was killed, the other would return for vengeance. Ernest knew it was nonsense. He wondered what the grannies would have to say if they knew male snakes had two penises.

Chapter Eight

A watermelon will grow in your stomach if you
swallow a watermelon seed.

Appalachian Folk Belief

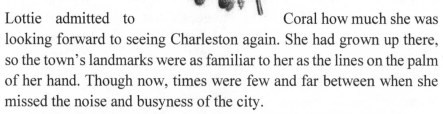

Lottie admitted to Coral how much she was looking forward to seeing Charleston again. She had grown up there, so the town's landmarks were as familiar to her as the lines on the palm of her hand. Though now, times were few and far between when she missed the noise and busyness of the city.

Living near Ernest, in the hills, Lottie's heart had discovered a new home. She missed him now. His familiar walk, his gift of song, his playful conversations, and his tireless efforts with the learners were treasures she had left behind. In the end, she hoped that her decision to leave Ernest alone for a time would draw them closer and wouldn't divide their loyalties.

The City of Charleston had experienced her own divided loyalties. During the Civil War, the allegiance of her residents split the state between the Union and Confederacy. When Virginia succeeded from the Union, the northwest portion of Virginia became its own state, West Virginia, with Charleston as her capital.

The penitentiary was located on the outskirts of the city. The two-story stone gothic building with a center turret looked ominous to say the least and was rumored to be haunted. Over the years, the white stones at the base of the building had been discolored by the red West Virginia soil. The locals referred to the hue as prison blood.

One of the well-known prisoners was said to have been tried by ghosts. A young husband was convicted of killing his bride based on the testimony of the victim's mother. The mother told the court that a ghost revealed to her the truth regarding her daughter's death; supernatural experiences held sway.

With the structure visible in the distance, Lottie and Coral walked a few paces behind Pastor Rex. Lottie tried to see the threesome as a formidable foe to anyone or anything wanting to harm them; yet she felt intimidated. In her mind's eye, Charlie had become a monster with fangs and claws.

Before setting out on their journey that morning, Pastor Rex and the young women had discussed in detail what their trip to the prison would entail. The elderly pastor then spoke with the warden and made the visiting arrangements. All set to go, the trio prayed. Coral had led them in singing the Battle Hymn of the Republic, which she said was fitting.

Mine eyes have seen the glory of the coming of the Lord; He is trampling out the vintage where the grapes of wrath are stored; He has loosed the fateful lightning of His terrible swift sword. His truth is marching on. Glory, glory, hallelujah! Glory, glory, hallelujah! Glory, glory, hallelujah! His truth is marching on...

Lottie's tough-girl heart was especially wooed by the last verse.

In the beauty of the lilies Christ was born across the sea, with a glory in his bosom that transfigures you and me; As he died to make man holy, let us die to make men free, While God is marching on...

A southern gal, Charlotte was taught the lyrics were penned during the Civil War by a young woman while visiting Union army camps. Some Southerners didn't care for the song, but Lottie felt differently. It was part of her country's history and contained a strong, solid, and substantial message. The truth about God was living and powerful to her. Christ died to make men holy and free.

Charlotte and Coral walked hand in hand along the narrow wooden sidewalk. It was important to stand close together. The shoulders of the two friends were touching. The road beside them was traveled by horses with riders on their backs, mule drawn carts, and automobiles whose drivers wore goggles and gloves. Each mode of transportation jostled for its own space.

She remembered talking with Ernest about the need to forgive Charlie. The words had come easily. Now, knowing that she would soon face her husband's murderer, forgiveness seemed far away and unattainable.

"Sister, since God is with us, nobody can be causin' us harm." As Lottie spoke the words, she realized they were as much for herself as for Coral.

"I'm agreein', but at the same time, my heart is racin', my hands are sweatin', and my mouth is so dry that it's hard to speak."

"Pastor Rex said Charlie will be chained. He won't be able to touch us."

"I'm understandin' such, but what happens if I made all this up in my mind, and we ain't really supposed to be here?" Coral then turned to Lottie, "Does the good Lord protect us even if we're bein' foolish?"

Lottie softly squeezed her friend's hand. "You ain't bein' foolish. You heard from God and are listenin' to His ways. We're like soldiers marchin' to tell the truth about God."

"I know what you're sayin' is true. I'm just scared. I'm like a rabbit lookin' for a hole. How do I go about startin' my talk with Charlie?" Coral asked. "I've been playin' the talk over in my mind. I know what I'm needin' to say, but I don't know how to go about startin'."

"I'm not sure," Lottie answered. "I'm battlin' some things in my own mind. I came to aid you, but right now I'm as empty as a bucket tryin' to draw water from a dried up well."

"Bein' with me is plenty help. I was painin' until you joined me and Pastor Rex on the train."

"I almost missed the departin'."

Coral's pale blue eyes smiled.

"I didn't tell you what happened, Coral, but I came across a mama bear and her two cubs. They was feedin' on blackberries. It ain't time yet for the berries to be ripe, but they was enjoyin' them just the same. I waited quiet like, hopin' not to be noticed. Them bears got good noses, though. The mama smelled me. I was worried and gettin' ready to draw my bow. But, when I looked at them babies, I couldn't to do. The cubs would die without their mama carin' for 'um. I prayed and asked God to keep me. I felt like someone else was rememberin' me at that moment. I wasn't even fearin' much. The mama looked right at me. She stared awhile and then took off with them cubs followin' behind."

"Sister, God was watchin' out for you. He was knowin' that I needed you. Trains are always leavin' the depot, Lottie, but He knew which one you needed to take, and He got you there just in time. That's what counts."

The warden's office smelled musty. The walls were stained with water marks. Worn wooden floors were dingy from neglect. It appeared that housekeeping was not a prison priority. Since the room was stifling and the windows remained closed, Coral assumed the barred dirty panes were painted shut.

The warden used a handkerchief to wipe the sweat from his brow. "He's refusin', and I can't make him. Now, he says he'll see the ladies one by one or together, but he ain't got no use for a pastor."

"Well, nobody will be visitin' then," Pastor Rex declared. "We've come a long way, and this is a mite disappointin'."

Coral felt a stab in her heart. Not a physical stab but a spiritual stab, and it wasn't just a prick but a penetrating perforation puncturing her heart. God had called her to tell Charlie about His great love. How could the warden be saying that Pastor Rex couldn't be present? She looked to Charlotte for strength, hoping that some secret message of encouragement and empowerment could be read on her friend's face.

Coral witnessed Lottie take a deep breath and slowly release the air from her lungs. It was as if she was saying, *all is well.*

The Ashby girls were known for their stubbornness and occasional bouts of anger. Coral felt that anger was a strong word for how she eventually expressed her pent-up frustrations. Annoyance, exasperation, vexation, displeasure, and chagrin seemed like better word choices to describe her general demeanor when it came to anger. Today, however, anger seemed like the best description. She was angry at Charlie. It was obvious that his manipulating manners had not changed. Of course, if he had changed and was serving Jesus there would be no need for her message.

"Pastor Rex, Warden, please forgive my interruptin'," Coral began. "I'm here on a mission, and I won't be givin' up on seein' Charlie."

Coral looked toward the warden, "Now if Charlie is willin' to visit me and Charlotte, there ain't no need for waitin'."

Pastor Rex look stunned. "Coral, your family entrusted you to my care. You can't be visitin' Charlie unless I'm by your side."

"God brought Charlotte. He knew this would happen."

"I can't be obligin'."

"Pastor, please, I'm needin' to see Charlie. I mean no disrespect. You're a good man, a good pastor, but the Holy Spirit is leadin' me. Now, I can't say no. I ain't wantin' to pain you. I'd rather you agreed and let me and Charlotte be about visitin'. I'm hopin' and prayin' that you'll do some considerin'."

"How old are you?" the warden interjected.

"Old enough," Coral answered.

The warden looked at Pastor Rex, "Pastor, she's a mite young for visiting the likes of Charlie, but with the other gal joining her, I'll allow it. There'll be an officer present, and you can stand outside the door with another one of my men."

Pastor Rex seemed to ignore the warden's words. He looked right at Coral. His lips were drawn tightly together. Coral could see the deep wrinkles around his eyes and across his scrunched forehead. He looked foreboding, but she knew him to be kind and gracious in speech and actions. His displeasure wasn't directed at her but at the situation at large.

"When David went to battle with Goliath," Coral began. "No one thought he was able. But, usin' only a rock, he hit the giant in the forehead. I'm thinkin' that the rock stands for the Word of God. I know some verses. David didn't even wear any armor because the armor Saul had didn't fit him. The Bible says that I've got armor. And, David didn't have a friend at his side helpin'; yet, I got Charlotte."

Because Coral was prone to quietness, it didn't bother her to wait and let her words sink in. Her sister, Emie, could talk a badger into being nice. Badgers were fierce animals. They could even fight wolves and bears. Coral, however, didn't want to argue with Pastor Rex. She respected him. She didn't want to convince or persuade; she preferred that the Holy Spirit speak to his heart and change his mind. She prayed in her heart for harmony. Music was beautiful to behold when everyone played their instruments and lifted their voices harmonizing in the same key.

"Coral, this is against my better judgment," the pastor began, "In my mind, it ain't right. But in my heart, I am knowin' that you need to listen to God. With the warden's permission, I'd like to share a word with the officer who'll be in the room. You have a powerful passion for what needs done, but I don't want those feelin's overridin' good sense."

Pastor Rex put his hand on Charlotte's shoulder, "I'm lookin' for the officer and for Charlotte to call an end to any foolishness from Charlie. He's a snake. He'll be shakin' his rattles tryin' to rattle everyone that's in the room. When he goes too far and a strike's comin', that's when I'm askin' that you leave."

Coral took Pastor's Rex's hand. "I understand about snakes. Rattlers live in the rocks in the holler. They like to take in the sun. The Bible says that it's worship. I'm guessin' that's between the snake and its Maker. I ain't beholdin' to snakes, Pastor."

Coral and Charlotte sat at a stained wooden table. Their chairs were rickety and splintered. The room was dark and dismal. The walls were greyish white. Except for the badge on the officer's chest, there was no adornment in the room, not even a dirtied window to let in a glimmer of light. Coral willed herself to look directly at the door. She could hear Lottie praying under her breath. She knew that Pastor Rex was waiting outside the door with a second officer, but she still felt frightened.

"Well, howdy do, Pastor."

Coral and Charlotte simultaneously shuddered. Charlie's sarcastic stammer was recognizable anywhere. After acknowledging Pastor Rex, he entered the door with a lopsided swagger, like he was king of the gloomy prison castle, like those in attendance–from petty thieves to the criminally insane–were his servants. He was dressed, however, more like a jester. Coral thought that the black and white suit should come with juggling balls.

With chains binding his hands and feet and a third chain connecting the two, Charlie struggled to sit. "Ladies, it's so nice that you came callin'. I wasn't expectin' such finery. Charlotte it looks like your grievin' is past, and Coral you is done grown and lovely for beholdin'."

The officer cleared his throat. Charlie, who had been playing the fool, quieted.

Authority is somethin' powerful, Coral thought. *God, thank you that you're all powerful.*

Before Coral had the chance to speak, Lottie rushed in. "Charlie, I'm workin' on forgivin' you. I ain't there yet, but I'm tryin'. Name callin' words are wantin' to escape my lips, but I'm holdin' 'um back. This visit is about Coral havin' a message for you, and I'm only here to be helpin' her."

Coral was relieved that Charlotte had opened the door on her behalf. She had heard about men working in elaborate hotels who opened doors for guests. They supposedly dressed in fancy dark suits with gold epaulets. Coral had trouble picturing Lottie in such a costume but instead envisioned her with bow and arrow in hand ushering weary travelers into the safety of a temporary home and hearth.

Charlie looked at Coral and raised his head slightly, gesturing for her to speak.

"I am bringin' a message, Charlie, a message from God."

Charlie burst out laughing. "Girlie, I done heard plenty of such messages. Mostly from cloaked men looking for a dollar for each word spoke. My pappy among 'um. While I still find your innocent ways refreshing, I ain't wantin' to hear the message you're bringin'."

"Charlie, please…"

"I'll tell you what darlin' Coral, you're a beauty for sure. When Emie did her dirty dealin', I was of a mind to marry you. So, I'll listen, but to stories about the holler. Tell me about them mulberry bushes. Are they ripe and ready for eatin'?"

She knew it was a sign–a sign from the Lord. Her first conversations with God about visiting Charlie had taken place under the mulberries.

Coral talked about the berries and their changing colors. She described the birds and squirrels who feasted on the fruit. She mentioned homemade jam and buttermilk biscuits. Charlie sat in silence breathing in her words.

"Mrs. Randolph once told the Big Creek learners that the game Here We Go Round the Mulberry Bush came from lady prisoners. They was exercisin' in the yard around a mulberry tree when one of them made up the ditty and game."

"Well, Coral, my lovely," Charlie snickered, "ain't that nice me bein' in prison and such?"

The officer, who had stood stoically and silently throughout the visit, raised his voice, "Visiting time is now over."

"Ladies, come back and visit real soon," Charlie said bitingly. "I've a final request," he added. "On my departin', I want you to sing me a song."

Coral's soft sweet voice rang true as the officer grabbed Charlie's arm, lifting him from the chair, and escorted him through the wooden door. The door represented the cause of Christ. It had a cross etched on the upper portion and a Bible reflected below.

The love of God is greater far than tongue or pen can ever tell. It goes beyond the highest star and reaches to the lowest hell. The guilty pair bowed down with care, God gave His Son to win. His erring child He reconciled and pardoned from his sin. Oh, love of God, how rich and pure! How measureless and strong! It shall forevermore endure – the saints' and angels' song..."

Coral began to shiver and shake. Charlotte was instantly at her side, holding her close.

"Lottie. I was so frightened."

"You did good, Coral. God told you to share His love, and I've never seen a finer display of preachin'."

Standing in the doorway, Pastor Rex nodded his appreciation, "I couldn't agree more."

Chapter Nine

To make it rain, kill a snake and
turn it belly up.

Appalachian Folk Belief

Since it was the last day of school, Ernest had several surprises in store for the learners. He wished that Lottie was present to join in the festivities. He missed his gal.

The day was warm. The sun shone brightly. Buds on the trees were opening, and a floral scent was in the air. From his desk, Ernest spied a red robin sitting on the schoolhouse window ledge singing a mellow song. Some hill folk believed that the robin received its red chest when it tried to take the pain of Christ while He was on the cross. The traditional belief was meant to bring comfort. Ernest understood, however, that Christ and Christ alone endured death for the sin of all mankind.

In times of lack when the holler families were hungry, even small sparrows were snared and eaten; but never the red robin. The bird was treasured in the hills. To see a red breasted robin was a sign of luck and blessing.

"Students, please come to order," the teacher began. "I have an interestin' friend who I am wantin' you to meet."

The students went to their assigned tables and sat on the benches.

A local man had built the benches from a fallen oak tree. Ernest enjoyed the symbolism that oak represented: strength, character, and knowledge. The learners were separated by age and height. The oldest and tallest learners sat in the back of the classroom next to the freshly washed windows. Ernest believed that an orderly and clean classroom created an orderly and virtuous environment for learning. The youngest and shortest learners sat closest to the teachers' desks. It felt odd for Ernest to gaze at Lottie's desk and not see her smiling face. He knew that the students missed her as well.

"Adam, would you please be escortin' our guest?'

"Yes, Teacher."

There was a fuss among the brothers about who would and who would not bring Bullseye from the teacher's quarters into the classroom.

Ernest turned to the three younger boys. "Beau, Claude, and Dean, please be remaining in your seats. You'll git your turn. I promise."

Adam quickly returned with Bullseye sitting on his shoulder.

"Hello, hello, hello," the parrot greeted in Lottie's voice.

There were gasps and awes. One student proclaimed that their teacher had died and come back to life as a bird.

Ernest permitted the students to talk and engage with one another about the parrot. He had learned something from Mrs. Randolph. Although free conversation created noise and sometimes confusion, there was a difference between naughtiness and curiosity in the classroom.

"Adam, please share with the other learners how you met Bullseye? Now, remember only share the beginnin's of the yarn. Your brothers each have a part to be takin'."

The students had been working on re-telling stories in the proper sequence. Now, Ernest was taking the opportunity to put their learning into action.

"Well, he wasn't named such when we met. We just called him the cussin' bird because he used foul language. Mr. Ernest told me, however, that I can't be sharin' the bad words. He said that it ain't

71

proper talk."

Adam continued to talk about meeting Bullseye when he and his brothers were on their way to school and how the bird flew into the tree. "We was plain worried that he was gonna fly on his way, and just then, Miss Lottie done showed up."

It was Beau's turn to continue the story, "We thought to hoist Teacher up into the tree, but she climbed on up on her own. Plus, we was worried about how to do the hoistin'…"

Claude stood up and stomped to the front of the classroom. Dean followed close behind.

"It's my turn now," Claude began. "Well, the bird took a likin' to Miss Lottie. He was sitting on her shoulder, calling her sweet nothings, and singin' her songs. It was somethin' to behold. Adam went to get Mr. Ernest, and Miss Lottie told us to sit real quiet like, so the creature didn't fly off."

"Claude, would you please let Dean be finishin' the story?" Ernest asked.

"Well," Dean started, "I saw teacher's underwear. I was tryin' not to look but couldn't help it with her sittin' in the tree an all."

The students started laughing. Ernest couldn't help but laugh himself.

"Dean, would you mind concludin' the story?" the teacher requested.

"Well, Mr. Ernest came callin', and we all walked back to the schoolhouse. Miss Lottie took the bird home and named him since he took such a shine to her and all. Me and my brothers are wantin' Bullseye to come live with us. Now that Mercy's back in her right mind, at least that's what my Daddy's sayin', and Bullseye's quit cussin', we're hopin' that it's time for him to move in with us. Now, let me be tellin' ya about how we're gonna take care of him and such…"

"Dean," Ernest interrupted. "Thank you and all the boys for the wonderful recountin' of what happened. I've also got some news to be addin'."

72

Ernest then proceeded to talk about Lottie going on a trip and how Bullseye was now in his charge. At appropriate and inappropriate times, the parrot added his own words. The learners sat on the edge of their seats when Ernest talked about Bullseye's snake warning.

"Teacher, is it true if you take to killin' a snake by cuttin' it up that at midnight the snake parts will come back together and bite ya?" asked one of the more curious students.

Ernest reached into his pocket and drew out the rattlers. "Well, if that's true," Ernest chuckled, "we got us a hill snake with its hind part missin'."

The students, along with their teacher, roared with laughter.

Ernest then proceeded to put things into perspective. "Students, once a snake is dead, it's done dead. The body ain't comin' back together."

Snakes were an ongoing subject of fear, intrigue, and enchantment in Appalachia. It was thought to be a bad omen if someone dreamt about snakes. It meant that someone was talking about you behind your back or was out to git you.

Ernest thought that education was one of the best ways to combat mountain mysticism.

He also used the snake lesson as an opportunity to discuss Benjamin Franklin and the early colonists. "Now England was sendin' prisoners to America. The king was sayin' that workers was needed to help build the new land, but ol' Ben Franklin felt different about America's new workers bein' criminals. He told the king, 'If you don't quit sendin' convicts, we're gonna start sendin' you rattlers.'"

Ernest stood on the schoolhouse porch. As each learner exited the building, he said his individual good-byes. He addressed every student by name, complimented him or her on a specific task that had been done well, and handed out final grade cards. He again wished for Charlotte's presence. She had a way with their students, and he knew they would have appreciated her well wishes.

He would have also enjoyed celebrating the last day of school with a rousing squirrel hunt and a delicious meal. One of the learners had talked earlier in the day about seeing a flying squirrel. Squirrels didn't really fly; They glided from tree to tree. But it would have been a treat to find the special species with the added membrane of skin on either side of its body.

At the end of the last day of school, Ernest rang the bell. A season passed; another was about to begin. In the hills, spring would soon be summer. The mountain men and boys had already plowed their fields and planted their seeds. Ernest hoped that the minds of his students had experienced the same careful tending.

"Ernest…"

He turned to see Mercy standing on the far end of the porch. Above her head, at the corner of the portico, a paper wasp was busy building its nest from plant material, dead tree fiber, and spittle. She followed Ernest's gaze upward. Seeing the danger, she moved to the other side of the porch to listen and was pleased for his concern.

The yellow spotted insects were extremely territorial and their sting painful. Ernest had once taught the learners the differences between a bee, a wasp, and a yellow jacket. Both the yellow jacket and the wasp can sting over-and-over-again. The venom can also mark the recipient as a target for other insects. A honeybee, however, can only sting once. It's unable to pull the barbed stinger back out. It leaves behind not only the stinger but also part of its abdomen.

Ernest had presented the lesson in hopes of squelching his students' fears. He had instructed them to hold still and pretend to be statues when bees were nearby. He had also told them if a bee landed on their skin, to gently blow it away. The best advice he had given was for the children to wear hats. Furry creatures were often honey stealers; human hair in a bee's world was fur.

"Well, Mercy, aren't you lookin' fine?"

"Thank you. I'm feelin' fine. I'm appreciatin' all you done to help me."

"Your daddy is a powerful prayin' man. He's who you should be thankin'. He wouldn't give up on you. You're his baby girl. So, he wanted you to have more than how you was livin'.'"

Mercy looked down. Ernest hoped that it wasn't guilt or shame causing her to hide her face. When Jesus set free people from sin, He also set them free from the guilt of their bad choices and from the shame of someone else's bad choices.

"Mercy, you're free now and that's what's matterin'.'"

"I know, Ernest. Somethin' latched on to me, and it became so familiar that I wasn't wantin' it to leave. It seemed to be helpin', or promisin' to fix things," she shrugged, "but I'm knowin' now that it wasn't helpin'. It was tormentin'.'"

Ernest nodded his head in agreement.

"I've some things that I'm needin' to tell you, Ernest. I am hopin' you got the time to listen."

"It's the last day of school, and the learners are done gone. I ain't got nothin' but time right now. Let's have us a sit and talk."

"Porch talkin' is the best kind. I brought a jug of cold spring water."

The artesian spring was a favorite source of refreshment for the local community. The water was icy cold. Even in August when it was too hot for the birds to fly or even sing, the water stayed cold. Mercy struggled a little bit to sit down on the steps. She took a drink from the glass jar, and, once Ernest was situated, passed him the container.

In the classroom, the students shared a common cup, but Ernest felt odd drinking after Mercy. He wondered what Charlotte would think about his lips touching where Mercy's lips had been. Then, he thought better. *It's foolishness not to take a drink.*

"Sharin' is nice, ain't it?"

Again, Ernest nodded his head.

"I know I done told some things that shouldn't been said, but I also said things that needed sayin'. I still care for you, Ernest. I know I ain't the girl I used to be, but I'm workin' on things. I want you to take me and this baby. I'm wantin' us to build a life."

Ernest took Mercy's hand. "I ain't the man I used to be neither.

Someone else has claimed my heart. I'm longin' for Charlotte. She left the holler to give me time. She was wantin' me to sort through some things."

"Well, maybe time is on my side, then," Mercy murmured. "How about I go about helpin' you with the schoolhouse like I used to? I know there's learners needin' extra care. Remember how we used to teach them brothers of mine?" Her words began to speed up as she clutched Ernest's hand.

Ernest paused and looked at his boots. "I ain't thinkin' that's a good idea, Mercy."

"Why? Are you fearin' that your feelin's might change?"

"Na, that ain't the reason. It seems disloyal. Disloyal to Lottie."

"You got it bad. Your gal ain't here and you're wantin' to be true. Most men I know wouldn't be thinkin' such."

Ernest let go of Mercy's hand. "You're a good friend, and I'm hopin' in time that you'll become Charlotte's friend, too. As far as most of the men you're knowin', you need to be changin' acquaintances. A good man loves his gal and is faithful whether they're together or apart."

"I don't know about bein' Charlotte's friend, Ernest. It's hard for two women lovin' the same man."

"I ain't understandin'. You turned me aside because of my skin color, and now that I'm with Lottie, you're wantin' me back?"

"Ernest, I didn't leave because I wanted to; I was worried about what others would be thinkin' about our differences. I wasn't brave enough. I was done scared. I was also worried about the law. But because of my continuin' affection, I'm thinkin' you're the best one to be protectin' me and this child."

"There'll always be others judgin' about this and that, includin' skin color and such, but then there'll be others who won't pay no mind. Mostly up in the hills, people are wantin' to be left alone and leave others alone."

"Can't we try, Ernest —me, you, and the baby?"

"Life moves on, Mercy. That spring water we're enjoyin' comes from water spurtin' up from the ground. It can't be seen, but it's movin' and flowin'. It's like life; it don't stay still."

Ernest stood and helped Mercy get up. She'd had an easier time sitting than rising.

"I best get goin', Ernest. I'm headed to see the granny witch."

"I ain't thinkin' that's a good idea, Mercy."

"I knows that she's full of mischief and stuff I shouldn't be messin' with, but when this baby comes, it's the granny witch who'll be helpin'. I'm wantin' to make sure that she's willin'."

"Don't be forgettin' your jar."

"Thank you kindly. Just leave it on the porch, I'll gather it on my way back." Mercy raised her eyebrows and smiled playfully, "The granny witch might think that jar is an invitation to mix me a powerful drinkin' potion."

The following morning, Ernest noticed that the jar was still sitting on the porch steps. He hoped that all was well with Mercy. He gathered the glass container and brought it into the schoolhouse. He then started re-organizing the classroom for the summer learners. Instead of having the children sit by age and height, he wanted them grouped according to skill level.

Out of the corner of his eye, he saw movement on the front porch. The school bell tingled softly like someone had tapped it with his or her fingers. Then, the door opened.

"I'm here for my mornin' lessons," Mercy jested.

Ernest smiled in response and jokingly waved his hand with a flair to usher her in.

"I forgot my jar last evenin' and stopped by for collectin'."

Ernest handed her the jar. "I was a mite worried that somethin' had happened."

"All is well. The granny witch thinks the baby should be makin' his or her appearin' at any time."

"That's good news."

Mercy sat down on one of the benches that Ernest had placed against the back wall. "I'm guessin' that's good news. My back is painin' me somethin' fierce."

Ernest noticed that Mercy's right hand was clenched in a fist. She was obviously in a great deal of discomfort. "Is there anythin' you're needin'?"

"If you done got time, sit with me a minute. Then I'll be headin' home."

Mercy clenched her fist tighter. Her knuckles were white.

"I'm thinkin' of namin' this baby Nimrod. The Bible says that he was a fine hunter."

"And if this baby is a girl?"

"Well, girls can be fine hunters, too."

"Yes, they can. I'm thinkin', Mercy, that gettin' ready to give birth is affectin' your mind. I ain't never heard of a child named Nimrod."

"How about Uz or Cush? Nimrod was a fighter, Ernest."

"I'm knowin' such."

"I've been fightin'. It seems to me like the name is fittin'."

"Mercy, a life of fightin' ain't never good. Nimrod fought against God. A name should be a blessin'. Each time a person hears his or her name, it should be a word from heaven."

Mercy bit down on her lower lip. She was obviously struggling. "Sing me a song, Ernest?"

"How about you sing me a song? It's been awhile since I heard your sweet voice."

"Are you kiddin', Ernest?"

"Nope. I'm thinkin' that you're needin' distractin'."

She rubbed the small of her back and rocked as she softly sang as best she could.

When you're smilin', keep on smilin'. The whole world smiles with you. And when you're laughin', keep on laughin'. The sun comes shinin' through. But when you're cryin' you bring on the rain, so stop your frownin', be happy again. Cause when you're smilin', keep on smilin', the whole world smiles with you. Ah, when you're laughin', keep on laughin'. The sun comes shinin' through. Now when you're cryin', you bring on the rain. So stop that sighin', be happy again. Cause when you're smilin', keep on smilin', and the whole world is gonna smile with you. The great big world will smile with you. The whole wide world will smile with you.

"Thank you, Mercy. I always liked your singin'. I hope you're smilin' some these days."

"I remember smilin'. It's where your mouth goes up at the ends. I'm tryin', and I'm askin' God for His help," she answered. "Singin' didn't work, Ernest. I'm still hurtin'. Somethin' just ain't right. I'm painin' somethin' awful."

"How can I be helpin'?"

"I ain't rightly sure. I'm thinkin' this baby might be comin'!"

Alarmed, Ernest guided Mercy from the bench. "Let's get you restin' proper, and I'll go for help."

Ernest escorted Mercy to his private quarters and assisted her in getting situated on the small bed. Bullseye, true to form, began babbling, then singing. Mercy smiled slightly.

Maybe the bird will occupy her till I get back, Ernest thought.

"Don't be leavin' me, Ernest."

"We're needin' help."

"I ain't talkin' about right now."

"Mercy, you're painin' and wantin' me to make promises. I'm wantin' to make them so you'll feel better, but it wouldn't be right. Enjoy acquaintin' yourself with Bullseye. I'll be right back. I'm thinkin' not to run for help, but to ring the school bell. I'm hopin' that others will come a mite quick.

He hurried to the covered porch and pulled the bell cord over-and-over again. It pealed strongly and urgently. Ernest was nervous. He'd seen piglets and puppies born but never a baby. He wasn't equipped to help Mercy; and, even if he knew what to do, it wouldn't be proper. As a single man to see her nether regions, would mean marrying her for sure.

It wouldn't matter in the hills that it was against the law for people of different races to marry. He crossed the racial boundaries every day: his closest friends were people of color. He taught black children; he bartered with the hill people both black and white; he and Charlotte shared meals with whomever they pleased; He was accepted as part of his distinct community. There was no lawman to uphold the rules and, even if there was, the people would chase him off for such nonsense.

He heard Mercy cry out in pain. He quietly prayed for someone to arrive quickly and headed to the back of schoolhouse.

Both Mercy and Bullseye were crying, then panting together. He wished that the bird wasn't so quick to impersonate. His mimicking wasn't helping.

The sheets were damp from sweat, tears, and fluid. Ernest felt panicked. *This baby's comin' soon.*

He pulled the worn chair next to the bed and took hold of Mercy's hand. The chair was generally his place of comfort; now, sitting down only added to his worries. Mercy's grip was powerful –more powerful than Lester's grip when they had arm wrestled.

"Mercy, try to be relaxin'. I know from workin' the hogs that a sow's first litter takes time."

"Are you comparin' me to a pig?!"

"Of course not, Mercy. I'm just sayin' that help will be here soon."

"I can feel this baby, Ernest," Mercy added. "It's comin' now. There ain't time. I'll be needin' your help."

She gripped even tighter. He thought his hand would break. He had no choice. He couldn't let her suffer.

He wondered who had helped Mary give birth to Jesus. *It must have been Joseph,* he thought. The two weren't married yet, so maybe it would be alright. He could use that as an arguing point with the men in the community. *Of course, they could argue right back that the couple was preparin' for marriage.*

Mercy was twisting in the bed. He knew she was trying to find relief. "Lay still, darlin'. I'm gonna help." He wrestled some with Mercy's clothing and finally had her undergarments removed. "Mercy, your baby is about to be born. I think you need to push as hard as you can."

Ernest held the baby's head. "Push again, Mercy." Next, the shoulders came. "One more time. Bear down, darlin', with all your might." He held the baby in his hands.

The piglets on his family's farm were generally born in farrowing pens. Mostly, the mamas did a great job without any human interference. On occasion, however, Ernest had cleaned a newborn pig's mouth and shook him good to get him breathing. Ernest cleared the baby's pink mouth and patted his pale bottom.

"It's a boy, Mercy. A beautiful healthy boy." Puzzled, Ernest added, "And as white as can be…"

The new mama laughed through her tears. "He won't stay that way for long. His color'll start changin' soon enough." The young woman looked at the ceiling. Sweat that only a mother understands poured like tears from her forehead into her eyes and down the sides of her face.

"Only God knows if he'll be the shade of the mornin' sun risin' among the clouds, or like dusk when the sun is settin' and the sky is turnin', or blue black like the night."

After a moment, Mercy lifted her head to look for her child. "Lay the baby on my belly, Ernest. I'll hold 'um whilst you cut the cord."

Just as Ernest readied to sever the umbilical cord, several local men arrived. The school bell had done the job in communicating that help was needed. He hurried to cover Mercy as best he could. He knew the granny witch had arrived when she whistled loudly from the other room. Her whistling supposedly summoned supernatural help.

The local men retreated to the schoolhouse while Granny Laurel got to work. When Ernest started to leave the room, Laurel encouraged him to stay. "Now boy, you done got yourself a baby. The mama is needin' you, so stay put."

When Ernest started to explain what happened, Granny shushed him and told him to take a seat. The baby's cord was cut. The infant was washed, swaddled, and handed to Ernest. Once Mercy released the afterbirth, Granny washed the mother as gently as she had the baby. A fresh gown was retrieved from Granny's bag, and the baby was placed in the new mama's arms.

During the process, Ernest tried to avert his eyes; Mercy kept looking at him. When he looked back, there was always some portion of her body exposed.

Ernest finally left the room and joined the men in the schoolhouse. Over and over, congratulations were given. Each time Ernest tried to explain that he wasn't the father, the men ignored him and continued their own chatter. Others arrived and the story was re-told. Questions were asked about the marriage ceremony and what the baby would be named.

"The mama is wantin' to call the baby Elisha Ernest, Eli as his small name," Granny Laurel said as she entered the schoolhouse portion of the building. She gestured to Ernest. "You might want to have a sit with your wife and baby."

Ernest wasn't sure what to do. He didn't want to leave Mercy alone, but he also didn't want to give the appearance that he was responsible for the mother and child.

When Justice entered the room, everyone cheered.

Granny put her arm around his back. "Congratulations, Pappy."

Justice started to cry, "It's a proud day. A mighty proud day. We've a new baby." His eye met Laurel. "Thank you for helpin' with the birth."

"Well, I cut the baby lose, but Ernest here done the birthin'."

Justice looked at Ernest slowly. Then, his gaze returned to Granny Laurel. "You weren't here to bring the little one into the world?"

"No. I heard the bell and run right over, but the baby was done born."

"That's odd," Justice spoke. "I thought I saw you and Mercy earlier today."

Granny gently patted Justice on the back. "Well, pappies are old men—old enough to be seein' things."

Chapter Ten

When you comb your hair, you must not let a bird
take a strand for nest building or you will have a
headache all summer.

Appalachian Folk Belief

Coral was trying to adjust to the noisiness of the city. In the holler, things were sometimes so quiet that she could hear the rhythmic beating of her heart. Ernest said if a person listened close enough, he or she could hear the sun set. Coral knew from her learning that the sun produced sound waves. She also knew that the waves couldn't be heard on earth.

The city was full of sounds: street vendors yelling, cart drivers directing mules, shop owners greeting customers, people arguing, and dogs barking. In order to rest at night, she sang herself to sleep. The commotion of the city was overwhelming. In Big Creek, people sat on front porch rockers. The men whittled and the women crocheted. In Charleston, people rushed from place to place. Even Lottie seemed busy.

"Sister, are you wantin' to tell me where you were this mornin'?" asked Coral.

Lottie blushed.

"It's okay if you ain't wantin' to tell. Part of bein' good friends is allowin' someone to take their time in tellin' or not even tellin' at all."

"It ain't that. It's hard to tell a story when the endin' wasn't what you had in mind. I was callin' the store in Big Creek."

"I'm guessin' you was tryin' to reach Ernest."

Charlotte smiled.

"I ain't never been in love but, if I was, I'd be callin' too, wantin' to hear my sweetheart's voice."

"I wasn't expectin' to hear his voice, but I was hopin' for a message. We had an arrangement of sorts. Ernest was to visit the store and leave me messages, then when I called, I was to answer his messages and be leavin' my own words."

Coral reached for her friend's hand. "Did he leave you some endearin' words?"

Charlotte shook her head. "I'm a mite puzzled. There was no message. Maybe with the school year endin', he couldn't get away, so I left some words."

"Just curious," Coral lifted her hands in jest. "Is Rudy's daddy takin' and givin' the messages or his mama?"

"Why, his daddy, Coral," Lottie laughed.

"I ain't bettin' such. His mama is doin' the takin' and givin'. If Emie has her way, she's helpin' too!"

"That baby is mine, Coral." Charlie's hands were clenched in fists. "I'm Jewel's daddy!"

Coral could tell that he was trying to keep his anger in check. If things got out of control, the officer would immediately take Charlie back to his cell.

She didn't want to be contrary, but part of her mission was being a truth teller. Even though she was intimidated, agreeing with Charlie would hinder what God was asking her to do. She was thankful that Charlotte was with her, that Pastor Rex was waiting just outside the door, and that Charlie was handcuffed.

She was also thankful that Officer Hadley was present. Coral found the officer's appearance and deep voice arresting. Officer Hadley's thick neck, mounding dark hair, and shoulders so broad that he had to turn slightly to enter and exit the door arrested Coral's attention. Coral couldn't help but notice the officer's powerful build and handsome face. When he spoke, her attention shifted toward him immediately. Looking more closely at him, she noticed his Cupid's bow. The dual curve of his upper lip along with his philtrum columns presented a prominent double arch under his nose.

Plain and simple, Coral was attracted to Officer Hadley. She was doing her best, however, to stay focused on her mission. Her heart needed to be captivated by God and doing His will.

Coral took a deep breath. "Charlie, makin' a baby ain't the same as lovin' the mama durin' the process. In the Bible when Adam knew Eve, it was an act of lovin'. Animals mate because of instinct. Most times there ain't love involved."

"I was lovin' Emie in my own way."

"You was takin' Emie like animals do."

Charlie's lumbering attempt to get up from the chair moved Officer Hadley to action. He pushed Charlie firmly back into his seat, and with piercing eyes, addressed Coral, "Are you done visitin'?"

"Just a few more minutes, please." Coral answered raising one eyebrow.

"Are you sure it ain't best we leave?" Lottie questioned betraying some anxiety. "Pastor Rex said if the snake started to rattle, then we needed to go."

"First, Coral called me an animal. Now you're callin' me a snake." Charlie spouted. "I ain't neither!"

"Alright, Charlie," Coral interrupted. "Tell me who are you?"

The question took the prisoner by surprise. He started to stammer, stutter, and stumble with his words. "Well, I'm… The reasons I was… You don't… I've always had ta…" Coral knew he was looking for the right words to describe his essence, but he couldn't find them. Coral had been very young, but she'd experienced, and been told repeatedly, how Charlie's preacher father had misrepresented the Creator and Savior all his fool life. Because the prisoner didn't know who Jesus was or how good his Maker was, Coral knew that Charlie didn't know who he was either.

"Charlie, you was a soul in heaven, created by God to come to earth and do and be somethin'. Your mama and daddy gave you life. Yet, when your mama died, your daddy done went crazy. He started preachin' lies and makin' you do his biddin'. You was little and didn't understand. You was used like an old rag, dirtied and dirtied again, never washed but discarded and left in the sun to fade. God cried every time you cried. He wanted more for you and still does. He loves you, Charlie."

Coral reached across the table to touch Charlie's arm. Her intent was to comfort him, but Officer Hadley quickly stopped her. "Visitin' time is over for today."

As the prisoner was escorted from the room, Coral loudly declared. "You didn't ask me, but I'm singin' over you today. I'm singin' a song that your mama would have sung to you as a baby. She would still be callin' you her baby and singin' for you if she was livin'."

All night, all day, angels watching over me, my Lord. All night, all day, angels watching over me. Now I lay me down to sleep. Angels watching over me, my Lord. Pray the Lord my soul to keep. Angels watching over me. All night, all day, angels watching over me, my Lord. All night, all day, angels watching over me. Lord, stay with me through the night. Angels watching over me, my Lord. Wake me with the morning light. Angels watching over me.

"Pastor Rex, are you sure about this?" Charlotte questioned. "I ain't never wore my Lottie the Legend outfit to a church gatherin', much less shot my bow and arrow while worshippin' the good Lord."

"Are you done worried about missin'?" Pastor Rex joked.

"No! I ain't worried about missin'."

"If she does miss and kills the pastor, do you think she'd be breakin' one of the commands?" Coral giggled.

"I ain't missin'!"

"Now, Charlotte, are you gonna shoot at the pastor while he's preachin' or before the sermon gets rollin'?" Coral said playfully.

"I wouldn't be too worried about me," Charlotte responded in kind. "You'll be too busy singin' to pay attention to my shootin'." Charlotte then paused for emphasis, "And don't forget about your bear mask."

"How can I be forgettin'?!"

"Coral, you know, I won't be actually shootin' at the pastor, I'll be shootin' at you."

"What?!

"That's part of the rouse. You'll be singin' and pretendin' to run, and I'll be shootin' at you."

"Girls, when we get back to Big Creek, I'm thinkin' the church family would enjoy this ditty," Pastor Rex spoke assuredly.

"No!" Charlotte and Coral responded in unison.

The pastor smiled, in a knowing manner. "Well, ladies, we can talk on this later."

The threesome traveled past the boundaries of town by horse and wagon. Not long after they passed the prison, the brick streets became rutted dirt roads. The streetlamps of the city disappeared. When night fell, the only light would be the stars in the sky. The trimmed lawns and rose gardens were left behind. Pastor Rex had previously explained that they would be visiting a tent meeting on the outskirts of Charleston.

The community's residents were obviously impoverished. The houses were clap board, tin, press board, and whatever materials the residents had found for building. Most windows were boarded over. Small pieces of scrap wood were readily available from the numerous building sites closer to the city. Glass, however, was hard to locate and even harder to transport.

Although Charleston was flourishing, somehow this community hadn't heard about new buildings, fancy clothing, and automobiles dashing about. Coral was puzzled. There were plenty of jobs available at the local coal mines. If the men in the community were working, certainly their families wouldn't be living in squalor.

It was early afternoon on a Saturday, but there were few adults in sight. There were, however, colored children running everywhere. Older children fussed at younger children who seemed to obey. The children wore no shoes and their clothing seemed to be too big or too small. Nothing seemed to fit.

We don't fit, Coral thought. *What are we doing here?*

When the wagon stopped next to a lopsided dirty white tent, Coral couldn't believe what was happening. Lottie looked as nervous as Coral felt. Pastor Rex was smiling and yelling greetings to a handsome looking man standing by a large, canvas, two-flap door that had been tied back with rope.

The man was light-skinned. His lips were full, and his nose was slightly broad. His eyes were dark brown, almost black, and his hair was less curly and lighter brown than most people of color. He quickly helped Charlotte and Coral down from the wagon and introduced himself as Thomas.

He hugged Pastor Rex and thanked him over and over again for coming to help with the mission. Thomas ushered the group into the tent. They sat on the edge of the makeshift platform and exchanged pleasantries for a few minutes. Coral couldn't help but notice that the tent sagged in sections and also had holes in the canvas, sizes varying from pin pricks to fist sized. There were possibly 25 chairs present in varying stages of disarray, numerous benches made from cast off wood, and several dirty mis-matched overlapping rugs in front of the platform.

"My mama named me Thomas because she doubted who my real daddy was," the young pastor began. "It soon became apparent that he was a white man. I didn't and don't fit in the white world or the black world. I'm prayin' that someday skin color won't matter in Charleston –especially in the House of God."

"Amen," Pastor Rex added.

"Most folk won't lend a hand because of my color or lack of color dependin' on who you're talkin' to. I'm grateful for your help." Thomas nodded in appreciation. "Adults won't pay me no mind, so I'm tryin' to share Jesus with the children. They come every Saturday, but I think it's mostly for the pieces of candy I try and give 'um."

"Thomas, me and the ladies got an excitin' time in store for you and the learners."

Pastor Rex, what have you done? Coral thought. *"As a man of the cloth you shouldn't have deceived me and Lottie."* Now Coral knew that the good pastor would never say that he had used deception, but didn't deception include the omission of important information?

"Are you preferrin' to tell me what you got in mind, or to wait and show me?" Pastor Thomas inquired.

Before Coral or Charlotte could answer, Pastor Rex spoke up once again. "I'm thinkin' showin' might be best. The ladies are doin' a demonstration about a bear. Does that bring to mind anythin' you can share with the little ones."

Thomas smiled, "I am thinkin' I know just the verses. Would you be willin' to offer aid?"

As the two pastors continued their discussion, Coral and Lottie started to meander around the tent.

"Lottie, what was Pastor Rex thinkin'?"

"I'm thinkin' that he wasn't thinkin'. But since we're here, let's have us some fun! We're in for a time, Coral –Lottie Legend and Little Bear won't soon be forgotten!"

Coral was puzzled. *How had Charlotte switched from being concerned to "let's have us some fun"?*

"Coral you're a country girl," Charlotte began. "A beautiful belle of the hills…"

"A belle of the hills, I'm likin' that," Coral giggled.

"Well, maybe I can be sharin' that with Officer Hadley?"

"Charlotte!"

"You was thinkin' I hadn't noticed, Sister. You're the only gal I know who can hold the attention of two men at the same time –both at a prison none-the-less. One starin' at ya straight in the face, and the other lookin' from the corner of his eye. You're makin' my life quite interestin', and I'm bidin' my time to tell Ernest all about our adventure."

"It ain't a compliment that men in prison might be likin' me. They ain't got much to do with women and are probably feelin' desperate. If I was chubby like a full-bellied baby, was playin' dead like a possum, or was as attractive as a buzzard, they might still want me for their gal."

Lottie laughed out loud. "Now, Coral, you know that possums only play dead when they is scared. I can see how Charlie could be a mite frightenin', but if you're afeard of Office Hadley, I'm thinkin' you're mistakin' alarm for love sickness."

Coral joined in Lottie's laughter. "Now, Sister, or should I say 'Doctor Sister', please be tellin' me more about the sickness of love."

"Some get a little love fever and others the fervent kind. If the fever is slight, the tummy might flutter and dreams of kissin' might come every few days but for the fervent kind, butterflies take up residence in the lower regions of the body, and lip smoochin' is a constant ailment."

Coral decided to change the subject. While she enjoyed laughing and carrying on with Lottie, she wasn't ready to talk about her feelings for Officer Hadley. Joking about love in general was one thing, but the matters of her own heart weren't clear enough for her to understand, let alone share with Lottie.

"Now, Lottie, we got other things that we need to be discussin'."

"Alright Sister, what was I sayin' before we started in about LOVE?"

"I think you was callin' me a beautiful belle of the hills…"

"Right," Lottie grinned. "You are a girl from the hills, a beautiful belle of the hills, but I grew up in the city. The children here ain't got nothin'. Their parents ain't lazy. They're wantin' to provide best they can, but times is hard. The jobs they can get don't pay much and sometimes what they're paid barely gets 'um to and from work. Most people here work six days a week and still can't feed, house, and clothe their children proper like."

"I ain't understandin', Charlotte. There is jobs everywhere in Charleston. The mines are beggin' for workers. Most folks is gettin' ahead."

"Black folk ain't paid the same as white folk. It ain't right, but it's how it is. Black men get the lowly jobs. Even then, they are paid less than the white men doin' the same work."

Coral wiped the tears from her cheeks. "I didn't know."

"It happens some in the hills, but we don't always see it cause, we live far and wide. Plus, our family don't tolerate such nonsense. The children, who are comin' here today need Jesus, and, Coral, we gotta do our best to tell them about God's love. This is a mission, just like seein' Charlie at the prison."

Coral and Lottie greeted the learners at the tent door. Lottie was dressed in her legend costume with her bow in hand and quiver strapped over her shoulder. Coral's face was covered with her bear mask. Coral started off growling at the children. When several littles ran away, she changed strategies and began giving big ol' bear hugs. Some of the children were still frightened. But as time wore on, the children began to view her as harmless. On occasion, Lottie shot tin cans she'd hidden in the trees. With each ping, the children clapped and cheered. The audience grew until the dilapidated tent was overflowing with children and youth of all ages.

Pastor Thomas instructed the children to remain seated. He and Pastor Rex stood off to the side in the front as monitors. After shooting the cans, Lottie had removed the tips from her arrows. There was still, however, some concern for the children's safety.

The program started with Coral leading the children in the tune

The Bear Went Over the Mountain.

The bear went over the mountain. The bear went over the mountain. The bear went over the mountain to see what he could see. But all that he could see, all that he could see, was the other side of the mountain. The other side of the mountain, the other side of the mountain was all that he could see...

Once the children were familiar with the song, Coral pretended to climb over a mountain, looking and looking for what she could see. When the bear spotted the hunter, she became frantic in her wonderings. Lottie the Legend, acting as the hunter, began shooting arrows at the bear. The bear dived and rolled, pranced and prattled, groaned and moaned, and occasionally grunted as she frantically ran from the hunter. The hunter pretended to hide behind trees and bushes taking exaggerated aims only to miss time and time again. The ruckus ended with both the bear and hunter collapsing in exhaustion.

As Pastor Thomas took center stage with Pastor Rex at his side, Charlotte and Coral quickly and quietly gathered all the arrows.

"Children, there's a story in the Bible about a gang of ruffians who was killed by two bears. Tell me, do you know people who are scoundrels, stealin' and takin' from others - criminals who hurt people for no good reason?" Pastor Thomas asked.

Some of the children yelled yes while others whispered the names of the people who frightened them. One boy stood and told a story about someone being mean and hurting his sister.

"A godly man by the name of Elisha was walkin' down the road. He was mindin' his own business. He wasn't botherin' anyone else, and a gang of no-gooders started makin' fun of his hair on account of the way he razor-cut it."

Pastor Thomas motioned for Pastor Rex to move closer. "See how our friend Pastor Rex has some hair missin'. Well, we ain't sure what happened to his hair, we just know it's done gone. Well, Elisha was missin' his hair, too. Some say it fell out; others say he cut his hair so people would recognize him as a special man of God. We don't know. But them ruffians started makin' fun of Elisha. They called him baldy and such."

Coral could see that the learners were enthralled by Thomas' recounting of the Bible story. Some were sitting on the edge of their seats. Others had their hands clasped together waiting to hear what would happen next. In anticipation of the story's conclusion, several children had their necks stretched as far forward as possible.

Coral was interested as well. She had made assumptions about the Bible story that were obviously not accurate.

"Now, it ain't never nice to be makin' fun of others," Pastor Thomas continued. "And I bet your mamas and daddies taught ya to run when no-gooders come callin'. Sometimes scallywags ain't content just to talk. They're aimin' to cause harm. Well, in our story. the scoundrels had trouble in mind. See they weren't just against Elisha, they was also against God. They were involved in nonsense that hurt God's heart. When the no-gooders wouldn't quit, God sent two bears to do His business."

Pastor Thomas paused for effect. "We need to be prayin' for God's help when scallywags come callin'. And, we also need to pray that we're on God's side and doin' His plans."

The children stood for prayer. Their earnestness moved Coral. She also thought about her own life. *Was she doing God's work? If so, why was Charlie so bent on not hearing the Lord's truth?*

As she prayed for the children, she also remembered Charlie in prayer. *"Lord, please give Charlie more time to respond to your ways. Please keep the bears away."*

Chapter Eleven

If you're having bad dreams, place a Bible under
your pillow. The nightmares
will go away.

Appalachian Folk Belief

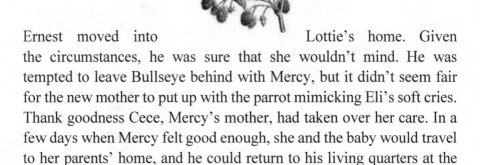

Ernest moved into Lottie's home. Given the circumstances, he was sure that she wouldn't mind. He was tempted to leave Bullseye behind with Mercy, but it didn't seem fair for the new mother to put up with the parrot mimicking Eli's soft cries. Thank goodness Cece, Mercy's mother, had taken over her care. In a few days when Mercy felt good enough, she and the baby would travel to her parents' home, and he could return to his living quarters at the schoolhouse.

Ernest wished Mercy had chosen a different name for the infant. He knew he should be honored that the baby was his namesake, but he also knew it wouldn't help him distance himself from Mercy and her child.

Sleeping in Lottie's bed felt improper to Ernest. Being there made his mind wander. Instead of sleeping in her bed, he began sleeping on a pallet on the floor in the small everything room. Looking at her what nots also seemed invasive, but he couldn't walk blindly through her home.

The items in her nature bowl reminded him of the love the learners felt for her. The students often brought Lottie treasures from the outdoors: rocks with gold veins, flower blossoms, and four-leaf clovers among other things.

The dishes in the kitchen reminded him of the meals they shared. The wood pile on the porch made him wish that Lottie would always feel warm, loved, safe, and cherished.

A bouquet of dried lilacs tied with twine were on an open shelf in the kitchen. The previous summer, Lottie had made lilac honey. Ernest still remembered the taste of the infused sweet mixture. He hoped the florets were from the wild purple lilacs he'd given Lottie at Rudy's insistence.

He yearned to talk with his gal. Of course, some would say which gal?

Before entering the room, Ernest knocked on the door. He wanted to check on Mercy and spend a little time with Eli before heading down the hill.

"Come on in, Ernest."

Mercy was suckling the baby.

"How did you know it was me comin' for a visit?"

"I know your walk, and your knockin' is softer than the boys, my daddy, or even Granny. Well, the boys don't really knock before enterin', but Mama's workin' on teachin' 'um."

"How's little Nimrod today?" Ernest joked.

"I don't know a Nimrod, but Eli Ernest is doin' just fine."

"Granny just took her leavin'," Mercy said. "The baby's good as day."

"I'm headin' to Big Creek. I'm thinkin' that I should ask Doc to come take a look. This baby ain't got much color, and Granny's got them mysterious ways and such."

"We done talked about the baby's color, Ernest. Eli is just fine. Besides, 'mysterious' is too nice a word to be describin' Granny's goin's-on."

"She means well. Granny witches are as old as the holler. I ain't disagreein' with everythin' she's a doin'. I'm appreciatin' her knowledge of herbs, plants, bark, and such. And I'm knowin' that she asks Jesus for help, but she's also askin' other spirits to aid in her healin'. That worries me."

"She won't like it none if Doc comes."

They sat in silence for a few minutes. One of the baby's arms had escaped his swaddling clothes. Ernest reached out for Eli's fingers and then quickly pulled back. He was becoming too familiar. Mercy's breast was partially exposed. With the baby so near her bosom, what was he doing? Ernest knew that Mercy sensed or possibly saw his withdrawal.

"Granny is stirrin' up a fuss, Ernest."

"How so?"

"She's tellin' others that we're needin' to marry."

"It don't surprise me none," Ernest added quietly. "I ain't sure what to do, Mercy. I care for you, but not like a husband should care for a wife."

"There's talk of forcin' a weddin'."

"Even if we was inclined, it ain't legal for us to wed."

"They'll have us jump the broom and call it legal." Mercy started to cry. "Not havin' a husband and havin' a baby will be like havin' leprosy. They will set me aside and not pay me and the baby any mind. My body won't decay like the ugly disease causes, but my heart will fall away piece by piece. I was foolish to think comin' back here would fix everthing."

"Not foolish, Mercy, but hopin' for better days. Maybe it's wishful considerin', but I'm thinkin' that we need to give the good people in our tiny portion of the upper holler more credit. They don't seem to be the judgin' kind."

Mercy scoffed. "They ain't gonna judge on skin color. There's been mixin' goin' on since slave days. In fact, some colored people with lighter skin moved to the hills to escape the ways of cruel folk. But the judgin' will happen cause I ain't got a husband. Usin' their words, they'll stone me like the woman caught in adultery."

"The woman wasn't stoned, Mercy. Jesus intervened. He wrote in the sand."

"But what did he write? Did he write judgin' words?"

Ernest took Mercy's hand. "I ain't rightly sure what he wrote. I'm knowin' that both the woman and the man caught sinnin' were supposed to be brought before the priest. Yet only the woman was there. The Pharisees weren't obeyin' what they knew. Some say that Jesus wrote down the names of the men. Whatever He wrote, the woman was protected. Jesus done kept her safe, and He's wantin' to keep you safe –you and Eli."

"Granny, there ain't no need to be hidin' in the bushes. Come on out." Ernest wondered if he would ever find peace and quiet again on the path to Big Creek.

Granny Laurel exited the trees. "I'm just seein' where you're headed."

"If you're in trouble and need to be hidin' Granny, don't be dartin' to and fro. You need to move quiet like. You also need to wear different shoes. Them boots you're wearin' gave you clean away."

"Well, thanks for the advisin'."

"And another thing: I thought you granny witches was supposed to walk quiet like in the woods when you're gatherin' all them weeds and such. If you want to know where I'm headed, you don't need to be spyin' like a sneaky cat. Just ask. I ain't up to nothin' bad." Ernest was frustrated.

"Now, Ernest, there ain't no need to be takin' that tone."

"Mercy just finished tellin' me that you was stirrin' up trouble."

"I ain't done such."

"Tellin' the good folk that I'm the baby's daddy and needin' to marry Mercy is stirrin' trouble. Save your stirrin' for your magic potions…" He wanted to add that whether Granny was stirrin' trouble among folks or stirrin' trouble in a witches' brew, that neither trouble had the long arm to grab him off course, but then he thought better of it.

"You better hush. I could make other types of trouble for you."

"Now who's not talkin' nice? Threatenin' to give me the curse."

"Givin' the curse is when a girl's havin' her monthly."

"I ain't really familiar with such, but what do you call your deceivin' ways?"

"A blessin'…"

Ernest heard something or someone rustling in the trees. "Granny, is someone with you?"

"No, I am by my lonesome. It's just the spirits, Ernest."

"More like a deer movin'."

"Now, I know you don't like me none, and I ain't sure why–but since we're havin' a chance meetin', I'm thinkin' we should settle a few things."

"Granny, this ain't no chance meetin'. You was followin' me!"

"Well, be that as it may, let's have us a sit down."

"There ain't no place to sit."

"Well, let's have us a stand down right here on the path."

"We're already havin' a stand down, but come a little closer so I ain't havin' to raise my voice."

As Granny Laurel approached, Ernest almost felt sorry for her. Her clothes were worn and torn. Her face was smudged with dirt, and her grey hair was pilled on her head with tentacles sprouting here and there. Her old fashioned faded blue dress with the greyish white overlay hung on her thin frame. He wondered about her age but knew it wasn't polite to ask.

"Granny, it ain't that I don't like you. It's just that your ways worry me some."

"There ain't no need to be worryin'. I'm just practicin' my type of doctorin' like my mama and her mama before me. My elders arrived in these hills from the old country with ideas in mind for carin' and helpin' their neighbors. At first, the Indians helped us, and we helped them. Then others came callin'. It's what I know, and it's what God gave me to help and heal."

"I ain't doubtin' your good intentions, but you're needin' to seek God and God only. You can't be talkin' to the dead and such. It ain't right."

"Our talkin' is done over," Granny interrupted and shook her finger at Ernest. "I can't be sharin' my secrets."

Ernest's hands went to his hips. He wanted to let her know he meant business. "I'm not askin' about your secrets. I'm just tellin' that you need to quit makin' mischief."

The old woman started to walk away.

"Granny, I'm askin' please don't be tellin' the folk that I need to be marryin' Mercy. I ain't that baby's daddy."

"You could be that baby's daddy if you was wantin'. Daddy, or not, when you done seen a woman's parts, and neither of you is married, it's time for gittin' hitched."

Ernest was exasperated. "I'm lovin' someone else."

"No matter. It has ta be. I have special knowin' that familiar feelings come and goes anyways."

"It ain't even legal for Mercy and me to marry."

"Ain't no law man in these parts. The black folk just jump the broom and call it done. The jumpin' is good. It'll ward off evil."

Deception was a terrible thing. Granny was deceived in believing that helpful spirits guided her. It seemed that when someone was deceived, that he or she couldn't help but deceive others. Whether Granny Laurel's intentions were good or not didn't matter. Deception hid the truth.

It also worried Ernest that Granny's words and Mercy's words sounded so alike. Whether Mercy knew it or not, Granny was influencing her.

Ernest's feet quickly carried him down the hillside. His mind seemed to race along with his steps. Generally, the beauty of the mountains called to him. Today, the overwhelming callings were for Lottie, Mercy, Eli, family, and friends. He also considered his students. Things were a mess. How could he live out his faith in the midst of such confusion, commotion, and lack of certainty?

He was clear about his feelings for Lottie and thought he was clear about his feelings for Mercy. The problem was Eli. Ernest was already attached to the boy. There was a connection that happened at the baby's birth. Because of an unseen tether, his range of emotional movement was now limited. He could feel the restraints. How could he have such deep feelings so quickly? Although, the baby wasn't his, Ernest somehow felt responsible.

Ernest was befuddled. His mind wouldn't stop. He couldn't quiet himself enough to pray. When he tried to talk with Jesus, the voices of others invaded. There was a battle for who would be in charge of his thoughts, his emotions, and his choices.

Ernest heard a whistle-pig. He couldn't tell if it was a male or female. Their warning calls weren't always distinct enough to tell the difference. Generally, a male ground hog had more than one female in his life at the same time. He would travel between the ladies each day, checking on their well-being.

He felt like a rodent and then wondered where such dark thoughts were coming from. He wasn't a rat, a squirrel, a woodchuck, or a beaver. He was a man who loved God and was loved by God.

"Ernest, I ain't never heard the likes of such," Emie muttered. "I'm glad the baby is good and Mercy's fine, but I don't know about marryin' and broom jumpin'. I ain't sure a white person can jump."

"Plenty of white people jump, Emerald."

"I ain't talkin' about jumpin' rope or jumpin' checkers. I'm talkin' about broom jumpin', Brother."

"I know what you're talkin' about." Ernest sighed. "I'm sorry. I just ain't knowin' what to do. Do I follow my heart, or do I follow what others is tellin' me is right? If I do the thing that's most right before God, maybe my heart will follow."

"Followin' your heart is right."

"I appreciate you sayin' such, but it ain't so, Emie, and you done know it. You're tryin' to bring me comfort, but the words ain't true. The Bible says that there's a way that seems right and it ain't such. I'm tryin' to hear from God, but He ain't talkin'."

"I ain't no expert, Ernest, but maybe you're doin' all the talkin' and there ain't room for God to speak. I was prayin'," Emie added.

"I'm was goin' on about this and that. Tellin' all my troubles like I was taught, askin' for help and such. Then I started wonderin' maybe God had somethin' to say, but I couldn't hear, 'cause I wouldn't be still. So, I done hushed and asked the Lord if he had somethin' on his mind. Well, he did, Ernest, and it didn't have anythin' to do with what I was talkin' about."

Ernest raised his eyebrows, "Well, I can understand about you goin' on and such, Emie…"

"Brother, I am tryin' to help. Now if God ain't talkin' and you ain't talkin', there could be others talkin'… talkin' in your mind."

"It's true. There's a fight goin' on in my thoughts."

"Well, just get rid of them folk!"

"I'm wishin' I could." Ernest said. His sister tilted her head and gave him the eye. "Well, since I ain't helpin', you might call on Rudy. He's at the farm workin' the hogs. We got us some piglets needin' help. The mama is wantin' to aid her littles, but she ain't sure what needs doin'."

Ernest thought about Mercy, remembering the offense she took in being compared to a sow. *Mamas are mamas,* he thought, *always wantin' the best for their babies and willing to fight and do most anything to keep 'um safe.*

Ernest knew the path to the farm as well as he knew the back of his hand. From the time he was a child, he had walked from the homestead to Aunt Ada's home each week. His mama and auntie had shared food, flowers, and friendship, and he had carried their messages and gifts. It did his heart good to know that Emie and her family resided close to Auntie now and could share life together.

After Emie was raped, he had moved his younger sister into their love aunt's home and arms. Then his weekly jaunts turned into daily visits, especially when Charlie was on the loose.

His thoughts shifted from Charlie to Coral and Charlotte. *Lord, I'm strugglin' to pray for myself and my difficulties, but I'm remembering those sweet gals that I love. Protect 'um. Help Coral in her mission of mercy and help Lottie.* Ernest's emotions got the best of him. His eyes filled, and he began wringing his hands –an Ashby tell that all was not well. *Just help my darlin' and bring her home safely to me..."*

He spied a dandelion that had gone to seed. Some called the whispers of white dream makers. Others considered the scattering like pestilence. Ernest saw the seeds as tenacious and tangible creations of God. The wind blew the seeds and seemingly planted them as willed.

May the wind of the Holy Spirit blow and Your will be done in my life, Ernest prayed.

The swell of Big Creek was at its peak. The ice and snow in the high country had melted. In the next few weeks, as the days warmed and the mornings and evenings remained cool, the liquid would turn to vapor, and a mist would rise from the water.

The apple trees in the field between the creek and the homestead were blooming. He was in a hurry but couldn't help but stand in the midst of the trees and enjoy the unusual rain that fell on his shoulders and head. *If only Lottie could see me now.*

As Ernest approached the barn, he yelled out to Rudy. "Brother, I've just left your sweet and sassy wife to come a callin'."

Rudy exited the barn and greeted Ernest wholeheartedly with a firm pat on the back. "She is sweet and sassy, but I do treasure her. I bet she was somethin' of a sister."

"She is still somethin' of a sister –givin' advice like she's lived to be a hundred."

"She'll get carried away on ya."

Ernest followed Rudy into the barn.

"I'm thinkin' this ain't a social call," Rudy said. "Have you been gatherin' wool and need to talk some."

"In a minute or two," answered Ernest. "Emie mentioned that you was havin' trouble with a sow and her littles."

"The mama is restless for sure." Rudy ushered Ernest to a small pen tucked in the very back of the barn. "The piglets is hungry, and the sow's wantin' to feed 'um. But, she's nervous and won't wait for 'um to latch."

"Do you mind if I give her some help? I've done this a few times."

"I know you have," Rudy chuckled. "Well, crawl on in there and see what's needin' done."

The sow's teats were full. It was obvious that she was miserable. Ernest approached her cautiously. His hand was filled with grain and his voice filled with song.

Wake up and end the day thinking of you. Oh, why does it do this to me? Is it such bliss to be thinking of you? And when I fall asleep at night, it seems you just tiptoe into all my dreams. So, I think of no other one ever since I've begun thinking of you...

He knew that Rudy was trying his best not to laugh. Ernest also knew that some sows appreciated a good love song. When he was a boy raising hogs with his father and brother, he had learned that a gentle touch and soft voice accomplished more than a hickory stick and harsh words.

The mama took the grain from his hand. Ernest began to rub the pig's back. His hand traveled lower toward her side. The sow laid down, and Ernest gently patted her belly. As the piglets drew near, he placed them each on a teat. As he continued to sing his love song, the mama relaxed, and her babies nosed and nursed.

"Brother, you got yourself a way with women and babies," Rudy chuckled.

Ernest sighed deeply. He closed his eyes and shook his head like he was telling the whole world "no."

"Rudy, are you sure you're wantin' to bear my burdens?"

"Let's take a sit. Emie made me some sweet tea earlier today and biscuits with bacon." Ernest didn't know how to begin. He felt like a jar of blackstrap molasses where the mixture was so thick the serving spoon stood upright. Molasses was made from sugarcane. The cane was mashed and boiled three times to create the dark mixture. He felt like he'd been picked, mashed, and boiled.

Ernest appreciated that Rudy didn't rush him. The two enjoyed Emie's fare, and when the time was right, he opened his mouth and the words began to trickle like molasses dripping from a dipper. The trickle then gave way to a tumult.

"Ernest, I know you feel pressed to help Mercy. I done know from what you said that the babe is in your heart. I also know that Granny Laurel is makin' trouble. Everythin' and everyone seem to be movin' in on you, but God is bigger than it all."

Rudy rested his elbows on his knees. "In these hills, marryin' has its own mind. With some, the daddies still do the arrangin'. With others, the boys just marry who comes along first."

Like Rudy, Ernest understood the unusual ways of the hill people.

"I married Emie cause I loved her. Her sweet nonsense drew me from the time we was little. I'm believin' that you love Lottie and that marryin' Mercy would break four hearts: you for marryin' when you love someone else; Lottie for being let loose, Mercy for realizin' someday that true married love can't be one sided, and Eli who will sense that you love him more than his mama and know somehow that it ain't right."

Ernest shifted positions on the stool.

"Some men can love more than one gal," Rudy continued. "I expect if God took Emie that maybe over time I might could love again. Like Lottie, maybe I could pass through grief. My granddaddy told me once that he learned to love my grandmama. Seems their marriage was arranged. I believe he loved her. He was faithful and true. He only had eyes for her. But I ain't sure that I could learn to love when lovin' Emie feels just like breathin'."

Ernest could hear the piglets in the back of the barn, nuzzling again. The mama grunted. It was her way of saying she was happy. He had sung a pig a love song meant for Charlotte. If that wasn't true love, he didn't know what love was. Loving Lottie felt right. To not be with her would be like drowning.

The idea of drowning brought back to mind an incident that he and his brother had shared in the flow of Big Creek. Growing up, Lester had almost drowned there. It was a hot summer day. The two brothers had worked the hogs all morning and were both tired and overheated. A cool dip in the creek seemed the best way to wash away their shattered strength, stink, and sweat. The swallow hole had surprised Lester. He went under once, then twice, on the third time his arms flailed as he fought the water.

Ernest still remembered the look of panic on Lester's face. Lester, who generally was self-assured, unruffled by trouble, and courageous in the face of danger, had fought with an invisible monster. He could have saved himself by swimming a few strokes and then standing on his feet.

Ernest, who stood on sure footing, was able to pull his brother safely to the creek bank.

Lottie was his sure footing. Ernest loved her. He knew God was in control, yet a part of him feared losing the gal of his dreams. What would happen if he fell into a swallow hole because of Mercy? Ernest felt panicked and imagined himself flailing at the bottom of the creek, searching for hope to survive.

Chapter Twelve

To get rid of warts, steal someone's dishcloth and
bury it. The warts will go away.

Appalachian Folk Belief

Coral didn't mean to look at the words from
her brother. Well, maybe she did, but only because Lottie was so quiet,
and that worried her. The note was confusing yet humorous, "Come
home. I done sung to a sow, and she ain't near as pretty as you."

When Coral glanced up, Lottie entered the room. "I'm sorry,
Sister. It ain't my place to be readin' your private words."

Lottie started laughing. "I'm glad I'm prettier than a pig."

Coral felt embarrassed. "Forgive me…I was worried."

"I wrote the note, Coral, so I would remember to tell you, word
for word, what Rudy's mama said."

"It still ain't right…"

Lottie smiled, "I've forgiven you, now forgive yourself. I'm
wantin' to talk about your brother. I'm thinkin' that he misses me and
wants me home."

"I'm also thinkin' as much." Coral sat on the settee and patted the
place beside her. "It's takin' longer than I thought with Charlie. We
done visited him a couple of times, and still he's actin' like a mule."

Lottie giggled while taking her place next to her friend. "It ain't
nice to be name callin', but is it really name callin' if there's truth in
the words?"

"I'm thinkin' that name callin' is name callin'," Coral answered. "I'm hopin' that today will be the day that Charlie talks to Jesus."

"Me, too." Lottie paused before continuing. "Coral, somethin' don't feel right. I'm thinkin' that somethin' might be brewin' in the holler."

"What kind of brewin'?" Coral asked. "Fermentin' or fomentin'?"

"I ain't thinkin' that moonshine's involved," Lottie answered. "More like trouble comin'."

The conversation was interrupted when Pastor Rex hurried into the room. "Ladies, I've just received word that Thomas is hurtin'. Hurtin' bad. The tent done collapsed on him. I'm goin' to his aid. He's at a house next to where we held the gatherin'." The pastor stopped to catch his breath. "Go on and visit with Charlie. The warden won't like it none if we start changin' the arrangements. I'm knowin' the officer will keep watch. Please be prayin' for Thomas."

Before the girls could ask a question, Pastor Rex left the room. Coral heard the door slam in the adjoining suite. She and Charlotte ran to the window where a pair of horses and a small wagon waited. The driver was the same man who had taken them to the meeting. The horseman pulled into the street without looking, forcing a passing automobile to swerve. The driver pounded the Gabriel. Coral knew that the horn was named after the angel in the Bible who delivered messages. The driver's message was loud and clear. *Get out of my way.*

Coral and Lottie were already seated and waiting when Charlie entered the visitor's room.

"Well, if it ain't my two favorite gals come a callin'." When neither of the girls answered, Charlie looked puzzled. "You two is a mite pretty, but today somethin' ain't quite right. Cat got your tongue."

Mrs. Randolph had explained the aphorism during Coral's schooling. In ancient Egypt, the tongues of judged liars were cut out and fed to cats.

Coral knew it wasn't very Christian, but at that moment, she thought the removal of Charlie's tongue might be a good thing.

She watched Officer Cupid help Charlie sit down in the chair. Even if it was only in her mind, she knew it was a problem to imagine him using an endearment. What would happen if she slipped in her speech? Office Hadley caught her gazing at him. Lottie also noticed and quietly cleared her throat.

"Charlie, I ain't feelin' too friendly today," Coral said. "We just heard news about a hurtin' friend."

"Well, tell girlie, tell."

Officer Hadley was at his post and looked just as disgusted as Coral felt. She and Lottie shouldn't have come to see Charlie. She was too worried about Pastor Thomas and didn't feel worried about Charlie at all. Charlotte was worried about Ernest and nothing seemed to feel right.

"We don't have hardly any news. There ain't much to tell." Coral acknowledged. "Do you mind if we talk about mulberries again?"

"I think we done exhausted that subject," Charlie snapped.

The shape of his mouth reminded Coral of the snapping turtles in Big Creek. Ernest said they were aggressive because it was hard for them to hide their heads and limbs inside their protective shells.

"Coral," Lottie spoke. "I know a thing or two about mulberries." She looked directly at Charlie. "If eaten at the wrong time of year, they could poison a person."

"Girlies," Charlie began. "I am not experiencin' your kindness today. I believe Lottie's got killin' on her mind."

Coral gave Charlie the stink eye. "Your sarcasm ain't becomin'."

"So, when I'm talkin' sweet, you find me becomin', little one? Why, I had no idea. Well, I'm tellin' you that the feelin' is mutual and wonderin' what we're gonna do about it."

Charlotte looked like she was ready to throttle Charlie. "Do you know that I'm an expert marksman? If I had my bow and an arrow, I could do some demonstratin'."

"I'm afeared, Lottie. It's a good thing I'm in prison where such harmful things ain't allowed."

Coral looked at Officer Hadley. His stance was stiff. His chest was expanded, and his hands were clenched. His eyes looked askance. Charlie was outdoing himself, and Coral worried that trouble would ferment between the officer and inmate.

When she was a child, each year her mama canned grape juice. Mama would boil the grapes and drain the juice through cheesecloth. Then she threw the skins into the garden for compost. Her mama told her the skins contained wild yeast that fermented if left in the juice, causing the canning jars to explode. The purplish red liquid would stain, and the broken jars would cut.

Coral quickly asked God to forgive her mindset and to redeem her and Lottie's time with Charlie. Just as the officer stepped forward, she started talking.

"Charlie, we're havin' a not-so-nice meetin' today, and I'm thinkin' we need to talk about pleasantries," she began. "Do you know why I'm likin' mulberries so much? I like the pies and jams and the berries picked fresh, but someday I am wantin' to touch silk. In other parts of the world, them silkworms do enjoy eatin' the mulberry leaves."

"You is done crazy," Charlie declared.

"Sometimes I am," she answered. "But among the women in the holler, there's a longin' for finer things. Not to get rich and leave their husbands and littles but just to know about and touch and see."

She could feel Lottie and Office Hadley looking at her.

Charlie shifted in his chair. "I'll be rememberin' that the next time I go courtin'."

"Tell me about courtin', Charlie. "I ain't never been."

"Well, if courtin' is meetin' gals in speakeasies and doin' unspeakables, I have plenty to be tellin'.""

"I ain't never been in a speakeasy either," she said.

She could see Charlie softening.

"Coral, gals like you don't belong in such places. They belong in churches wearin' white and marryin' men who will treat 'um right."

"Charlie, men like you don't belong in such places neither.

There's a better way. You belong in church wearin' your finest, waitin' for a pretty gal to say 'I do.'"

"That ain't gonna happen'. You and me both knows it."

"Lottie," Coral spoke as they exited the main door to the prison, "we are tryin' to keep Charlie out of hell, not poison him and send him into the clutches of the devil."

"I know, Sister. I just couldn't help myself."

"Well, truth be told, I was thinkin' of cuttin' his tongue out."

"We're a fine pair, Coral. We're supposed to be spreadin' the love of Jesus, and we done got killin' on our minds."

"I was only gonna maim him, Sister, and maybe the mulberries would have just given him a bad belly ache. Now, about the bow and arrow, I ain't rightly sure how to justify that one."

Shocked by her own words, Coral put her hand over her mouth. When Lottie started to tee-hee, Coral couldn't help but join in.

The pathway between the two barbed wire fences led to the guard house located just inside the prison walls. Coral was surprised to see Officer Hadley standing next to the mud-colored hut. She felt her face warm and knew that her light complexion made blushes more visible.

Coral greeted the officer who returned in kind.

"Ladies, you did a fine job today of keepin' the prisoner in his place."

"Thank you," Coral replied and then wondered if thanks were in order. She didn't know what else to say. Coral glanced at Charlotte who had an unusual expression on her face. When Lottie raised her eyebrows slightly, Coral understood that her friend was encouraging her to engage the officer in conversation.

"It's a nice day, ain't it," Coral faltered.

"Yes," Office Hadley answered. "I was wonderin' about your friend. The one who is hurting. Is there anything I can do to help?"

Coral had always been shy. She was bold in talking with Charlie because God had impressed upon her the importance of her delivering a message of deliverance. Talking with a man she found attractive was a new experience. When Lottie spoke up on her behalf, Coral felt relieved.

As Lottie explained about Pastor Thomas, Coral stood nervously with her hands clasped together at her waist. Because she was concerned about the officer seeing her blush again, she kept looking at the ground. She also was worried about Thomas, Lottie, and whatever Lottie thought was happening in the holler. She was even worried about Charlie.

Officer Hadley's compassion brought some relief to Coral. He even volunteered to accompany her and Lottie to the outskirts of town.

Coral was impressed by Office Hadley's Tin Lizzie. She knew that Henry Ford had worked his way from manufacturing the Model A to the Model T –twenty models in all. The motor car was black and very tall. The wheels had wooden spokes. A spare wheel was attached to the side of the car.

No one in the holler owned a car. Ernest had told her once that most roads were unfit for a mule and cart let alone a car. Her brother Lester had driven in the moonshiners' stock car races. In fact, that was where he met Lottie.

"Coral, would you like to join me in the front?" Office Hadley asked.

Coral was sure that she would be more comfortable in the second seat. Before she could politely refuse, the officer opened the back door ushering Lottie inside. He then rounded the car and opened the front passenger door for Coral. How could she refuse?

He started the car with a crank and climbed into the driver's seat. Somehow it felt scandalous to be sitting in such close quarters with a man.

The sedan seats were black leather and slightly worn. Coral was fascinated by the wooden steering wheel. In the holler, reins were used to guide the horses. She giggled quietly when she thought about Amos and Andy with a steering wheel attached to their backs. She wasn't sure how the numerous gauges and long stick coming from the floorboard were used.

It didn't take her long to figure out that the stick coming from the floor had something to do with moving faster and slower. Coral began pointing to this and that and asking questions about the buttons, gauges, and levers. She admired Officer Hadley's patience in instructing her about the automobile's operation.

"I bought the Leaping Lena used. I'm hoping that you like her."

The what? Coral thought. Then, the meaning dawned on her. "I do like her, but I'm wonderin' why vehicles on four wheels are referred to as women."

"I don't know, but it may have to do with a man's sense of affection. I prefer that she's a she."

As they exited the prison grounds, Coral directed the officer to turn right.

"Thank you, Officer Hadley, for helpin'."

"Coral, please call me James. After all, I'm addressing you by your given name."

Coral knew that there were four different Jameses in Scripture and wondered if James had any of the attributes of the other men. She hoped that he wasn't like the father of Judas Iscariot. Of course, the father could have been fine and the son still might have betrayed Jesus. There was James the lesser because he was small in stature. That certainly wasn't this James. There was nothing small about him. Then there was James the brother of John. Both brothers, along with Peter, had shared a special relationship with Christ. There was also a James who was the half-brother of Jesus.

"Do you have a middle name?" Coral asked.

His face flushed slightly. "I'm only answering on account of you being you. It's Valentine, if you must know."

Coral smiled. Now, it would be even harder not to think of him as Officer Cupid.

"Well, at least you didn't laugh. I've thrown a few punches because of my name."

She was slightly taken aback. She knew that Lester had been a fighter. Her daddy had also thrown punches and done other things in the Great War. Ernest believed that there were things worth fighting for but admitted that he hadn't come across too many. She couldn't imagine Rudy with raised fists unless he was worried for Emie or Jewel. "Defendin' your honor is one thing, but I have a hard time imaginin' you fightin' over a given name. It's unusual, though. I'll hand ya that."

James glanced at Coral strangely. She assumed his look had to do with her comment about fighting.

"My parents named me Valentine because I was born on Valentine's Day. My mama wanted Valentine to be my first name, but my daddy wouldn't have it. He'd only agree to it bein' in the middle."

After a slight lull in the conversation, Coral broke the silence. "This is nice. I'm enjoyin' automobile ridin'. At school, Mrs. Randolph told the learners that Henry Ford hoped that everyone could purchase a car and enjoy God's great open spaces."

Between shifting gears, James briefly took her hand. "You make me happy, Coral."

She didn't know what to say and turned back to look at Lottie. Her friend was gazing out the window. The noise from the car had more than likely prevented Lottie from hearing the officer's confession.

Coral cranked down her window. The breeze felt good on her face. Her dark blond hair that was generally tied in a knot broke free and started blowing in the breeze. "I like this. Your name's like churned ice cream on a hot day."

"Maybe we could share ice cream together some time. Do you like just the cream or the cream with berries?"

"That would be fine," she answered nervously. "I'm thinkin' that mulberries or even blackberries would be nice."

It wasn't hard to find the house that Pastor Rex had referenced. The horses were tied to a hitching post in front of a tired looking residence. Two children that Coral recognized from the meeting were sitting on the sagging porch steps. When she and Lottie exited the car, the young ones rushed to meet them and began singing,

The bear went over the mountain. The bear went over the mountain...

James looked confused, but Coral didn't take the time to explain.

Lottie knocked on the front door which was answered by a woman who looked as tired and worn as the house in which she stood.

"We're lookin' for Pastor Rex and Pastor Thomas," Lottie said.

The older negro woman opened the door wider and stepped aside. "They's in the back."

The house was small. There were only three rooms. Coral could see Pastor Rex from where she was standing by the front door. She quickly took the few steps to reach him.

Pastor Rex turned as she and Lottie entered the room. "I'm surprised to be seein' you." He then nodded to Officer Hadley who was standing just outside the doorway.

The older pastor shifted so Coral and Lottie could reach the bed. Thomas' face was bloodied. His shirt had been removed and Coral could see lacerations on his arms and upper chest. There were several deep gashes oozing blood. One cut was extremely deep, exposing tissue and muscle. Thomas was moaning yet appeared to be sleeping.

Pastor Rex gestured toward the younger pastor. "I looked him over good, mostly cuts and bruises. I ain't thinkin' nothin' is broken. A doctor did come callin."

"Some of the cuts is lookin' deep. Why didn't the doctor do stitchin'?" Coral asked.

"He was a colored man and said that negro doctors work on dark folk and white doctors work on white folk. Since Thomas wasn't neither, he didn't know what to do other than give 'um a couple tablets."

Lottie squeezed past Pastor Rex and went to the other side of the bed. Simultaneously, Pastor Thomas' hands were enveloped by the young women. When Lottie prayed for healing, Coral closed her eyes and nodded in agreement. Coral had only sung in front of others while visiting Charlie, but she wanted to encourage Thomas in song as well as prayer.

Why should I feel discouraged? Why should the shadows come? Why should my heart be lonely and long for heaven and home, when Jesus is my portion? My constant friend is He. His eye is on the sparrow, and I know He watches me. His eye is on the sparrow, and I know He watches me. I sing because I'm happy. I sing because I'm free. His eye is on the sparrow, and He watches over me…

"Thomas, a lady wrote that song while visitin' her ailin' friend. God is watchin' over you. His eye is on you," Coral added.

Charlotte looked at Coral. "His breathin' don't sound quite right."

James drew closer and stood behind Coral. She could feel the weight of his hand on her shoulder. "I know someone who could maybe help. He's a doctor at the prison and doesn't care about the color of a man's skin. Let me fetch him. I'll be back soon as I can."

There was nothing to do but wait. Earlier, Coral had smelled wood burning. Now the scent of brewing coffee permeated the air. Her mouth began to water.

She heard rustling outside the bedroom window and pulled back the washed-out blue rayon curtains to find the two children from earlier grinning ear to ear. The boy and girl looked to be siblings. The girl was younger than the boy. Since her two front teeth were missing, Coral guessed her age to be about seven. The pair were rolling ice cubes in their mouths and hands. Water from the melted ice had left streaks on their dirty faces. Across the street, a delivery man carried a small block of ice to a neighbor.

Coral smiled slightly at Pastor Rex and motioned for Lottie to join her by the window. Lottie pantomimed nocking an arrow and shooting a bow. Coral pretended that her hands were bear claws and drew her face into a scowl. The boy and girl giggled all-the-more. They only ran off when the woman who had opened the front door came into view and put her index finger to her lips, signaling the children to be quiet.

The woman carried three glasses of what appeared to be coffee with ice. The earthy, nutty aroma reached Coral. She had never heard of coffee being deliberately chilled.

Pastor Rex introduced Mae as the children's grandmother. She also worked at a diner just outside Charleston that served iced coffee. The mixture had been sweetened with sugar and contained a small amount of cream.

In an effort not to disturb Pastor Thomas, everyone talked in hushed tones. Pleasantries were exchanged before Mae repeated to Coral and Lottie the account of what had happened to the young pastor. Thomas was inside the tent when some area troublemakers began pressing on the exterior posts. The tent collapsed, holding Pastor Thomas hostage. The men who came to his rescue found the pastor unconscious and bleeding. The wounds came from the wooden frame that supported the interior walls as well as the weight of the tent itself.

Mae washed Thomas' face, shoulders, and arms with cool water. Her loving touch brought tears to Coral's eyes. She remembered Pastor Thomas saying that he wasn't appreciated in the community where he served. Mae's gentle gestures spoke otherwise.

When James returned with a young, dark-haired, brown-eyed doctor, Coral sighed with relief. The physician had a no-nonsense presence and immediately ushered everyone from the room.

The small group waited in the cramped living room. There weren't enough chairs, but it didn't matter. Comfortable bottoms gave way to anxious hearts. James stayed by her side. Occasionally he would reassuringly pat her arm or back. Even the two young children, Tim and Trudy, were subdued.

It was dusk. Coral worried that the lighting in Pastor Thomas' room wasn't sufficient for proper examination. Like the homes in the holler, there was no electricity. Kerosene lamps were lit. She heard Thomas softly cry out. The tablets from earlier had to be wearing off.

When the door creaked, all eyes turned toward the dim hallway.

"The prognosis is good," the doctor began. "Thomas will fully recover. He has two broken ribs that should mend with time. I stitched two of the deeper wounds, but there will be scarring. It would have been better if the stitching had been done earlier. You're fine folk for takin' care of him."

Chapter Thirteen

If you drop a fork, a man is coming to visit you.

Appalachian Folk Belief

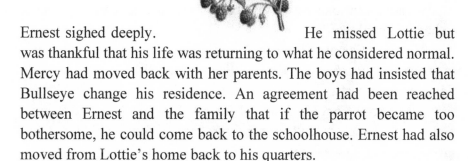

Ernest sighed deeply. He missed Lottie but was thankful that his life was returning to what he considered normal. Mercy had moved back with her parents. The boys had insisted that Bullseye change his residence. An agreement had been reached between Ernest and the family that if the parrot became too bothersome, he could come back to the schoolhouse. Ernest had also moved from Lottie's home back to his quarters.

The summer session for the learners started today. Ernest was ready and looking forward to spending time with his students. At the end of the school year, there had been some teasing within the class about who would and would not be attending the sessions. Ernest had decided to make his summer scholars feel like the favored ones. He'd prepared biscuits and stolen a jar of jam from Lottie's cupboard. He hoped to repay her with kisses as sweet at the berry concoction.

When the schoolhouse door opened, Ernest looked up from his desk expecting to see the learners. Instead, one of the holler men, accompanied by Justice, was at the threshold. Now, Samuel was a natural leader in the community and though not officially elected, he and several others generally enforced the local laws and settled any disputes among the people.

Samuel was a tall man and broad as a beam. By the determined look on his face, Ernest assumed that he wasn't visiting for pleasantries

117

but with a specific purpose in mind. The man had a good heart, but a sharp tongue: sharp as a needle, sharp as a razor, and sharp as a tack.

Ernest appreciated that Justice was present. He was a friend, kind and fair, not prone to anger, and wise beyond his years of schooling. In fact, Justice fit the biblical description of an elder. If a church was ever established in the region, Ernest hoped Justice would be one of the founders and leaders.

Samuel didn't mince words. "We ain't come for niceties."

"Now, we agreed that kindness should be prevailin'," Justice interjected.

"Be as kind as you want, but the truth is the truth. The teacher ain't got no choice but to marry Mercy, and the sooner the better."

"I'm thinkin' that we need to gather us a law man and a preacher to hear advisin' words."

"Justice, it's your kin we're talkin' about. Your daughter needs a man, and the teacher is the one." Samuel raised his eyebrows, "He done seen her parts."

Ernest rose from his desk and extended his hand, first to Samuel and then to Justice. "Gentlemen, I figured you'd come callin', and, by-all-means, you're welcome. I am askin', however, that you take a seat and prepare yourselves to join our local learners for a schoolin' session."

Justice motioned to the man standing next to him. "Samuel, I tried my best to be tellin' you we should visit later in the day,"

"Time is wastin', but I'm appreciatin' that what we got to say ain't fit for our young ones. We'll be back, Ernest, after the schoolin's done for the day."

Prior to the pledge and morning prayers, one of the young learners raised his hand. Just as Ernest started to give instructions to wait, the handsome chatty child began to prattle. "My daddy says that you is feudin' with the holler men and that it's gonna be bad like them Hatfields and McCoys."

Ernest felt anger rise in his chest but pushed it down. "The

Hatfields and McCoys was an arguin', fightin' bunch for sure." He grinned and began tickling the boy. "Let's say our allegiance and pledge our hearts first to God and then our country."

It amazed Ernest how news could spread so quickly in the holler. Without telephones, telegraphs, and teletypes, how did gossip travel so far?

Because of the young student's inquisitiveness, all the learners were now curious. Ernest knew that in some situations it was best to let a sleeping dog lie but when it came to his students, teaching moments often presented themselves in the most unexpected ways.

"The Hatfields hailed from West Virginia and the McCoys from Kentucky. Some of 'um fought for the Union and some for the Confederates."

The older children knew about the Civil War, but the younger children didn't understand. So Ernest, in as simple terms as possible, explained the complexities of the War Between the States.

"The families was fightin' each other about moonshine and money. They called their hooch the water of life. One of the men was even named 'Devil.'"

The learners gasped.

"Now he wasn't the real devil, just named after him for his meanness."

Ernest leaned against the corner of his desk. "There ain't gonna be fightin' like the Hatfields and McCoys. That's just a long tooth example of what can happen when people don't settle their differences."

Ernest enjoyed his day with the youngsters. One of his greatest pleasures in life was teaching. He was born a teacher. It was his calling. Sure, the littles could be disgusting, distasteful, and displeasing with their gas letting, belching, nose picking, and nail biting, but their unconditional love, desire to learn, and unacquittable curiosity made him smile.

Justice arrived before Samuel. "Ernest, I'm a mite sorry about this mornin'.""

"I knew it was comin'. Ain't no need to be sorry."

Ernest had an important question to ask but wasn't quite sure how to phrase his words–frustrated, he gently bit down on his lower lip.

"I am wonderin', Justice," he stammered. "Why did you suggest callin' on Sheriff Robbins and a preacher?"

"I am knowin' that there's somethin' amiss, Ernest. I was thinkin' that the sheriff and preacher could be helpin'. It's botherin' me that on the day Eli was born, I saw Granny and Mercy talkin', but when I asked Granny about it, she said I was seein' things."

"Why would she deny visitin' with Mercy?"

"I ain't rightly sure, but there's some kind of nonsense goin' on. Secret keepin' ain't generally a good thing."

"Thank you, Justice, for tellin'."

"I wish it weren't so. I already care for you like a son and given a choice, I would be welcomin' you into my family–but not through deceivin', trickery, and forcin' someone against their wishes."

"Is there talk of forcin'?"

"If you ain't agreein' to marry Mercy on your own, Samuel plans to bring his shotgun. Some is thinkin' it would be better if Mercy could be sayin' that she's a widow."

Ernest was stunned. "So, Samuel is gonna shoot me with bird shot?!"

"Well, first he's wantin' to use the gun to convince, and if convincin' don't work, shootin' would be next. The pain from the pellets would be persuadin'."

Ernest could see Samuel in the distance, "Justice, did you ask Mercy about her visit with Granny?"

"Ain't had a chance yet. The babe's just a few days old, and my girl's recoverin'."

Ernest looked his friend in the eye. "Who's being deceivin'?"

Justice looked away and lowered his head. "Ernest. I ain't asked because there's a part of me that ain't wantin' to know."

"Would you be mindin' if we talked to her together?"

As Samuel approached, Justice answered, "That's probably best."

Lord, I am needing the wisdom of Solomon, Ernest thought.

He patted Samuel on the back. "Glad you came visitin' again. The learners have done left and now we can be havin' our conversation."

Ernest directed Samuel and Justice to two chairs beside his desk. The chairs were reserved for children who occasionally needed to be reminded about proper behavior. "I got us some biscuits and jam. I can't brag on the biscuits since I made um, but the jam is mighty fine."

In the holler, sharing food and sharing conversation went together. When delicious morsels filled the mouth, harsh words were often forgotten.

"Samuel, while you and Justice is enjoyin' a sweet bite, I'm wantin' you to know that I appreciate your concern for the holler folk. It's men like you that keeps things in order and helps us all to be gettin' along."

Samuel opened his mouth to say something, but the biscuits had sat out all day and were quite dry. He tried to swallow but was forced to continue chewing.

"Justice and me was just talkin'. As soon as our visitin' is done, I'm headin' to talk with Mercy about our future."

Samuel finally emptied his mouth.

"Would you like another?" Ernest asked.

The large man wiped his mouth with the back of his hand. Dried crumbs fell to the floor. "I'm thankin' you, but one is a plenty. I'm glad you're seein' the truth of things, Ernest, and I'm hopin' we can done get this behind us."

"Mercy, this ain't time for foolin'," Justice began.

Mercy closed her lips tightly and clasped her hands.

"Your hands ain't big enough to be holdin' your future, Eli's future, and Ernest's future."

Mercy remained silent.

"Your not talkin' is sayin' a lot," Justice continued. "Ernest and me is needin' to know what happened between you and Granny."

"It's my time to be sucklin' the baby," Mercy said. "You best be leavin'."

"Now, Daughter, you're usin' the babe to help with your secret keepin' and manipulatin' ways. Eli is sleepin'. His tummy is full, and he ain't wantin' to be disturbed."

"There ain't no secrets and no manipulatin' on my part."

"If you're hidin' somethin' for Granny's benefit, Mercy, it's still called secret keepin' and deceivin'," Ernest said. "I ain't wantin' to speak out of turn, but God done set you free from one form of mischief, so don't be invitin' another."

Mercy started to cry, so Bullseye started to cry. His cries, however, mimicked Eli and were more like mews.

"I'm a considerate man," Ernest continued, "but I ain't so considerate that I'll marry you and give Eli my name based on lyin' and cheatin'. You best speak up now, or I'll be callin' Granny and the holler men into this very room and be exposin' the darkness."

"Ernest, you're scarin' me." Mercy bewailed.

"It ain't me that you should be fearin'."

"You is being a mite harsh."

"Harsh, Mercy, is turnin' our neighbors against me. The men are threatenin' to shoot me."

"It can't be!"

"Yes, Mercy, it can be."

"My needs is great, Ernest. I got me a baby that needs tendin'. You loved me once. I'm thinkin' you could love me again."

Ernest shook his head and started to leave the room. "I'll be back. First with Granny and then with Samuel."

Mercy reached toward Ernest. "Alright, alright…"

Ernest sat on one side of Mercy, Justice on the other. Their positions brought to remembrance the game that Mercy had previously played. The rules and players were different, but the end result the same. The Bible talked about not participating in witchcraft, but, at some point, God's people must have looked to divination, or it wouldn't have been necessary to have rules against it.

"I went to see Granny about helpin' birth the baby," Mercy began. "I told her that I'd just come from the schoolhouse. We shared some raspberry tea. Then I didn't see no harm when she wanted to rub ointment on my belly. She said it would help get me ready for birthin'. I was expectin' somethin' sweet smellin', but it stank–stank real bad."

When the baby started to stir, Ernest gathered Eli in his arms.

"I was nervous," Mercy continued. "I kept hearin' things and seein' images behind Granny's curtains. When I asked, she said it was just the spirits movin'. Then, I was more than nervous; I was done scared. The next mornin', I saw her on the road. She was sittin' under a tree like she was waitin' for me. When I told her about forgettin' my jar, the water jar I brought when I came to visit you, Ernest, she said it was a sign and that sealed inside it was my desire to be marryin' Ernest…"

Justice rose from his chair, took Mercy's hand, and then kissed the top of his daughter's head. Ernest had witnessed Mercy kiss Eli in the same fashion.

Justice encouraged her. "Go on, Girlie. You done started, now finish the story."

"Granny was carryin' a basket filled with buttercups. I could see them bright yellow petals. Them three leaves, too. She had the roots and all. She broke off a root and chewed on it a bit, then offered me a chaw. She was convincin', tellin' me that the root would help the baby."

Mercy started to cry. The crying turned to sobbing. Her lips quivered and mucus started running from her nose.

Ernest knew that buttercups were poisonous. Every farmer in the hills knew that the flowers would sour a goat or cow's milk. He had no idea about the roots. It was a mystery to him why the Lord created a flower that when cold formed a cup to draw warmth from the sun, yet it was filled with poison.

Mercy reached for Eli. Maybe it was the way of mamas and babies that each gave comfort to the other.

"Just after seein' Granny, did you head to the school?" Ernest asked.

Mercy pursed her lips and nodded yes.

He continued questioning her. "How much of the root were you eatin'?

She lifted-up her pinkie finger.

"When did the pains start?"

"There was a little painin' as I was walkin', but when I got to the school, it started hurtin' bad."

Granny had begun her ministrations by giving Mercy raspberry tea to induce labor. Ernest recalled his daddy had taught him to feed raspberries to the sows past due in bringing their littles into the world. The berries worked, but the process was slow. The ointment Granny made likely contained primrose. Primrose flowers were deceptive in that they looked like roses but smelled nothing alike. The ointment made from them would have only assisted, but not brought on sudden labor. The buttercup root was a mystery—whatever it contained succeeded in bringing Eli into the world quickly.

He wanted to ask Mercy if Granny Laurel mentioned nipple massaging. His daddy had sworn by that as well. He knew, however, that the question would be inappropriate and also, asked out of exasperation, not concern.

"Mercy, did you know that Granny was timin' things so I would help with the birthin'?"

Her shoulders sagged. "I thought as much but wasn't sure."

Ernest made eye contact with Justice and left the room. As he walked through the threshold, he heard Mercy call after him. He didn't answer. He couldn't. Whatever had happened to Mercy seemed to have driven all her morals into the ground. She had once held his heart in her hands. He was aggrieved beyond reason. God's mercy had changed his life but there were no words to describe how the woman named "Mercy" also had changed him.

A mosquito buzzed around his head, a sure sign that summer had arrived. He had once read that the thin tube the insect used for drawing blood was actually comprised of six different needles: two of the needles punctured the skin, the second pair held the skin apart, an additional needle found a blood vessel, and the final needle stimulated blood flow.

Granny Laurel and Mercy working together were like giant

mosquitoes siphoning life from him.

He swatted at the mosquito. It was relentless. When it finally landed on his left forearm, Ernest squished the blood sucker dead with his right index finger.

For the past several days, Ernest had lived in a state of disillusionment. His disappointment in Mercy, his distrust of Granny, his disbelief in Samuel and the holler men had all taken their toll.

Enough was enough. He wasn't without power. God's spirit resided inside him.

He had choices to make. He could choose to let others dictate his life, choose to direct his own life, or make the right choice and allow God to dominate his thoughts and actions. He knew that God was always the right choice, but it was hard to release Mercy and let her make choices and live through the consequences.

Chapter Fourteen

It's bad luck to close a pocketknife unless you
were the one to open it.

Appalachian Folk Belief

"I ain't understandin', Warden," Coral said.

"There's been an outbreak of influenza. It ain't safe for you to be here."

"Is Charlie strugglin'? Has he taken sick?"

"He is in the infirmary, ma'am."

Coral quickly prayed. *Lord, please don't take him. Not now. Not when he doesn't know you.*

"I need to see him."

"It ain't possible. You and your friend need to leave."

Charlotte took hold of Coral's arm. "Listen to the warden. We best go."

"Please, I just need to see Charlie one last time. I won't come back."

Charlotte gripped Coral's arm more firmly and tried to direct her from the room. "Coral, this ain't the time to be bargainin'. I'm a little older than you. I remember people dyin' from the Spanish Fever. It came when the soldiers returned from the war."

"I ain't wantin' to make trouble…"

"We have an emergency here. I'm needed for other business. I don't have time to argue. Your insistence is takin' more time than givin' you what you want."

The warden rose from his brown chair. The leather was worn on the arms and front of the seat. The material was damaged from the constant rubbing of the warden's hands and arms, the seat cushion exposed because of his continual rising and sitting. A part of Coral felt uncomfortable for adding to the warden's problems. He was obviously a man who worked daily under a tremendous amount of strain. Now with the outbreak of flu and pneumonia, she couldn't imagine what he was thinkin' and feeling.

He walked around the desk. "Only one of you can come."

Coral looked at Lottie, "Please don't be angry. I'm askin' that you wait here whilst I do my visitin' with Charlie."

"Pastor Rex won't like this, Sister."

"I'm knowin' such, but he ain't here to ask. He's helpin' Thomas as we're helpin' Charlie."

Coral followed the warden down a flight of stairs and through a dimly lit corridor that led to a prison wing she didn't know existed. Her shoes clicked on the time-worn wooden floor. She walked briskly to keep up with her guide.

The infirmary smelled like bleach powder. She saw Doctor Daniels in the corner of the room talking with a nurse whose uniform included a pale blue dress with a white apron and hat. When their eyes met, he immediately turned and headed her direction.

He nodded at Coral and addressed the warden. "This isn't safe. Influenza is extremely contagious."

"I tried," the warden responded. "Short of physically removing her from my office, nothing was gonna work. We got an emergency here, and I haven't the time to fight with this stubborn young woman. We've gone a few rounds, and so far, she's always been the winner and me on the receiving end of something I don't like."

The doctor took Coral by the shoulders and lifted her slim body off the floor. "Let me escort you from the building."

Although she had no clear recollection, she was certain as a baby or toddler her mama had picked her up and playfully held her in the air. Then as a schoolgirl, Ernest had once or twice mischievously swung her around in circles. She had undeniably, however, never been lifted off the ground by another man.

"Put me down," she clamoured. "You helped Pastor Thomas. Now I need to be helpin' someone."

Annoyed, Doctor Daniels placed Coral's feet on the ground. "He's in the next room on the far right…Officer Hadley told me about your visits."

The room was crowded with beds. They were in rows from one end to the other. Most of the patients were too ill to notice her. As she carefully walked through the infirmary, she stretched out her hands and touched each bed praying for those who were suffering. The second room was smaller and held fewer patients. The comparison in room size and identification of the patients could be calculated; the amount of suffering, however, could not be measured.

Charlie was pale. His half-hearted smile made her cry. "I knew you would come," he whispered.

"Are you ready? Are you ready to talk to God?"

"Not quite yet, Girlie. I'm thinkin' of holdin' out until the end."

"Why?"

"I'm too tired to be sayin' much. Do your prayin' and go, Coral, and don't be comin' back."

She touched his forehead. He was sweating and fevered. She offered him water from a glass that was sitting on a small ledge just above his bed. He refused and closed his eyes. She brushed back his hair and prayed for salvation and healing. In an effort to soothe him, she softly sang.

What a friend we have in Jesus, all our sins and grief to bear! What a privilege to carry everything to God in prayer. O what peace we often forfeit. O what needless pain we bear, all because we do not carry everything to God in prayer…"

When Charlie fell asleep, she left his bedside and wished that she had sung a different song. The writer had experienced such grief, torment, and pain that there was suspicion that he had taken his own life. Some thought that he had penned the song for his mother, believing that she would find it after he died. *How sad for someone to have known Jesus yet be so discouraged that life didn't feel worth livin'. Lord, please be givin' Charlie the will to live and to serve you.*

Doctor Daniels opened the infirmary door for her. "I only have a moment. The men are needin' me. Don't come back here. Influenza is going to sweep through this prison like a new broom with fresh bristles that won't miss a speck of dirt. There's a comfort room just down the hall. Wash your hands and arms with soap and water. Let the water get as hot as you can stand."

Coral did as Doctor Daniels instructed and then headed back to the warden's office. She had never walked the prison hallways unaccompanied. It felt odd to be alone in such a desperate, desolate place. Though the halls were lit by buzzing overhead lights, there was a darkness present. There was also the stench of death: not just physical death from the influenza but also spiritual death. It was as if hell had seeped into the walls of the penitentiary and covered those who lived in the crowded quarters.

She thought of a passage in the Book of Romans. How can people call on Jesus' name when they don't even believe in him? How can they believe if they don't understand? And, how can they understand if no one tells them?

She had explained such things to Charlie, but what about the other inmates? They were prisoners in body, in soul, and in spirit. Their bodies were held in physical cells. Their souls were confused, and their spirits were dead in their sin.

Lord, I listened to your voice. Coral prayed. *I came for Charlie like you done told me. I spoke the truth. I'm askin' again. Charlie needs a Savior. Help him to believe and understand. And what about the others? Hell has a foothold on some and a stronghold on others. Deliver them from its hold.*

She saw him before he saw her. James was outside the warden's office pacing. Her heart skipped a beat and she felt her face flush once again.

"Coral, I was so worried. It's not safe for you to be here."

"There ain't no need for concern."

"You are my concern."

No one had ever told her such things. She was embarrassed and looked down only to notice that James' knuckles were bruised and skinned. "What happened to your hands?"

He put both hands in his pockets. "Nothin' really. Just a little scuffle."

She was concerned about James' hands and worried that he was hiding something.

"Looks like more than a scuffle. Your hands is raw."

She thought she saw a fleeting glimpse of irritation on James' face but wasn't sure. *Why would my question of concern be bothering him?*

"I already said that it ain't no cause for worry, Girlie."

The way James said "girlie" unsettled her. Ernest called her "girlie" as a form of endearment, and it made her smile. Her sisters called her "girlie" when they were teasing and giggling together. Charlie had called her "girlie" once or twice. Her heart raced with trepidation. James' tone wasn't as unnerving as Charlie's had been; yet she didn't like how he made her feel. It was almost as if he was trying to exert authority when no authority had been authorized. She felt demeaned.

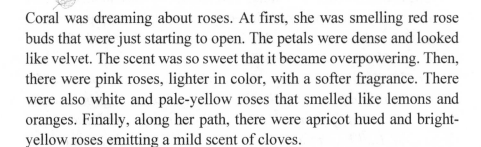

Coral was dreaming about roses. At first, she was smelling red rose buds that were just starting to open. The petals were dense and looked like velvet. The scent was so sweet that it became overpowering. Then, there were pink roses, lighter in color, with a softer fragrance. There were also white and pale-yellow roses that smelled like lemons and oranges. Finally, along her path, there were apricot hued and bright-yellow roses emitting a mild scent of cloves.

Two days after visiting Charlie, Coral's initial symptoms began. Lottie sent word to the prison asking Doctor Daniels for help. She had made the difficult decision not to contact Pastor Rex. She knew the kindly, aging minister would come immediately, but she also knew that Thomas needed help.

Lottie stood next to Coral's bed. Her friend looked so innocent, so helpless. There was nothing more that she could do. She'd bathed Coral in rubbing alcohol, had applied cool compresses to her head, and even in Coral's state of delirium, had tried to give her sips of water. The liquid had dribbled down Coral's chin and dried, blemishing her night dress.

Lottie's hair was tangled. Her face was covered in sweat. Her clothes were wrinkled. She was a sight but didn't care. Her thoughts were only of Coral and how to make her well.

Fear gripped Charleston. Officials kept telling residents the tumult was nothing like the pandemic of 1918. Citizens were quick to remember the dishonesty of the government regarding the dire consequences of the previous outbreak.

Lottie knew Coral was contagious, but how could she leave her friend? Ernest would never forgive her. She would never forgive herself for abandoning Coral in her time of need. She knew, however, that out of fear, people would walk away from the sick and dying. Patients would be forsaken who, under a healing hand, might have recovered. Others would face death without the prayers and tender care of a loved one.

To disregard someone hurtin' must bring grievin' to the heart of God, she thought.

Coral's fever, nausea, and aches had quickly worsened. When the dark spots started to appear, Lottie combated her fear with continual prayers of faith, asking God for a miracle.

She didn't have the gift of music like Coral and Ernest, but she sang little ditties to her friend. Silly songs that she had used in her Lottie the Legend performances came to mind, like the popular one that circled on the radio after harvested bananas began being shipped into the east coast harbors.

Yes, we have no bananas. We have-a no bananas today. We've string beans, and onions, cabbages, and scallions, and all sorts of fruit and say. We have an old fashioned to-mah-to. A Long Island po-tah-to. But yes, we have no bananas. We have no bananas today.

On one occasion, though sick and silent with fever, Coral had gently tapped her index finger in rhythm.

The prison had become its own breeding ground for the virus. The area had been initially quarantined. As the sickness reached other parts of the city, the confinement had lifted, and Doctor Daniels had sent word through James about how to best care for Coral.

Although Lottie followed his instructions, Coral's fever spiked, and her cough worsened. The phlegm now contained streaks of blood.

When James first visited, Lottie tried to keep him at bay. She spoke to him through her side of the door, and he answered through his side, but eventually the communication process seemed ridiculous. It was hard to hear, and their raised voices only added to the already difficult situation. She wasn't sure how her friend would feel about being seen in such a state of illness and disrepair by a man she barely knew.

James Hadley stood over Coral holding her frail pale hand. As if trying to memorize the shape and structure of Coral's hand, he had turned her palm and fingers gently this way and that way. He also interwove their fingers. His deep voice had resonated through the room. Lottie sat off to the side wishing Ernest was present to hold her own hand. She knew Coral's hands were smaller and softer. Lottie's hands were firm with muscle from drawing her bow and arrow. Her fingertips were also slightly calloused.

James explained to Lottie that he was a believer in the Good Book but struggled with his faith. "It's not easy working in a jailhouse. The good becomes blurred with the bad. Sometimes I can't tell the difference."

It was obvious to Lottie that Coral was attracted to James and that the feeling was mutual; and yet, the two had only visited once outside the confines of the prison walls. At the jailhouse, conversation had been directed at Charlie, not the officer.

During James' next visit, he brought good news from the penitentiary. The virus that had spread quickly among the inmates appeared to be easing. Those who remained ill mostly had pneumonia symptoms like Coral. Charlie was improving slightly but was still in the infirmary.

There was, however, a change in James' demeanor. He spoke to the sleeping Coral about despising Charlie for how he had spread the virus to her. Lottie knew that Coral had willingly made the choice to visit Charlie. As soon as she said, "James, it was Coral's risk, and Coral's choice…" trying to explain the situation to James, he grew tense, turned away from Lottie, and spoke to the wall in a low, strained voice. Seeing his shoulders stiffen, she coaxed. "James, James…" When James finally turned toward Coral again, his incipient expression disturbed Lottie.

Lottie knew that Coral was very naïve about men. Other than church, young women of faith living in the holler had limited opportunities to meet and interact with peers of the opposite gender. So, Lottie felt relief when James left. She determined not to entertain him again.

Coral was dreaming about the repentant thief on the cross. Jesus was demonstrating his indescribable love toward the two men hanging on the crosses beside him. The one thief asked Jesus to remember him. She could only see the body of the man who received the promise of being with Jesus. When she stepped closer, however, and looked up, his face came into view. It was Charlie. Charlie had received forgiveness for his sins.

Lottie prayed for help. Coral was still fevered, her cough persisted. Charlotte knew that recovery from the Spanish Fever knew no rhyme or reason. At times, patients would seem to recover only to face death hours later. She was thankful that the flu was milder in form than the pandemic and that the death toll was far less. People were building immunities against the strange virus. Yet, Coral's frailty continued.

Lottie heard voices in the hallway. She breathed a sigh of relief when she recognized Doctor Daniels' voice. James was with him.

"You say that Charlie's dead? Good riddance," James said. "I'd have taken his life myself for what he did to Coral."

"She wouldn't advocate murder," the doctor answered. "She made her own choice to visit Charlie."

"No one chooses the flu."

"She's young, James, and innocent in many ways."

"I'll do right by her."

Lottie knew it was wrong to eavesdrop. Yet the two were talking just outside the door. Their voices raised, she couldn't help but listen. In fact, she wondered if she should interrupt the conversation. Though Coral's health was at risk, when Coral recovered physically, her emotional health would then be at risk with the likes of James.

"You can't take care of her–not like she needs. She's tender. You're too angry a man–angry at the world."

"I ain't angry," James' voice rose to a new level.

There was a pause in the exchange.

"It's the prison. It's the men and their evil ways," the voice of James confessed. "Prisoners like Charlie…"

"You and I both know that's it more than working at the penitentiary. We started working there about the same time. You were angry even then."

Another pause.

"Alright," James admitted. "It is more, but I can't and won't be angry with Coral. I couldn't."

"No? I am betting that you've been angry with other women." Charlotte silently cheered on the wise doctor's message. She didn't want to be the one who had to turn James away from seeing Coral. Doctor Daniels' voice continued, "You can't control your rage, can you?"

Charlotte heard a sudden scuffle and quickly opened the door. James had Doctor Daniels by the throat, pressed against the wall. When the officer saw her, he turned and stormed from the hallway, out the exterior door, and into the street.

She stared in disbelief and then began shaking. Doctor Daniels was immediately at her side.

"It's alright. He's gone. We have to focus, Lottie. Coral needs our help."

She felt nervous about the possibility of James returning, yet the doctor was right. Coral was the priority. There would be time later to discuss James.

In the midst of Doctor Daniels' examination, Coral opened her eyes. Her breathing ragged, her words were hard to understand. "Did Charlie die?"

"Yes, ma'am. He passed," the doctor answered with a curt professional nod. "But, you're strong. You can fight this, young lady."

"I dreamt about him." Coral started coughing. She weakly wiped her mouth with the back of her hand and showed obvious alarm by the small streak of blood.

"It's alright, Coral. Just that you're awake is a good sign," Doctor Daniels spoke to encourage them all.

Lottie breathed a sigh of relief and gently placed her hand on Coral's arm.

Coral's voice was barely above a whisper, "He was the thief. Charlie was the thief who went to heaven." Her eyes closed. She fell back asleep.

Chapter Fifteen

Eating honey on the day of the funeral of
someone you know will keep his or her spirit tied
to the earth.

Appalachian Folk Belief

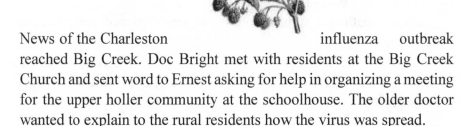

News of the Charleston influenza outbreak reached Big Creek. Doc Bright met with residents at the Big Creek Church and sent word to Ernest asking for help in organizing a meeting for the upper holler community at the schoolhouse. The older doctor wanted to explain to the rural residents how the virus was spread.

The 1918 pandemic had hit the holler but not as severely as in the bigger cities. In the backwoods, people lived a more isolated lifestyle. Homesteads were sometimes a mile or more apart, separated by farmlands, wooded areas, open fields, and streams. Outside visitors were always welcome but were few and far between.

Whether city or holler, the young and old were the most affected by the flu. Millions died- babies next to bosoms, children tended by careful hands, aged arthritic aunties, and granddads whose families had gathered for final good-byes. Soldiers also died in fabricated hospitals and trenches dug by hands. Bodies were buried in city cemeteries, treed meadows, homestead hill lands, and even foreign soil.

With concerns about the influenza in his forethoughts, worries about Mercy and Granny Laurel had been pushed aside. Each time

Ernest felt anxiousness rising in his heart, he prayed. He had also grown tired of the constant strain and confusion about his future. Thankfully, he had reached the conclusion that God, and only God, could fix the conflict, chaos, and constraints of his life.

He was also praying for Lottie, Coral, Pastor Rex, and the people of Charleston affected by the Spanish Flu.

Doc Bright didn't believe that the flu originated in Spain. The wise man told Ernest that during the Great War, the wartime censors minimized the reports of the illness. The U.S. and her allies controlled the press in hopes of keeping up morale and patriotism. Spain was a neutral country. Newspapers freely reported about the deadly disease which created the false idea about the pandemic's origin.

The holler people were good folk. He hoped they would listen to Doctor Bright and do their best to protect themselves, their families, and their neighbors. Ernest understood that they were frightened. The earlier epidemic had claimed more lives than World War I.

News of the meeting was far reaching. The schoolhouse was full of young and old alike. Ernest opened the session in prayer. The "amens" resounded. Most community residents were familiar with the warm-hearted doctor, but Ernest introduced him none the less.

"Good afternoon," Doc Bright began. "Thank you for joinin' us. As most of you know, influenza has reached Charleston. There's need for concern, but it ain't as bad as before."

Ernest wished that Auntie Ada had joined her husband for the trek up the hillside and community meeting. Doc Bright, who preferred that Ernest call him Uncle Christian, explained that Ada, concerned about an influenza eruption, had stayed behind to prepare the needed medical supplies.

Flu was such an odd word, Ernest thought. He understood that it was short for influenza, but most English words were shortened by using the front or back of the longer word. Flu came from the middle of the word. Just like the virus–it came from odd places and was hard to contain.

Doc taught a brief lesson about germs and reminded the community about the importance of hand washing and not sharing eating utensils. Ernest had witnessed first-hand households in the upper holler where a cookpot was the only plate and one fork or spoon was passed between the family members. Some homes had shallow wells with a water pump in the yard. Other families still drew water from nearby streams. When water had to be carried, sanitation suffered.

Doctor Bright patiently answered questions and did his best to encourage the community to be diligent in protecting one another.

Toward the end of the meeting, Granny Laurel appeared at the back of the schoolhouse. She interrupted by telling the attendees that influenza came from evil and that she already had potions mixed to help.

Although the medical professional didn't always agree with Granny's doctoring ways, he didn't embarrass or demean. He agreed that the Spanish Flu did come from evil and said that natural herbs, if administered correctly, could help with the virus. *Uncle Christian is wiser than ever,* Ernest thought.

As the meeting disbanded, Samuel approached Ernest. "I saw Mercy today. She did some truth telling. I'm sorry for your troubles, but she's still needin' you. Since you was there for the birthing and there ain't no other daddy, not marrying ain't an option."

Ernest's heart started to race. He silently prayed, asking for the peace of God to be present. "Bigger matters is at hand. Let's be waitin' on talk of marryin'."

Samuel nodded his head. "I'm agreein' for now."

"I checked on Mercy and the baby."

"Thank you, Uncle Christian. I'm hopin' all is well."

"You did a fine job of bringin' the baby into the world. Eli is healthy, and his mama is recoverin'."

Doc Bright went on to explain how women needed to take care of themselves after giving birth.

"They have baby after baby without considerin' the cost to their own well-bein'."

Ernest knew how babies were made, but he wondered how to keep a married woman from having baby after baby. Lester had once told Ernest about an illegal serum that could be used.

"Those gals will be back workin' in the garden, scrubbin' floors, choppin' word, and haulin' water without proper rest. When the food is scarce, they will do without and give to their little ones, not realizin' that the littlest will lack nutrition if the mama doesn't eat."

Uncle Christian was on a roll, but Ernest didn't mind. He wanted to learn all he could about taking care of Lottie. He hoped that Uncle Christian's indirect advice would be beneficial one day. He wanted to be a good husband and a good father. First things first. He, however, needed God's help in figuring out the situation with Mercy, and Charlotte needed to come home.

"And some husbands won't wait the time needed for marital relations," the doctor added.

The two were sitting on the front steps of the schoolhouse porch. As the afternoon grew late, Ernest knew his uncle would soon leave for the holler below. He imagined Auntie Ada's wonderful cooking and wished again for Charlotte's quick return. He missed their fried squirrel dinners.

Some believed, the way to a man's heart was through his stomach. There was probably some truth to the saying. Right now, with or without the savories, he longed for happiness sitting with Charlotte and watching the sunset.

"My favorite part of doctorin' is helpin' a mama give birth."

"It was certainly somethin' to behold," Ernest answered. "I was done scared, but the joy of holdin' a little livin', breathin' bein' will always remain."

"Yes, it will, son."

Ernest couldn't remember his daddy ever calling him "son." Lester had been the honored one. His daddy also wasn't prone to endearments. I love yous and sweet nothings were never exchanged between his parents in public. On occasion, Ernest could hear his parents in their room. Once or twice before the romping began, he'd heard his daddy refer to his mama as "dear."

Ernest had a number of sexual questions he desired to ask Uncle Christian about, but it felt awkward. In the holler, it was considered immoral to discuss mating. Ernest knew, however, that Uncle Christian was of a different mindset. He believed that not asking for help was a sign of ignorance. Maybe down the road, when he and Lottie were closer to the fact, he would approach his uncle.

Lester had mentioned a few things to Ernest about sex, but he wasn't sure if they were true or not. *Was having sex with your socks on truly a bad thing, and, if so, why would it matter?*

There were a number of endearments Ernest wanted to say to Lottie. Some of them would be meant for public ears and some for private times between the two of them. He was proud of his girl and wanted the world to know that they belonged together. He also wanted special names for special times behind closed doors.

"Emie told Ada and me about the broom jumpin'. I've never heard such nonsense. If it comes to that, send someone you trust to come and get me. I have already talked with Sheriff Robbins. We'll do our best to intervene."

In Ernest's mind, Uncle Christian and Sheriff Robbins were heroes. Uncle Christian was like Babe Ruth hitting home runs, and Sheriff Robbins was like Lucky Lindy flying solo across the Atlantic. They were both sensations in their own right.

Early the next morning, Ernest was roused from sleep. He recognized the voices of Adam, Beau, Claude, and Dean. Mischief abounded when the boys were present.

"Wake him up, Adam. You's the oldest," Dean said.

"I ain't wakin' nobody," Adam responded. "Mercy done got that crazed look in her eyes when by accident we woke the baby."

"It weren't no accident so don't be lyin', Adam. You know you was tryin' to wrestle with Beau," Claude corrected. "Daddy done told you where liars go, and I ain't thinkin' it's a nice place with all that fire and such."

"Daddy also told you not to be talkin' about hell. He says you done got a fixation with fire. If you're fixin' your mind, it should be about heaven," Adam spoke with authority.

"I'm thinkin' we should be singin' teacher a song. A good mornin' tune." Beau started humming and then broke into verse.

Good mornin', the bees are hummin'. Mornin', a new day comin'. Mornin', your heart's drum drummin'. Wake up, wake and see the...

When Ernest heard Bullseye whistle in the background, he'd had enough. He tapped on the window of his room to let the boys know he was awake. He quickly put on his trousers and headed out the back door of the schoolhouse.

"Teacher, I ain't never seen you without a shirt on."

It was just like Claude to make an unnecessary comment. Of course, what an adult viewed as unnecessary might not hold true in the eyes of a child. Ernest decided to ignore the lad's remark.

"What brings you boys a visitin' so early in the mornin'?" Ernest asked.

The brothers started talking all at once. Ernest chided himself. He knew better than to pose a question to the four of them. He let them ramble for a minute or two. When all the boys had lost their wind except for Claude, he interrupted.

"I'm needin' one of you to tell the goin's-on. Adam, would you please be sharin' the information?"

"Yes, teacher. Since I'm the oldest, I should be the one sharin'."

Beau gave Adam the stink eye. Claude crossed his arms in frustration, and Dean kicked the dirt with his foot.

Ernest knew that most siblings rivaled for attention. As young boys, he and Lester had often challenged each other in front of their daddy.

"Our daddy says Bullseye can't be stayin'. Mercy's cryin'. Eli's cryin', and Bullseye is cryin' even more. He can even be duplicatin' the baby's eruptin's from both ends."

Ernest closed his eyes and sighed.

"Mr. Ernest, are you prayin', ponderin', or pretending to sleep?" Claude asked.

Ernest had continued teaching the summer learners about synonyms and antonyms. He was currently thinkin' about synonyms–synonyms for the word annoyed: irritated, cross, vexed, exasperated, irked, displeased, disgruntled, aggravated, riled.

Hot under the collar and foaming at the mouth didn't really count. They were descriptive phrases, not synonyms.

Bullseye wouldn't be quiet. He was a quick study and had learned to imitate the four boys as well as Justice, Mercy, and Eli. He had yet to mimic Cece. Ernest knew Cece was quiet by nature–besides, how could she get a word in edgewise with a house that was overrun by noise?

The parrot started to cry and wouldn't stop. Ernest was at a loss about what to do. The lamenting was in the form of Mercy's voice. At first, Ernest wanted to shout in frustration. As Bullseye carried on, Ernest's attitude began to change. He felt a crack of compassion. He chided himself and played over and over in his mind Mercy's ongoing deception. He didn't want to feel sorry for Mercy. She didn't deserve his pity.

"God, forgive me. Please forgive me," Bullseye mimicked. "Forgive me. Forgive me."

As Bullseye said the words over-and-over again, the crack grew. It was like cracking a window for fresh air when the breeze felt so invigorating that the window needed to be lifted higher and higher.

The sorrowful words reminded Ernest of a bleating lamb needing the help of a shepherd.

The tale of Mary's Little Lamb was based on a true story. While walking to school, Mary heard the lamb bleating and called for her pet to join her.

Mercy was calling for the Shepherd. In return the Shepherd was calling for Mercy to join Him.

Ernest prayed, "Lord, please be helpin' Mercy. Please be helpin' me…"

A plan began to formulate in Ernest's mind. As the idea took shape and depth, he mulled it over again and again. *God, is this you guiding, or is my imaginings running wild? Show me…*

His learners tended to let their minds run away with them. Some of the students were great storytellers. Like most of the holler residents, Ernest enjoyed a good yarn. Storytellers often elaborated for effect. It was common for the teller to use voice and physical form to act out a tale and draw attention.

He didn't want to spin a yarn for Mercy and give her false hope. He wanted to present a concise and clear plan for helping her and Eli.

He needed to visit with Mercy and wanted Justice and Cece present for their conversation. Everyone had to agree. The first step, however, would be convincing Mercy and her parents his idea was more than an imaginary adventure. It wasn't a tall tale but a legitimate plan. He had his own doubts. If the others, especially Mercy, didn't agree, he wouldn't push but would step away and continue to pray.

Justice was by the barn working with Amos and Andy. "I am hopin' that you didn't come with that ornery bird. I ain't never seen the likes," Justice said. "I'll be takin' my stubborn mules any day over a chattin', crazy parrot."

"Don't be worryin'. I left him at the schoolhouse." Ernest patted Amos, then turned his attention to Andy. He knew the mules had a jealous streak and didn't want to endure a nibble of naughtiness from either mule.

"What brings you callin'? You know you is always welcome, but things is a mite odd these days, and I wasn't expectin' a visit any time soon."

"I'm needin' to talk with Mercy and wanted to be welcomin' you and Cece to join in."

Justice closed the corral gate. "Cece's in the house. Them boys is off lookin' for snipes."

"Am I right in thinkin' that you is the one who told them about snipe catchin'?"

"No, it was their mama. She'd done had enough of their nonsense and noisiness and sent them out for a hunt."

"It's a mite early in the day for snipe catchin'. Did they take a poke and a stick?"

Justice smiled. "It ain't early when the mama says that it's time. She's the one who gave 'um a poke, and she cut a switch off the tree. I'm thinkin' that they was just thankful the switch wasn't cut for them."

Ernest smiled. Snipes were a legend in the holler. Not a one had ever been caught, but numerous tales had been shared about the adventures of the hunt.

Justice called out as he and Ernest stepped onto the porch. "Ladies, Ernest has come callin'!"

Mercy was sitting in the front room holding Eli. "Hello, Ernest."

"Mercy, you're lookin' fine. How's Eli?" Ernest extended his hands for the baby. It had only been a couple of days, yet the babe seemed slightly heavier.

"Doc Bright declared him fit. Thanks for sendin' him to visit."

The conversation was stilted. Things had been left unsettled. Ernest hoped their visit would clear the air. In the winter when the holler residents burnt wood or coal for warmth, a heavy dark smoke would settle in the low places. Some of the learners suffered from what Doc called asthma. They coughed and had trouble catching their breaths.

Ernest wanted to cough up the sputum of unforgiveness. He wanted to breathe freely spiritually and emotionally. When a strong cold winter wind blew through the mountain trees, the smoke would clear. His suffering students would return to their running, skipping, and playing. He silently prayed that the fresh wind of the Holy Spirit would blow and clear away helplessness, hopelessness, and hard heartedness.

The yellow curtains mounted above the two small windows on either side of the front door started to blow in the breeze. The material had tiny white dots that seemed to dance in the wind.

Cece served chicory coffee and biscuits. Coffee plants didn't grow in the hills, and beans were hard to come by. Most folks supplemented

144

with chicory or even used it outright. Though chicory plants weren't native to Appalachia, with care, individual plants would grow and multiply. The bright blue flowers were admired for their beauty. The leaves were eaten raw or cooked with other vegetables, and the roots were ground and brewed in hot water for drinking.

"Nice biscuits, ain't they Ernest?" Justice asked. "Soft and moist…"

Ernest couldn't help but chuckle. "Now, Justice, if I didn't know better, I'd be thinkin' that you was tryin' to make me feel bad about my cookin'. I was only being hospitable to you and Samuel. I was sharin' from the bounty of my table."

Even Mercy laughed when Justice described Ernest's dry biscuits and how they were useful in silencing Samuel.

Additional pleasantries were exchanged. Ernest commented that Mercy was looking fine. The weather was discussed and snipe hunting adventures recalled.

Ernest knew that it was time to put fun and niceties aside and discuss his purpose for visiting. "I've been prayin' on a few things."

"I've been prayin', too." Mercy added. "Please forgive me…forgive me."

The words were identical to the phrase Bullseye had mimicked. Ernest stood and placed Eli against his shoulder. He used one hand to hold the baby in place. He touched Mercy's arm with the other. "I'm workin' on forgivin'. That's why I came callin'. If you is partin' from deception and willin' to work together, I'm thinkin' it's best."

Trickles of tears fell down Mercy's cheeks. Ernest felt his own eyes swell.

He returned to his seat and fumbled with the cup of chicory. It was hard to add the milk and molasses one-handed. When Eli started to fuss, Ernest instinctively patted the baby's back. He remembered the way his mother could work in the house or garden while carrying a baby on her hip with two more young ones at her feet. The memory was sweet and added to his already unsettled emotions.

Mercy wouldn't look him in the eye but softly spoke. "Ernest, it was wrong not to be tellin' the truth. I won't be withholdin' anymore.

I'm knowin' that you and Lottie is meant. But I was dreamin' about what we used to have between us. I ain't always knowin' what's right, but I know schemin's wrong. I'm prayin' and askin' God for help."

"I'm thinkin' the Lord done talked to me. Mercy, I'm believin' that there's a man for you in these hills," Ernest began. "It's a strange idea, but I'm knowin' that the Bible is filled with strange ideas."

Ernest paused. He wasn't quite sure how to continue.

"Go on, Ernest. We're needin' to hear your thoughts," Justice said.

"I feel like God has a husband for Mercy right here, and I am wantin' to help find him. I'm thinkin' that the holler is filled with men needin' a wife. Mercy would be a good one. Some men would be seeing Eli as an added blessin'."

Justice and Cece looked shocked, but Mercy smiled. "Now, Ernest, let me be tellin' you the kind of husband I'm wantin'…"

"This is good. I see you're appreciatin' my plan," Ernest answered.

"He is needin' to be tall, with fair skin, red hair and an abundance of them freckles…"

Ernest's shoulders sagged. Mercy's lightheartedness didn't come from relief and thankfulness but scoffing.

"I'm also thinkin' that he is needin' money."

"Mercy, I'm knowin' that the word freckle means scattered. Mrs. Randolph taught us learners about it in school. One of the boys had some freckles and was teased. I am wantin' you to think on what I'm sayin'. Scattered among us is men needin' a wife, needin' a son, and, with your permission, I am bound to be findin' him. I ain't gonna pick 'um for ya, I'm just gonna have a look see and bring a report."

Mercy had quit laughing but seemed to be at a loss for words. Justice looked dumbfounded, and Ernest couldn't tell what was going on with Cece. He decided to sit quietly for a minute or two and let his words sink in.

Though the baby was settled, Ernest continued to pat his back. Eli's murmuring and soft cooing were sweet and soothed Ernest as he waited.

Surprisingly, it was Cece who broke the silence. "Abraham sent his servant man to be findin' a wife for his son. Isaac loved the girl. The Bible says that she was a comfort to him."

Justice looked at Cece, "Wife, you ain't thinkin' this is gonna work?"

"I'm thinkin' that it's time to be doin' somethin'," she answered. "We done raised Mercy as a good woman. She fell some by the wayside but is back doing good, and Eli is a light down from heaven. Mercy would do a man right, and I know that Ernest would be lookin' for a man who would be treatin' her and the baby right."

Ernest smiled and looked directly at Justice. He then quoted his friend's words, "When the mama says that it's time…"

Chapter Sixteen

It is bad luck to burn apple tree logs
in a fireplace.

Appalachian Folk Belief

Ernest was sweating under the collar for more than one reason on this warm day. Earlier, he had decided to ask his learners, discretely, about possible husbands for Mercy. He knew the summer scholars would know men living in the outlying areas. Maybe there was an uncle, older brother, cousin, or even a family friend he had never met. The trick was making inquiries without his students really being aware of what he was asking.

The previous evening, he had made a list of potential candidates but had checked them off one by one. None of them had seemed to be the right fit for Mercy and Eli.

Fitting properly was important. As a boy, he outgrew his shoes. There was no money to purchase a new pair, so his mama cut off the backs of the old pair. They felt good on his feet. He could even wiggle his toes a little, but while running and playing, the shoes flew off the bottom of his body like a bird in flight.

He began by talking to learners about Uncle Christian. Most of the students were familiar with Doc Bright. Ernest extoled the generous doctor's attributes and talked about his love for family.

"He and my aunt done got married late in life. He left jars of fireflies on her stoop. In the mornings, she would release them back to nature where they belonged."

He should have known that his comment about the unusual bugs with red, yellow, or even green lights would bring all kinds of stories and questions. Fireflies were a mystery. When Ernest was a student, Mrs. Randolph had tried to explain the uniqueness of the flying insects that could light up a field or forest. He admired their beauty but was at a loss about how to explain the workings of their lights.

He knew some female lightning bugs couldn't fly. Males would seek out the opposite sex for companionship.

Mercy couldn't fly. She couldn't physically fly, but she was also in a vulnerable position. She had landed and landed hard. A man with godly love in his heart would hopefully help Mercy heal. He could also provide protection from additional wounding from the community folk.

"Learners, God done created special beetles to light up when they is lookin' for love. Their colors is sometimes different because different things are attractive to different people."

"Teacher, I thought we was talkin' about fireflies not peoples."

Ernest was in over his head. He could feel sweat running down his back. "Yes, we was discussin' fireflies, but attraction is also holdin' true for people."

He did his best to redirect the scholars. "Now, we was talkin' some about Doc Bright. He is a man that I'm admirin'. He loves God and his family and is kindly to his neighbors. Is any of you knowin' a nice man like Doc Bright? A man who is lookin' for a family to love."

Ernest had to remind his students to raise their hands and not shout out their comments. It was a good sign that the learners were eager to share.

"My uncle, he is missin' two front teeth. He can spit tobaccy through the space on his uppers, and his aimin' is pretty good."

"My daddy's friend raises coon dogs. Them rascals can tree a racoon quick as anythin'. He done loves his dogs. My mama says that he loves them critters more than any woman."

"I'm knowin' a man that can cook up mighty fine pig whistler.

He's especially likin' the paw. I'm thinkin' that part takes lots of gnawin', but he says that's what makes it fine. The longer you is chewin', the more it fills your belly."

"My cousin. I'm admirin' him cause he don't take a shine to bathin', and I don't neither."

Though things hadn't gone well with the learners, Ernest wasn't dissuaded. He decided to draft a notice to place on the board at Rudy's mama and daddy's store. The couple had assured him of their support.

When Rudy and Emie wanted to marry, Rudy's parents were among the first to offer their blessing and assistance. They knew Mercy's situation and wanted to help.

Ernest was struggling, however, with writing the communication. Since it was illegal for a black person and white person to marry, he felt like a description of Mercy should be included. Ernest didn't think the government should have any say in matters of love. It didn't seem right for a couple to have to hide their love from the law.

Mercy was a beautiful woman. He wanted his phrasing to do her justice. Words like creamed coffee, cinnamon, nutmeg, and chocolate all came to mind. Yet it didn't seem appropriate to use words about food to describe her loveliness.

He thought about descriptive words for the great outdoors and pondered the beauty of the hills, especially spring season when the wildflowers bloomed and birth among the animals was prevalent. *Mercy's attractive skin was the color of a fawn.*

Ernest quickly put pen to paper and recorded his thoughts.

Matchmaker wanting to help a lonely man find a good godly wife. Kind and lovely lady with skin the color of a new-born fawn could be the gal for you.

On a date specific, the note instructed potential candidates to meet him at the store for an interview. Mercy helped Ernest design needed questions. The two discussed what she viewed as appropriate responses. Then, upon Ernest's approval, the men would meet with Mercy, Justice, and Cece.

Ernest decided not to include Eli in the post. The baby was too precious to include as an after-thought. Plus, he wanted to see first-hand the men's expressions when they heard about Mercy's newborn.

Ernest didn't sleep the night before the big matchmaking day. The moon was full in the sky. When rest wouldn't come, he gathered the curtain to one side and opened the window slightly. The breeze was warm. The night sky seemed lit up like the city lights he had once seen in a photograph. He thought of Lottie in hopes that the moon, as well as the city lights, were blessing her.

The holler folk believed during a full moon that the spirits of the dead walked through the graveyard. Protection from evil came in the form of a graveyard rabbit foot. The whole notion bothered Ernest. It was another superstition that put fear in the hearts of good people. Besides, if someone believed it was best not to visit the graveyard, how would he or she get a rabbit from there? It also seemed very morbid to kill a cemetery rabbit only because its foot supposedly brought safety and good luck.

When morning came, he roused himself from bed. It seemed like only minutes passed between sleep and the sunrise. Ernest was nervous. He followed the path to Big Creek with trepidation. *What would happen if a suitable husband wasn't found? Where would that leave Mercy?*

He had glossed over Mercy's description of being a single mom in the holler, but part of him knew that what she had spoken was true. She and Eli would be shunned. There would be whispers and outright judgments made against her. Eli might eventually believe what others believed about him. Rejection was a horrible thing. He wanted life's best for Mercy and her son.

A learner once told the story of Daniel and the lions' pit. The young boy attested to his teachers and fellow students that Daniel ate all the lions. Ernest wondered if the lad believed that Daniel would only be safe if all the lions disappeared. Although Ernest wanted all the lions gone, he knew that life's lions didn't always vanish. At times,

God in his divine wisdom, kept the lions present but closed their mouths.

Mrs. Randolph explained to the Big Creek students that male lions marked their territory at night when everyone was fast asleep. As Ernest walked, he contemplated the need to be alert, to stay awake, and watch for lions who wanted to mark their territory in his life and in the lives of those he cared for.

As Ernest approached the store, he could see several men waiting in a queue. Since none of the men knew that he was the matchmaker, he joined the line and made initial observations about the potential husbands. It was still early in the day, and there was a slight chill in the air. Rudy's mama, known for her hospitality, had poured the men coffee. He could smell the brew and noticed steam rising from the white enamel cups.

Mercy had made it clear that she wasn't interested in a dawn-dusk relationship. Two of the men were aged and possibly looking for a nursemaid instead of a wife. He felt bad for the elderly men. He knew if they were living on their own that life's basic provisions challenged them.

He also knew if Mercy met the men, she would, likewise, be overcome with sympathy. Grieving for someone was not the same as loving a person the way a husband and wife should feel for each other. Compassion could cause people to make strange decisions and then regret the consequences.

He listened to the mutterings of the men. No one in particular caught his attention, which was probably best since initial impressions could be deceiving. Ernest often prayed for discernment but understood that when matters were close to the heart, discernment could be clouded.

He meandered from the front of the store around the corner of the building when he saw Samuel take a spot in line. Ernest couldn't help but grin. *This should prove interesting.*

He knocked on the back egress of the store. To his surprise, Emie answered.

"Girlie, what are you doing here?"

"I done saw the notice. Now, don't be gettin' angered up at Rudy's mama. I started askin' questions and could tell by her eyes dartin' here and there some of the goin's-on."

"Emie, if Mercy was wantin' your aid, she'd have asked."

"Brother, I'm only plannin' on escortin' the men in and out of the store. I won't be botherin' unless, of course, you're askin' for my advice and womanly wisdom."

Ernest frowned and gave Emie a disapprovin' look.

"Please, Ernest. I'm promisin' not to git in your way."

He shook his head in frustration. Emie stepped aside, and he opened the screen door and entered the building.

Rudy's mama had organized a small private room toward the back of the store. The room was used for storage and contained feed sacks of flour, sugar, buckwheat, and cornmeal. His mama had used similar sacks to make clothes for her children. Two chairs sat in the center of the room.

Ernest rolled a wooden barrel filled with goods of some sort next to his seat. He planned to use it as a make-do table and placed paper and a pencil on the top. He took a seat in the straight-back, hand-hewn chair facing the doorway and tried to look official.

Emie escorted in the first candidate and closed the door. Ernest stood, shook the man's hand, and offered him a seat. He was dressed in city clothes, unusually tall, and handsome with dark eyes and dark wavy hair.

The man was a gambler by trade and had recently moved to Big Creek, hoping to start a new life. Ernest didn't view him as husband material for Mercy and wasn't swayed by his good looks.

The next several candidates also didn't fit the bill. One disliked children and another smelled of moonshine.

When Samuel entered the room, Ernest didn't bother to shake his hand but instead simply smiled.

"I should'a been knowin' that Mercy was involved in this nonsense," Samuel said.

"If it's such nonsense, why have you been standin' in line?"

"You're knowin' that my wife done passed. I'm in want fer

another and a good woman ain't easy to find."

"Well, let's be proceedin' with the interviewin'."

"Ernest, you is more than aware that Mercy ain't the gal for me. Her past foolishness would be more than I could bear. Now, I'm understandin' why you're matchmakin'; it lets you off the hook. Like a big ole catfish swimmin' at the bottom of the creek, I'm thinkin' that you're restin' hope on another fish comin' to the top."

"It ain't quite what you're sayin', Samuel. I'm carin' for Mercy and Eli best I can, but I ain't the man for her."

"A wedding's comin'. Time will be tellin' if you're the groom."

Samuel grinned. Abruptly, he left the room slamming the door behind him.

Next, Emie ushered a woman into the storeroom. Lester had once told him about such relationships. It was hard not to stare. The woman was robust and older. She wore unlaced leather boots, a faded red cotton oversized dress with a hankie tucked into the right sleeve, and a shawl around her shoulders. Her grey hair was tightly pulled back. Her skin was wrinkled from age, exposure to the elements, and strenuous work. Her hands were large and strong. Her lips were thin. Her eyes, they had lost their sheen.

"I'm knowin' this is a mite unusual, but I'm hopin' that you'll be givin' me the chance to tell my tale," the woman began.

Ernest wasn't quite sure what to do but nodded for the woman to continue.

She introduced herself as Florence and went on to explain her situation. "I got me some ginseng growin'. It's been a labor of love for a mite few years. It's a small crop, but I also hunt the roots amongst the trees. I was doin' just fine 'til my husband up and died and his no-good brother decided to take my land."

Ernest knew that ginseng was valuable. The Shawnee, Mingo, Tutelo, and Tuscarora tribes had all treasured the hard to find root. The granny witches often prescribed the essence for a variety of ailments. Holler folks often sold their ginger to city slickers for pennies on the dollar. The potent plant was even imported to other countries.

Florence had no children and no family to speak of other than her accusing abusive brother-in-law who was threatening her. Before mischief could take place, Florence wanted to transfer ownership to a responsible person and assumed that a young woman, rumoured to have a baby out of wedlock, would be a good choice. She believed if the settlement wasn't in the family name that her accuser would be thwarted.

Ernest had once read about a tribe in Africa where older widowed women, in order to preserve their homes, married younger women. Big Creek, however, wasn't Africa. Florence, being intimidated, needed the help of Sheriff Robbins. He told her as much.

At the end of the day, Ernest wasn't any closer than before in his quest for finding Mercy a husband and Eli a father. Emie had generously offered her opinion to Ernest and agreed that none of the men were suitable.

Chapter Seventeen

If the bottom of your right foot itches, you are going on a trip.

Appalachian Folk Belief

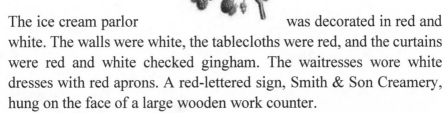

The ice cream parlor was decorated in red and white. The walls were white, the tablecloths were red, and the curtains were red and white checked gingham. The waitresses wore white dresses with red aprons. A red-lettered sign, Smith & Son Creamery, hung on the face of a large wooden work counter.

Coral thought the red letters displayed on the sign were beautiful. She had heard about red-lettered Bibles but had yet to see one. It was ingenious for someone to think of putting the words of Jesus in red. Pastor Rex had once given a sermon at Big Creek Church about the symbolism of red in Scripture. It was during the fall, when the leaves on the trees were turning shades of yellow, orange, and red.

An older man was busy dipping ice cream from containers behind the counter. Coral was curious about the workings of the creamery. She sat at a small table for two in a metal chair with a red vinyl seat cover. She was waiting for Doctor Daniels who now insisted that she call him by his given name, Kenneth. She was still slightly weak, but for the most part had recovered from the influenza.

She felt grateful for many things: her physical renewal, Charlie's spiritual renewal, and the blossoming of a friendship with Kenneth.

She was also thankful for Lottie's healing hands and Pastor Rex's prayers. He was initially upset about not receiving word of her illness but soon refocused on encouraging her physically and spiritually. She was relieved that Thomas' broken ribs and wounds were mending.

It was a warm spring day. In fact, so warm it felt like the early arrival of the dog days of summer. Mrs. Randolph had explained in school that the term came from Roman and Greek astrology and referred to mad dogs and bad luck. As a child, Coral however, had decided to put aside Mrs. Randolph's lesson and to instead think of dogs lying in the shade in an attempt to escape the August heat.

She grieved for James. It was not the type of grief where she longed for his presence but rather a grief that drove her to mention him continuously in prayer.

As a child, almost daily, she, her siblings, and her mother experienced her daddy's bouts of anger. There was a constant fear that her daddy would become enraged and violent. Her mama had made excuses for him. Even as a young girl, Coral knew that there was no excuse. Her daddy's hostility finally resulted in knocking over an oil lamp and creating a house fire, causing his own death and the death of Coral's mother.

Coral chided herself for ignoring James' anger. She had allowed her physical attraction to override her common sense. She compared it to a time in the holler when she had bitten into a well-shaped and deliciously ripened apple only to find a worm inside. She considered the empress-witch who gave Snow White the poison apple. She remembered the variety of apples in the holler that in late summer and fall tantalized her taste buds. She was learning once again the necessity of carefully examining the fruit before taking a bite.

Coral eyed the menu with delight. Her mama had made ice cream on occasion, freezing the cream, egg, and sugar mixture with ice collected from the creek and stored in an underground dugout. Salt was precious. By taking a love pinch here and there, mama had saved enough salt to make ice cream for special celebrations. Coral remembered Mama and Emie filling a large outside bowl with crushed ice and salt, placing inside it a small bowl that contained a combination of cream and honey. Then, the stirring began.

The variety of flavors offered by the confectionary surprised Coral. She didn't know what to sample. Kenneth soon arrived and together they selected three varieties: strawberry, peach, and black walnut.

"How was you knowin' that I'm partial to ice cream?" Coral asked.

Kenneth looked hangdogged like he had done something wrong. "James told me that he was planing to bring you here."

Hoping to ease the doctor's discomfort, Coral smiled. "My mouth is waterin'. I ain't wantin' to wait."

The waitress carried the dishes on a platter placed on the palm of her hand. Coral couldn't wait to demonstrate to Lottie how the sweet treats were carried to the table.

Sharing food was common in the holler. Families would take bites from each other's plates, and tastes were often offered on someone else's fork or spoon. Initially, it felt odd for Coral to dip her spoon in the same bowl as Kenneth. Soon, she cast aside her reticence as she savored the sweet, creamy, cold mixture. She couldn't decide which flavor she liked best.

"Coral, I enjoy being a doctor. I am good at it. I care for my patients. At times, however, I can appear brisk and indifferent. I'm not like Thomas who, when given opportunity, could freely express himself."

"Kenneth, I admit that initially when meetin' you, I felt uncertain. But I felt your gentle hands carin' for me even when I was fadin' in and out. I could sense you there."

Coral felt herself flush. From the time she was a little girl, her blushes gave away moments of awkwardness. Her mama used to sing her a made-up ditty about rosy cheeks. Then, when her siblings learned the tune, they sang it as well.

Blushing baby, cheeks so pink, mama loves you so. Sweet kisses on your forehead more than let you know. Eyes so blue and hair so fair like gifts from God's own heart. Mama wishes every day for us to never part.

She felt her scarlet cheeks burn even more when she recited the song to Kenneth. "I'm rememberin' your bedside manners in aid to my recoverin'."

"Any doctor would have done the same."

"Yes, but not any doctor would be takin' me for ice cream."

Kenneth smiled.

Coral was pleased to see Pastor Thomas. He was slightly bent over and walking with a cane for support but was clearly on the mend. Lottie had invited her to visit the tent site. Thomas and Pastor Rex were there as well.

Once hugs, cheek kisses, and health inquires had been exchanged, a discussion started about Thomas' future plans for ministry.

"I'm not rightly sure what to do," Thomas said. "I told you that my mama named me after Doubtin' Thomas in the Bible, but now I'm doubtin' myself and what God is wantin' from me."

Pastor Rex placed his hand on Thomas' shoulder, "All of Jesus' disciples were prone to doubtin'. Thomas is just the one remembered."

"Maybe, it ain't about what God is wantin' from you, as much as what He is wantin' to do for you. I'm knowin' that He has a plan and will be showin' you where to be goin' and what to be doin'," Charlotte added.

"Coral, would you mind leadin' us in song? I'm thinkin' we could all do with some encouragin'," Pastor Rex queried.

Her voiced quivered a bit, but Coral was determined to do her part in uplifting Pastor Thomas.

All to Jesus I surrender. All to Him I freely give. I will ever love and trust Him. In His presence daily live. I surrender all. I surrender all. All to Thee my blessed Savior, I surrender all. All to Jesus I surrender. Humbly at His feet I bow. Worldly pleasures all forsaken. Take me Jesus, take me now. I surrender all. I surrender all. All to Thee my blessed Savior, I surrender all…

The atmosphere seemed to shift. The environment felt different. It reminded Coral of a still day when a breeze mercifully started to blow. Her senses were sharpened. There was an overwhelming feeling of peace. The time of worship started with the idea of encouraging Thomas, asking the Lord to guide him and help him on life's path. Yet, God was speaking to her. She wasn't under a mulberry tree like before, but the presence of the Holy Spirit was touching her in the same manner.

She knew the blossoms from the mulberry had already showered the ground and that the white berries had started to appear. From a distance the berries would be hard to discern, but with close examination the fruit would be exposed and hold a promise for the future.

What God was asking Coral to do wouldn't be easy. It would be just like before when her initial plans to visit Charlie were misunderstood and met with opposition. She was confident that she had heard from the Lord but not so confident that she could explain to her family about her future.

"Lottie, I know I was agreein' to be Eve in our performin', but I ain't takin' off my clothes," Coral said.

Charlotte smiled.

"When Adam and Eve was in the garden, they were naked and not ashamed. Now, I'm knowin' that we enter the world naked, and I'm thinkin' that babies naked or clothed, chubby or lean, are all a mite pretty. But if I'm naked, I would done be ashamed."

When Lottie didn't respond, Coral continued her one-sided conversation.

"I been wonderin' about several things, Sister. I heard someone say today they needed to iron their shoelaces. It don't make sense. Why iron somethin' only to wrinkle it again when you're weavin' the string through the shoe eyes? And how can shoes have eyes? They ain't decidin' which way to go. It's the person in the shoes who gets to decide. Plus, ironin' is a lot of work. You gotta gather the wood, build a fire, set the iron on heat until it's a mite hot. That's a lot of trouble for shoes laces—"

"Coral, why are prattlin' on like Emie?"

"You're makin' me nervous. Since this mornin' you ain't been talkin', and I am wonderin' what to do. I know it's plain selfishness on my part. I don't like worryin' and am wantin' you to feel better so I can feel better, and that ain't right."

Lottie placed her hand on her heart. "My heart's hurtin'."

The worry Coral felt was compounded. "Hurtin' how, Sister?"

"I done called the Big Creek store this mornin' and got a message from Ernest. He said that Mercy and the baby was fine and that a weddin's comin'. I'm thinkin' in my absence that he decided to marry Mercy."

Charlotte started to cry, and Coral soon joined her. Together they sounded like a mournful song. Lottie was the melody and Coral the harmony.

"Ernest loves you. He wouldn't be marryin' Mercy."

"I'm knowin' he loves me. He told me such with words and works, but he is of a compassionate nature. I'm thinkin' Mercy could be convincin'. They have history, you know. And with a babe involved, that just might make Ernest change his mind."

"Did you return a message?"

"I couldn't, Coral. I wasn't sure what I should be sayin'."

"I'm thinkin' that you need to return to Big Creek and sort this thing through. Charlie's done gone. You did your part in helpin'. It's time to be goin' home."

Lottie sighed. Her shoulders sagged like the weight of the world rested on her.

Coral knew that Atlas was condemned by Zeus to carry the sky, but Jesus freed the condemned. He carried her friend's burdens.

"Coral."

"Yes, Sister."

"Ironin' your shoelaces means that you need ta use the toilet."

Both ladies broke out in laughter.

161

Appalled by the look of herself in costume, Coral wondered why she had ever agreed to wear tan clothes with her vital parts covered in leaves. She was the quiet one. Lottie was the performer. Of course, it hadn't helped that Pastor Rex could winnow a bone from a dog by chattin' it up. Then there was Thomas. All his talk about doubting his future had played on Coral's sympathies.

Children were gathered at the tent site. Lottie, dressed like a snake, was handing out sweets. Coral couldn't take it any longer. She motioned for Lottie to join her, but the children hemmed in her friend. Coral didn't want to discuss her concerns in front of the boys and girls. Now she didn't have a choice.

"Lottie, give me them sugar buttons!" Coral spoke emphatically. "It ain't proper for the devil to be giving anything nice."

"Coral, I ain't really the devil. It's just a costume—a snake costume."

"The snake is representing the devil. You're gonna scare the children."

Lottie continued distributing the sweets. "The youngsters ain't seeming upset to me."

Before the two friends could settle things, Pastor Rex motioned that the service was about to begin. The canvas tent, holes and all, had been placed on the ground as a covering. Chairs were set up for the older children. The younger ones would sit on the recycled tent tarp toward the front of the skewed plywood platform.

Pastor Thomas greeted the children and set the stage for Lottie and Coral. "Someone once told me that the devil was clever and handsome. Now learners, he might be clever but not as clever as Jesus. On occasion he might look handsome, but ain't nothing attractive about tricking and deceiving."

Coral pretended to be Eve. She was wandering in a make-believe garden when approached by Lottie, in her snake costume, holding a bow and arrow. A discussion about the fruit of the garden ensued.

At first, Eve ignored the snake. Then, using his deceptive voice he connived his way into her thoughts. Eve listened to the evil and was trapped. The snake placed an apple on Eve's head. He notched an arrow, lit it on fire, and shot the apple from the top of his victim's body. The children screamed but thankfully remained in their seats.

Thank goodness, Lottie's a good shot. Coral thought.

Pastor Thomas proceeded to talk about the devil and his fiery arrows. The youngsters were mesmerized. He then used an object in nature to discuss the deceptive plans of Satan and his helpers.

"The devil mantis looks like a praying mantis. One of them bugs that holds their front legs together looking like they is asking God for help. But this devil mantis disguises itself as a beautiful flower when really it's meaning mischief. It can even be shifting its wings left to right out of trickery."

Now, Coral was mesmerized. She would have to ask Thomas later about his reference to the praying mantis.

The time with the children ended on a sad note. There were footnotes, banknotes, keynotes, headnotes, and endnotes, but a sad note was the most heartfelt, notable word of the "notes." Coral knew that the English language was vast and that there were words for every shade of sadness: but the term "sad note" seemed to resound in her heart.

Pastor Thomas explained to the children that he was leaving Charleston for an indefinite amount of time. With the meeting tent destroyed and a lack of funds to replace the structure, Thomas was at a loss. The rains peaked in June and July and, without a covering, it would be difficult to meet with the learners. Thankfully, a local church had agreed to continue ministry to God's little lambs. Both Pastor Thomas and the children were heartbroken.

Coral knew that life constantly changed. Transformation was stressful but often ended on a positive note. The metamorphosis of the butterfly was a wonderful example of variance: egg, larva, pupa, and adult. Her own life was changing. She didn't feel like a butterfly and knew she wasn't an egg. Maybe a larva or a pupa?

"Coral, where did this notion come from?!" Pastor Rex thundered.

Lottie looked dumbfounded. Coral didn't know if her friend was more surprised about her announcement or Pastor Rex's loud voice.

She waited a moment before answering the Big Creek pastor, who was boisterous and a bit bossy but a truly kind-hearted, gentle soul. Once he overcame his initial reaction, Coral knew that he would be reasonable.

She put her hand on Pastor Rex's arm. "You're knowin' my heart. You been my pastor for a time now. I ain't prone to wildness or wanderin' off the path..."

The godly man placed his hand over Coral's. "I'm knowin' such, but your family entrusted your well-bein' to me. How am I to tell them that you're stayin' in Charleston and not comin' home?"

"It's just for a time," Coral humbly answered.

"Are you certain God is talkin' to you, Coral? It's not a desire that you're wantin' and sayin' the Lord told me so?"

Instantly offended, Coral reminded the man that she took the guidance of God very seriously. She wanted to respond in righteous anger. Then, she remembered something Ernest once told her.

Girlie, if someone's words are upsetting, put them aside and do your best to trust and believe that the person has intentions of love.

She knew Pastor Rex wanted God's best for her. "Pastor, you taught me that takin' the Lord's name in vain included pretendin' that somethin' was from heaven when it's not. I ain't exactly sure why God's askin' me to stay a spell in Charleston, but I'm wantin' my ways to be pleasin' Him."

Pastor Rex placed his index finger over his lips. Coral knew he was pondering the situation at hand.

Coral was accustomed to waiting in silence. It didn't bother her to sit quietly, but when she glanced at Lottie, her friend was fidgeting. Coral took a seat next to Lottie and began humming. Lottie hummed along and soon the two were singing softly while Pastor Rex paced back and forth.

Breathe on me, breath of God. Fill me with life anew. That I may love what Thou dost love and do what Thou wouldst do. Breathe on me, breath of God. Until my heart is pure. Until with Thee, I will one will, to do and to endure. Breathe on me, breath of God. Blend my soul with Thine. Until this earthly part of me glows with Thy fire divine...

"There ain't no use arguin'," Pastor Rex concluded. "I'll be concedin' to tell your family such. I want assurances though, Coral, that you'll be stayin' in a safe place and have means for money. Truth tellin' your family or not, I can't be leavin' you otherwise."

Coral nodded her head in agreement. "I'll be doin' just as you said."

Lottie still looked dazed. She hadn't spoken a word, but when Pastor Rex left the room, it was only a matter of seconds before her lips loosened.

"Which is makin' you stay, Sister, the ice cream or the doctor?"

"Neither. Although the ice cream was a mite fine."

"I'm thinkin' you're thinkin' that Doctor Daniels is also fine."

"Charlotte!"

"Coral, this is disturbin'. You've never lived on your own. Besides, it ain't proper. Where will you be stayin'? What will you be doin'?"

"I ain't rightly sure, but I promised Pastor Rex to have some answers before the two of you leave for Big Creek. I'll be keepin' my word. If God is directin', He will make things right."

Chapter Eighteen

It is bad luck to sit a hat on a bed.

Appalachian Folk Belief

The summer screamers had arrived. Male cicadas attracted their lady friends by singing. Some liked to sing alone, while others enjoyed harmonizing. The females responded to the males by softly sweeping their transparent wings. Ernest listened to the adult cicadas living in trees feeding on sap. They spent most of their lives as nymphs in the soil, but it was due time to sing.

Ernest wondered if he should include song lessons as part of his matchmaking project. Things weren't going well. Not well at all. He had yet to find a man for Mercy, and Samuel was continuing his threats. Most recently, Samuel had mentioned the need to clean his shotgun. The situation was deteriorating, and fast.

Doctor Bright once treated a patient who suffered hearing loss from a nearby cicada's song. Ernest could believe it 'cause the noise was deafening. According to Granny Laurel, the insects tasted good, but no way could Granny fry up enough of them to stop the screaming roar.

Ernest hadn't sampled one himself but considered it might be fun to take the learners on a nature walk and let them enjoy some food from the land: berries, roots, bugs, and the like. Besides, he was certain that Granny would have fun offering samples of her cicada recipe to the learners. He could also show them Lamb's Ear, the ground cover plant which had been used for a drinking tea by Native Americans and also used as toilet tissue. Anything related to going to the bathroom seemed to entertain the students. He smiled. Lamb's Ear had to be softer on the hindquarters than old newspapers or circulars.

Ernest had met with Mercy yesterday to discuss the husband situation. She was taking his matchmaking difficulties as a personal affront. She also was worried Ernest was being too particular. When he gave examples about the personal hygiene of the interviewees, Mercy was aghast.

Somehow Mercy's four brothers had gotten word of the whole sordid business and had decided to take matters into their own hands. They'd even paraded a couple of men through their home for Mercy's viewing.

If the situation wasn't so dire, Ernest could laugh. Stan Laurel and Oliver Hardy were slap-stick comedians known now to most of the holler folk by name. He wasn't sure that even the funny men duo could do justice to the comedy of errors surrounding his search for a husband for Mercy.

"Ernest, have you found a husband yet?" Emie inquired.

"Sister, I am not lookin' for a husband for me. I'm lookin' for a husband for Mercy!"

"Well, have you found one?"

"No. It's provin' harder than I thought."

"I ain't surprised, Ernest. I'm thinkin' you need my help. In fact, I've got two gentlemen in mind –Orville and Homer."

"The twins that live outside of Spencer?"

"I'm thinkin' one might work."

"Have you mentioned this idea of yours to Rudy?"

"He's reasonin' that I shouldn't be comin' to your aid. But Ernest, it's plain obvious that you're needin' help."

Ernest chuckled. He loved his sister, but she could get a crazy idea every now and then. "Girlie, how would this be workin'? The two lookin' alike and all? And wouldn't it be a mite offensive for Mercy to pick one over the other if they was standin' side-by-side."

"Just 'cause they look alike don't mean that they're alike in other ways."

"Let me think on this a bit," Ernest answered.

"I know your ways, Brother. You've no intention of considerin' this matter at all. The two is even famous. Their mama says they're related to Chief Logan of the Mingo tribe."

He put his arm around his sister. "I love you, Emie."

"I've got other news if you're inclined."

"Emerald, I know that look. You're wantin' me to draw it out of you. It's a game we've been playin' since we was little."

Emie smirked.

"Is it big news or little news?" Ernest asked.

"I'm thinkin' it's big." Emie answered.

"Is it painful or joyful?"

"Definitely joyful!"

"No more questions, Emie. I got stuff to be doin'. I'm wantin' to see if Lottie left me a message at the store."

His sister reached into the pocket of her tan dress and pulled out a piece of paper. "I've got a message, but it ain't directly from Lottie…" She teasingly held the note high in the air.

Ernest easily took the paper from Emie's hand. Pastor Rex had talked with his daughter who sent word to Rudy.

Grandpappy will be home in time for the church picnic. Says he's got lots of news to tell.

"They're comin' home, Sister. Comin' home."

Emie smiled.

"And just so you're knowin', when it comes to Lottie, I'm like the cicadas. I like to sing alone."

Ernest whistled as he started up the hillside. Lottie would be home soon. He was grinning from ear to ear and could hardly wait.

With each stride, however, worry began to crawl and creep. Chelones, chameleons, crocodiles, and cobras were all crawlers and creepers. Babies also crawled with their tummies on the ground and creeped with their tummies off the floor using their hands and knees.

He felt both relieved and worried. Relieved that he would see his gal soon but worried about the situation with Mercy. He had felt confident that the Lord had spoken to him about a husband being present in the holler for Mercy. Now, he began to doubt.

Ain't it just like a man to be thinkin' God's at work, but when things don't happen right off or obstacles come along, the doubting begins, Ernest thought.

He wished he had responded differently to Emie about Orville and Homer. In hindsight, maybe one of the twins was the perfect man for Mercy; or maybe it was his sense of desperation wanting a quick resolution.

When he took the learners on their nature walk, they could gather flowers and grasses from the fields to plant around the schoolhouse and Lottie's home. The horticulture lesson would help his students understand what specific plants could be uprooted and replanted. Ernest knew that Charlotte would appreciate their efforts and that he, along with the children, would enjoy the welcome home preparations.

He had been reviewing adjectives with his students. Maybe a sign could be prepared listing Lottie's attributes:

L –loving, luscious, lusty

O –one and only, out-of-this-world, optimal

T –tantalizing, tasty, tender,

T –touchable, thrilling

I –impassioned, intoxicating, invigorating

E –enchanting, enticing, evocative

On second thought, maybe the sign wasn't such a good idea.

Among Lottie's many attributes was patience. She had left the holler so that he would have time to sort out things with Mercy. Now time had made things even more complicated. Ernest knew a person's patience could only last so long. He remembered a poem from his schooling with Mrs. Randolph.

Patience is not sitting and waiting, it is foreseeing. It is looking at the thorn and seeing the rose, looking at the night and seeing the day.

He hoped that Lottie wasn't sitting and waiting but foreseeing their future together.

As Ernest approached the school, there seemed to be a great deal of activity. Since it was Saturday and lessons weren't in session, he wondered why parents and students were in the schoolyard. As he drew closer, he could see Granny Laurel in the middle of the group and could hear her rambling on about Charleston. Everyone seemed angry, and Granny appeared to be encouraging the ruckus.

"There's our boy!" Granny shouted. "Back from Charleston bringin' the disease!"

All eyes turned toward Ernest. There was pushing and shoving. Some folks even had their fists raised in the air shouting. Unless riled, the holler folk weren't generally prone to violence against their neighbors.

"Granny," Ernest yelled above the throng. "What are the goin's-on?"

She seemed to have the crowd in the palm of her hand. When she gestured for the people to quiet down, they listened and parted a path for her to approach Ernest.

"The flu's done come to the holler! You brought its deadliness from Charleston!" Granny jousted at him with her forefinger.

The crowd jeered.

"I ain't been to Charleston. I've only been gone since this mornin'. I was doin' business in Big Creek."

Granny Laurel put her gnarled fist in front of Ernest's face. "Just 'cause your body's done been present don't mean you ain't the cause of the influenza here. You done carried it by your thoughts, boy. You ain't been dwellin' on Mercy and the baby. No, you been thinkin' of the gal in Charleston, and it opened the door for the evilness to be brought here."

Ernest gently pulled Granny's fist down. Placing her hand at her side, he patted the wrinkled skin a couple of times. His gesture seemed to take the wind out of her sails. It seemed the older woman didn't have any oars in her boat for reserves in the fight, so it was only a matter of time before everything calmed and was silent.

Ernest made his way to the stoop. There was a notice on the schoolhouse door, "Quarantined." Flu had come to the upper holler. He turned to face the angry crowd. Thankfully, they had settled some and no longer seemed like a vicious mob.

"We're needin' to let common sense prevail," Ernest began. "Contagious infections can't be carried by thoughts. Most of you done heard Doctor Bright's lesson."

Inside the schoolhouse, makeshift beds had been set-up. Two adults and four children were being tended by a woman. He assumed the patients were all from the same family. The caregiver's back faced Ernest. It would only be a matter of time before other patients came into the quarantined area. Ernest understood that fear was the motivator for the anger witnessed outside.

When the nurse turned around, Ernest was startled by her appearance. The woman was younger than he originally thought. She was probably in her late teens and had a cleft lip. She wouldn't look at Ernest. Chances were that she had been hidden away since infancy. Ernest wondered about Granny Laurel's involvement and relationship with the young woman. He knew the granny witch believed that any physical deformity meant the presence of evil.

The door opened with Granny stomping into the room. Her steps were like the call of the mighty blue whale. Mrs. Randolph had told him that the giant creature was the loudest mammal on earth. Ernest had talked with Granny before about her stomping. It wasn't the time, however, to issue a reminder. Plus, he had noticed earlier that her boots were far too big. This had to be contributing factor.

"I see you done met Minerva," Granny spoke.

Ernest addressed the young woman, "Thank you for tendin' the sick."

"Minerva's been with me for quite a time. I'm teachin' her my doctorin' ways."

Ernest nodded. "I ain't recognizin' these folks. Where did they come from?"

"While choppin' wood, Samuel found 'um amongst some trees. Seems they come from outside Charleston."

"Granny, you and I will be talkin' later about scarin' folk and stirrin' trouble, but right now we're needin' to send for Doctor Bright."

"Minerva and me has got things in order."

"There's order in the schoolhouse, but outside it ain't nothin' short of bedlam. Those people need to be sent home 'cause we need to be preparin' for others who will soon be comin'. Uncle Christian and Auntie Ada will bring aid for the infirmed."

Ernest had avoided Samuel for several days but breathed a sigh of relief when he heard him outside directing the folks to return to their homes.

Chapter Nineteen

It is bad luck to swim in a river during the Dog Days of Summer.

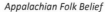

Appalachian Folk Belief

Ernest bathed Granny's face with cool water. The elderly woman, along with Minerva, had worked tirelessly in caring for the infirmed. So far there had been no deaths, but Ernest worried the Grim Reaper would come for Granny Laurel. The figure of death cloaked in black had originated from the black plague which ravaged Europe. The death of one of God's children was precious in His sight. Death, when someone didn't know Jesus, was a travesty like no other.

Samuel had done his best to keep the upper holler residents calm. He also tenaciously aided the suffering. Aunt Ada and Uncle Christian stayed in Lottie's home. They worked in shifts helping the frail.

Influenza had settled in Granny's chest. Doctor Bright's diagnosis was direct and concise. "Only time will tell if she recovers or not."

Aunt Ada shushed her husband. "Christian, my love, don't be declarin' death."

"Darlin', I'm a doctor. It's my job to tell the truth and to prepare others for what might come."

There was also Minerva to consider. She was somewhat of a mystery. No one seemed to know her. Due to the deformity of her mouth, her speech was impaired. When she did speak, which rarely happened, her meaning was extremely difficult to understand. Ernest could tell she was smart but had no formal learning. Where did she come from? And why had she been entrusted to Granny's care?

The young woman was shy and kept to herself. She seemed attached to a worn pale blue scarf that was tied around her neck. If people looked at her curiously, she used the scarf to cover her face.

Granny coughed pervasively. When Ernest started to wipe her mouth, she pushed his hand away. Fighting for air, she was nevertheless determined to speak. Ernest drew close to hear the rattling, raspy words.

"I'm dyin'. I done know it, so don't be sayin' otherwise."

Ernest wanted to disagree but chose to honor Granny's request. He also didn't want to interrupt her words. He wasn't sure how many she had left.

"I'm needin' a promise, Ernest. Watch out for Minerva. I call her Mini. She's like a broken flower that won't bloom."

Coughing wracked Granny's body. She was suffering. Beads of sweat were on her brow; her hair was damp from perspiration. He wiped her face and offered her a sip of water.

She declined the water, but Ernest was persistent. "It's sweet water from the spring."

Her lips touched the rim of the metal cup; Ernest wasn't sure if any moisture reached her mouth.

Between Granny's bouts of wheezing, Ernest learned that Minerva was her granddaughter. Mini had been born out of wedlock. Because of the status of her birth and her cleft lip and palate, her mother had been ashamed and hid her away. Granny had finally intervened and brought her to the holler.

"I did her wrong, Ernest. I kept thinkin' that it was evil that made her such."

Granny took his hand and closed her eyes. Her chest rose and fell. Ernest remembered a verse from the Bible, *Life is like a vapor.*

He patted her hand and tried to soothe her, "Granny, I'm knowin' that you think that I don't like you but, in truth, I admire you," Ernest began.

The weary woman opened her glassy eyes and immediately closed them again. The weight of her chin rested on her upper chest.

"You've been strong in tough times. You've lived in the wilds and did your best to be helpin' others. Now, I am wantin' to help you. I know you believe in God, but it's important to believe that God sent His Son Jesus to save us. Your time on earth might be comin' to an end. I'm gonna pray. I'm wantin' you to pray with me."

Ernest motioned for Minerva to join them. They made a hand circle. He closed his eyes and prayed a simple prayer. When he opened his eyes and looked at Granny, she had released Minerva's hand. The wrinkled worn weathered hand was raised in the air like Granny was reaching for someone. She gasped and let go of life on earth. Ernest believed she was reaching for the angels who had come to escort her to heaven. He serenaded her home.

There's a land that is fairer than day, and by faith we can see it afar. For the Father waits over the way to prepare us a dwelling place there. In the sweet by and by, we shall meet on that beautiful shore. In the sweet by and by, we shall meet on that beautiful shore. We shall sing on the beautiful shore, the melodious songs of the blessed. And our spirits shall sorrow no more, not a sigh for the blessing of rest. In the sweet by and by, we shall meet on that beautiful shore. In the sweet by and by, we shall meet on that beautiful shore.

Samuel played the last verse followed by the chorus on his harmonica. Ernest knew that for all of Samuel's bluster, he cared deeply for the upper holler folks. His ways were peculiar, but he took his responsibilities as a leader seriously.

Ernest ambled from the schoolhouse to Lottie's. The flowers that he and the learners had gathered and planted were wilted from neglect. Hopefully, with tender care, they could be brought back to life.

The Bible said that there was hope in God. Ernest was thankful for the hope of salvation. He was also thankful for the opportunity to share the Lord's hope with Granny and Mini.

He knocked on the front door of Lottie's home.

"Come on in, Ernest," Aunt Ada responded.

"How did ya know it was me?"

"You got them quiet steps. I'd be recognizin' your walk anywhere. I practically raised you, my boy."

Ernest smiled. "Yes, you did. You done raised me and my brothers and sisters, and I'm knowin' that we could be rascals at times."

"Bein' a rascal myself, I never noticed the likes."

Ernest's smile grew bigger. "Auntie, that's nice of you to be sayin', but I'm knowin' it ain't true."

"I just made some milk tea. Would you like some? I'll lace it with honey like you're preferrin'."

Ernest nodded. "Auntie, I'm needin' a favor. I want a pair of shoes for Granny Laurel."

"That's a fine idea. Them boots she wears is a tad big and a mite noisy."

"Aunt Ada, Granny's passed. She's walkin' on gold now."

Ada wiped a tear from her eye. "Why are you needin' shoes? People ain't usually buried with 'um."

"Granny Laurel ambled the earth with make do shoes. She rambled about tryin' to help others. I'm thinkin' a nice pair of shoes is befittin'."

When a week passed without any new cases of Spanish Influenza, Aunt Ada and Uncle Christian returned home, taking Mini with them. Uncle Christian knew a surgeon in Charleston who could possibly reconstruct Mini's mouth and lip. Minerva, however, had lived a very sheltered life. Just traveling to the lower portion of the holler had overwhelmed and frightened her.

Ernest was so thankful for his aunt and uncle's gentle ways. He had experienced their kindness, over and over, again. His siblings and many others in the community also had been the recipients of their lavish love.

Uncle Christian was concerned about who could assist Mini during her stay in Charleston, especially during her time of convalescence. She would need ongoing treatment to help her with her speech. Ernest had committed to keep the matter in prayer. He knew God was faithful. Mini had heard Ernest share the Gospel with Granny. He believed seeds had been planted in her heart; not just any seeds, but heirloom seeds–tried and true seeds passed down from generation to generation.

Ernest scrubbed the schoolhouse from top to bottom. He wanted everything clean and in order before the learners continued their summer session.

Samuel worked beside Ernest. Doctor Bright had mentioned the disinfecting powers of alcohol, and Samuel had taken it upon himself to procure several sizeable jugs of moonshine. Though liquor was illegal, Samuel believed the benefits of protecting the holler's citizens overrode prohibition.

"Ernest, I done heard Granny tell you her story about Mini." Samuel said.

"I thought as much."

Ernest felt Samuel was a little heavy-handed with the moonshine. The school was starting to smell like a backwoods still.

"I now understand some of Granny Laurel's ways. She didn't want Mercy and Eli to be shamed, even though her desire to help caused trouble. I'm sincerely wishin' that you didn't need to marry Mercy." Samuel swished some additional alcohol on the students' desks. "I'm knowin' that it don't seem fair, but with you seein' her parts and the baby needin' a daddy, we ain't got no choice."

Ernest turned to face Samuel and saw him take a swig from the crock he was holding. When Ernest looked concerned, Samuel only laughed. "Might as well be enjoying the fruit of the vine."

Ernest who was thinking about the shine's ingredients almost gagged. "I'm thinkin' that refers to wine, and this moonshine, I'm betting it is made from rotten potatoes."

"Emie, I have been gettin' caught up in your mischief since you was little." Ernest declared.

"Now, Brother, this ain't the time to be talkin' about the past. We are on a mission, a mission to find Mercy a husband," Emie answered. "I sent word so Orville and Homer are expectin' us. I'm wishin' you would have worn finer clothes. We need to be makin' a good impression. We're representin' a mama and her baby."

Ernest grunted.

"You sound like a buck searchin' for a doe."

"Emie, I am searchin' for my red-headed, blue-eyed doe. I'm ready for her to come home. And about my attire. I ain't ownin' a suit. Plus, we're ridin' mules."

"I was thinkin' that Amos and Andy would be a way of showin' the bounty of takin' Mercy as a wife."

"These ornery things ain't bounty. If anythin', there should be a bounty on their fool heads, Emie. I done been bit twice. I'm thinkin' that we need to trade."

"Brother, I chose Amos on purpose. Justice told me Andy was the biter. I ain't tradin'."

The meeting with Orville and Homer had been disastrous. The brothers looked alike and had similar speech patterns and mannerism. They also wore identical clothing, and if that wasn't off-putting enough, their mother participated in the interview. The process started with her discussing in detail their famous ancestor, Chief Logan of the Mingo tribe. Most folks in the area knew the history of the famous chief. Ernest didn't require a lesson about bygone days. He also knew about the establishment of the smaller county of Mingo.

Marrying Mercy seemed agreeable, and they didn't have a problem with Eli. In fact, there was excitement about having a baby in the family. The puzzlement came when Emie asked which brother wanted to marry her. Both were eager to tie the knot. The mother suggested Mercy and Eli stay with them in the family home. Mercy could tend things, clean house, wash clothes and cook, and then after a time, it would be decided which brother took a bigger shine.

Emie had gotten riled, "I'm tellin' you boys and your MOTHER that Mercy won't be takin' a shine to any of you all. You best be puttin' an advertisement in the local paper about needin' a maid, and I'm bettin' that girl won't take a shine neither…"

Ernest had to physically guide his sister out the door and lift her onto one of the mules. He knew the slight differences in the beasts and sat her on the back of Andy.

Chapter Twenty

It is bad luck to kill a ladybug.

Appalachian Folk Belief

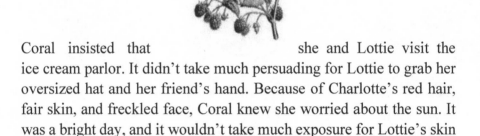

Coral insisted that she and Lottie visit the ice cream parlor. It didn't take much persuading for Lottie to grab her oversized hat and her friend's hand. Because of Charlotte's red hair, fair skin, and freckled face, Coral knew she worried about the sun. It was a bright day, and it wouldn't take much exposure for Lottie's skin to burn.

Hand-in-hand, the twosome walked the short distance to the confectionary. Coral had already described in detail the red and white interior of the parlor, the expansive delectable cold and creamy items on the menu, the clothing worn by the waitresses, and the unique way the serving trays were held.

"I'm gonna miss you, Coral. Who will climb mountains and visit the Garden of Eden with me?"

"I promise that we'll enjoy other travels, Sister." Coral smiled.

The day felt too wonderful to be true. Although there were loose ends to be tied, somehow Coral felt confident that everything would be in order before Lottie and Pastor Rex headed back to Big Creek. She didn't want her family to worry. She also didn't want Ernest or possibly Rudy to make an unnecessary trip to Charleston to check on her.

Coral's pulse raced when she saw the Help Wanted sign posted in the window. She didn't believe in chance and wondered if God was providing an opportunity for her. Four-leaf clovers and horseshoes were only inanimate things. God brought good fortune, it said so in His Word. Opportunities and blessings were from Him. His symbol of goodness was found in the cross of His Son, Jesus.

Lottie also noticed the sign, encouraging Coral to make inquiries.

"First things first, Sister. We're samplin' sweetness. Then, I'll be askin' about the job."

As the friends oohed and aahed over their sundaes, Coral expressed her apprehension about being a waitress. "I don't have any experience, Lottie. Look at me. I know I'm slight. They won't think I can manage carryin' heavy glass things to the tables."

"Your imagination is runnin' wild, Sister. Settle your mind and take another bite. I am enjoyin' this concoction."

The owner of the creamery was present and available to visit with Coral. Mr. Smith was an older gentleman. In some ways, he reminded her of Pastor Rex. He smiled easily, but Coral could tell he didn't tolerate mischief. When he spoke about the guidelines under which his business operated, his tone dropped to a no-nonsense warning. Such formality indicated that his business was something he took pride in. He stressed that quality ice cream and service were of the utmost importance.

The conversation ended with what Coral assumed to be an important question from Mr. Smith, "Why is the word sundae when referrin' to ice cream spelled s-u-n-d-a-e?"

"I ain't rightly sure," Coral answered honestly, "but I'm thinkin' that if it was spelled like the Lord's day, Christian folk might be takin' offense. Now, I like a good S-u-n-d-a-y service, but I'm also thinkin' that an ice cream sundae is mighty fine."

Mr. Smith stood to his feet, shook Coral's hand, and said, "The job is yours."

"Lottie, thank you for walkin' with me to the prison."

"It's a lovely day for strollin'. Besides, I haven't seen the goodly

181

doctor in a few days, and I'm wantin' to see if love is in the air."

Coral giggled. The sun felt warm on her face. She and Lottie had walked the distance from the boarding house to the jailhouse on several occasions. It felt odd, however, that today their path wasn't leading them to visit Charlie.

She was anxious to tell Kenneth about her decision to remain in Charleston. She also wanted to tease him a little bit about any future visits he might have in mind to the Smith & Son Creamery. The older gentleman was the son in Smith & Son which Coral found interesting. She was certain all types of interesting knowledge and experiences awaited her.

"I've been thinkin' a little bit about love," Coral said. "Harsh words are sometimes used for describin' what should be tender: crush, hit it off, love to pieces, head over heels, tie the knot, and get hitched."

"Love is both–tender and harsh. Moments sweet as can be and times when it hurts to the bone." Lottie appeared to be lost in thought. "My mama used to say, 'tender to the bone.' I'm wonderin' if that ain't a good picture of love–so tender that everythin' falls to pieces, yet so delicious that a person wants more."

The girls passed by the guard shack. Coral could see James sitting inside. She waved, but he looked away. She stopped in her tracks and turned around.

"Coral, no!" Lottie burst out.

She knocked on the door before entering. James rose to his feet but didn't move toward her or even extend a hand.

"Charlotte told me you visited and sat by my bed. I'm wantin' to offer thanks."

"I'm sure she told other things as well," James answered.

"She did, but thanks is still in order."

He stepped forward and took her hand. "I have feelings for you, Coral. We can work this out. I've been dreamin' of you and your beauty. You're the girl for me. I know it, and I believe you know it, too. Give me a chance. I'll do whatever it takes to win you over."

Coral drew her hand back and shook her head no.

"It's the job. The men in this place are vile and violent. I've become like them. I can change…"

"I'm sure that guardin' criminals ain't easy, but don't be blamin' others for your struggles. Sheriff Robbins in Big Creek is tough as nails, but anger ain't part of his being."

"Forgive me, Coral. It won't happen again. I promise. The Bible says you need to forgive me…"

"Don't be usin' God's word for manipulatin''." She turned and walked away.

"You forgave Charlie but won't forgive me. That ain't Christian, Coral."

She didn't answer. She kept walking and didn't look back.

Lottie took her hand and, with heads held high, they entered the expansive front door.

It was obvious the warden had had enough of Coral and Lottie. When Lottie mentioned her upcoming return to Big Creek, he seemed to sigh with relief. He didn't bother to question why the young women wanted to visit the infirmary. He simply asked the officer standing outside his door to usher them to the separate wing. He also gave specific instructions that the ladies were not to enter the clinic but to remain outside the facility until Doctor Daniels had the opportunity to speak with them. They were not to interact with other officers or be in the presence of inmates.

It was apparent to Coral that Kenneth was pleased to see her and Lottie.

"I'm not accustomed to having visitors. This is a pleasant surprise. Let's talk in my office. The patients are a bit surly today–well, really every day."

Lottie smiled and nodded at Coral.

Coral knew from her previous visit that Doctor Daniels' office was located just outside the infirmary. She was relieved to know visiting Kenneth wouldn't require them to see any of the incarcerated men. Her mission to Charleston had been for Charlie. She prayed for those imprisoned but knew that her time of ministry at the facility was over.

"I apologize, but I haven't much time," Kenneth announced.

"I hope it wasn't wrong to come," Coral indirectly questioned.

"I would rather see you in the sunlight or moonlight than under the green vapor lights," he answered.

And he said that he didn't have a way with niceties, Coral thought.

"I promise to be quick. I've come with some startlin' news."

"Good news," Lottie interjected.

"I've done decided to stay in Charleston for a bit. I've even found a job."

"This is good news—wonderful news, in fact." There was a knock on Kenneth's door. "Please excuse me, ladies. May I take you both to dinner this evening? I'm anxious to hear all the details and would like to offer my assistance if needed."

Coral smiled coyly. "Would it be possible to visit Smith & Son Creamery after dinner?"

Coral whispered in the dark an Emily Dickinson poem that she had learned in school

I felt a cleaving in my mind, as if my brain had split. I tried to match it seam by seam but could not make them fit. The thought behind I strove to join unto the thought before. But sequence raveled out of reach like balls upon a floor.

Her thoughts were scattered like balls hitting the floor, but she didn't care. Ice cream with Lottie, a new job, a shared dinner with Kenneth, more ice cream, and a special gift. At the confectionary, Kenneth had presented her with a hat box. She had wishfully held the box wondering if it contained a cloche, fedora, bowler, boater, toque, or even a pork pie hat. Inside was a stunningly beautiful, cream-colored, brimmed sailor hat with a large black bow.

Sweeter than the berry ice cream and Kenneth's lovely and generous gift had been his words. "I noticed your sun-kissed skin today. I hope my gift offers you shade when you need it most."

Coral couldn't sleep. It had been a deliciously delightful day.

Coral stood on the platform at the train station waving goodbye to Pastor Rex, Lottie, and Pastor Thomas. Although she had experienced first-hand Pastor Rex's ways of persuasion, it still surprised her that Thomas had agreed to travel to Big Creek. Coral wondered if the young pastor knew how long his adventure in the hills would keep him away from the city. She also wondered about her time apart from home and family. How long would she remain in Charleston? She and Pastor Thomas had essentially swapped places.

The night before, she and Lottie agreed to leave phone messages for each other at Rudy's parents' store. The friends were anxious to keep in touch. The plan had worked, for the most part, between Lottie and Ernest. Coral had encouraged Lottie not to draw conclusions before seeing Ernest; Lottie had encouraged Coral to enjoy her time in the city and to keep her heart open to whatever the Lord had in mind.

At the station, Pastor Rex insisted on a word of prayer. Pastor Thomas requested Lottie and Coral sing their special rendition of *The Bear Went Over the Mountain*. This along with the repeated embraces she and Lottie shared and the repeated well-wishes created quite a stir.

She wondered how so many emotions could be experienced at the same time. On one hand, she was excited for her independence. She had gone from her parents' home to living with Aunt Ada and Uncle Christian. With Emie, Rudy, and little Jewel living next door, her moments alone were few and far between. She craved time by herself to ponder the past, to preside over the present, and to carefully and prayerfully consider the fullness of her future.

On the other hand, she felt unprepared. Hopefully, her time away from home wouldn't reflect Lemuel Gulliver's travels. She clearly remembered Mrs. Randolph reading the satirical story.

It brought some reassurance that Pastor Rex had not merely agreed to, but had wholeheartedly approved of, her job and living arrangements. Mr. Smith and the pastor had struck up an immediate friendship, and he had also deemed her rented room at a boarding house operated by Kenneth's aunt and uncle safe and secure.

She wasn't alone. God was with her. He was directing her life. He would hold her in His hand and keep her safe. He had also blessed her with friends and confections to help along the way.

Chapter Twenty-One

Knock three times on wood after mentioning
good fortune so evil spirits
can't ruin it.

Appalachian Folk Belief

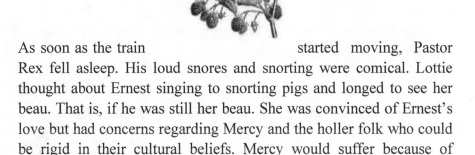

As soon as the train started moving, Pastor Rex fell asleep. His loud snores and snorting were comical. Lottie thought about Ernest singing to snorting pigs and longed to see her beau. That is, if he was still her beau. She was convinced of Ernest's love but had concerns regarding Mercy and the holler folk who could be rigid in their cultural beliefs. Mercy would suffer because of unforgiving traditions about having babies out of wedlock.

Last spring, Ernest and the learners had conducted an experiment. They planted two trees in front of the school. One tree was firmly staked to the ground. The other tree, unstaked, was given freedom to sway, move, and bend with the wind. When the students returned to school in the fall, they assessed the well-being of the trees. The staked tree had grown taller, but its trunk was smaller. The other tree had a thicker base. Dancing in the wind had caused the root system to develop. The rigid tree didn't fare as well as the swaying sapling.

Charlotte understood the importance of standing firm in her faith. However, Christian beliefs and cultural traditions were not the same. The Pharisees thrived on tradition but lacked the love of God. Not all tradition was bad. In fact, she looked forward to building family traditions with Ernest. She never wanted historical convention, even good things passed down by others, to override the importance of loving freely and unconditionally.

She smiled at Pastor Thomas. He looked to be as nervous as she felt. There had been some confusion on the train about where he would sit. Colored people sat in one compartment and white people in another. Since Thomas didn't consider himself white or black, he'd explained to the ticket man that he was neither. Charlotte could tell it wasn't the first time the young pastor had such a conversation. Patiently, he did his best to describe his unusual situation. Pastor Rex had quickly intervened, quoting Scripture about mankind and explaining that the term mankind referred to people of all shades, the negro people, white people, and Indian people. The ticket man eventually shrugged his shoulders and walked off being it was three to one.

Charlotte and Thomas sat across from Pastor Rex whose slouching form took an entire bench.

"Lottie, you look a mite worried."

"I was just thinkin' the same about you."

Pastor Thomas smiled. "We've got a ride ahead of us. Tell me what's on your mind, and I'll do the same."

She talked and talked, and then talked some more. She told Thomas about Lottie the Legend, Lester, and his death. She talked about the learners and the upper holler. She spoke about her love for Ernest and about Mercy messing with evil. She also mentioned Mercy's pregnancy and the recent message from Rudy's mama. Pastor Thomas listened. He didn't interrupt or ask questions. Lottie felt secure in sharing her heart.

When it was Thomas' turn to speak, he was brief and to the point, "I'm worried that, once again, I won't fit. People won't understand who I am, and I'll be shunned, or worse yet, ignored like I don't exist."

"I ain't thinkin' that will happen," Charlotte said. "Different shades ain't always about color. A tree or building will shade a person from the heat. If the sun is hot, shade is a mite welcoming, don't you think? If it's cold, the shade makes it colder. In Big Creek, especially in the hills where people are sometimes wantin' to escape the hardships of the past or live quiet lives without others ruling over them, shade only matters if it's hot or cold. In general, mountain folk don't rightly care about the shade of a person's skin. It ain't like the city where roles are defined by color. In the holler, where life is hard and harsh, if people don't work together, ain't no one gonna survive."

Lottie then clarified a portion of her earlier story. "Thomas, I don't think that I rightly explained that Mercy is dark-skinned. Her baby is part negro and part white."

Thomas looked bewildered but didn't pursue the conversation further. Charlotte gave him peace and was content to look out the train window and view the beautiful Appalachian scenery. Some of the hills were marred by logging and coal mining. She willed herself not to complain about the ugly scars on her Appalachian earth. Families needed to eat.

Some companies in West Virginia seemed to be prospering. Charlotte hoped the workers within the companies also were prospering. Logging was hard work. Lumberjacks lived in remote areas and used hand tools to fell trees. The work was dangerous. Coal mining was also dangerous. For some, black lung stole their lives. Miners were sometimes paid in company script which could only be used at company-owned stores. Miners often spent their money before they earned it. The Battle of Blair Mountain was still discussed in the holler. Big Creek wasn't too far from Logan County where the most hostile battle of the coal wars had taken place.

People in the holler needed jobs. Even if it was dangerous, she knew the mountain men would welcome work. She had known helpless, broken-hearted men struggling to take care of their families.

Thomas, not understanding Charlotte's fallen smile, tried to encourage. "I've been ponderin' some, your situation and mine. I'm hopin' that your words of encouragement are true. I've also been thinkin' about Ernest. I'm bettin' your beau is just like his name. He's earnest about matters of the heart and won't take his carin' for you lightly. I'm thinkin' that his feelings for you are serious and sincere. Men like Ernest don't change their minds about love and marriage."

Before reaching Big Creek, the train made a stop in Ripley. It was sprinkling rain when Lottie and Thomas exited the steam machine. Pastor Rex yawned as the train stopped and shuffled around a bit, but in the end, decided to wait on board.

Everything was wet and soggy. Ripley was located where two creeks came together. Sycamore Creek and Big Mill Creek were generally shallow enough for wading, but the late spring runoffs from the higher elevations and recent thunderstorms had caused the creeks to overflow. The town wasn't flooded but pools of water were abundant. The three traveling companions watched as children played in the muddy streets and oversized puddles.

"Lottie, would you mind fetching your bow?" Pastor Thomas asked. "Let's join in the children's fun!"

When she returned, Thomas was already surrounded by a group of children. He also had a pail of water next to his feet. The youngsters were obviously curious about the young pastor's looks. Lottie could see a small handprint on Thomas' cheek, and his hair was mussed.

She wished there was time to don her Lottie Legend costume. The stop, however, was only 45 minutes long.

Pastor Thomas quietly asked Lottie to pretend to be blind. She accommodated him by grasping his arm and fumbling her steps. He then began to tell the Bible story about the man who was blind from birth.

"Some said it was a curse that made him blind."

Charlotte wanted to stay in character, so she kept her eyes closed. She could, however, hear the children gasp. It was a common belief in the hills that the loss of sight was a curse.

"Jesus told his friends that it wasn't a curse or sin that made the man blind, but it was so God could do a miracle." Pastor Thomas drew Lottie close.

Looking down, she could see beneath her lashes, Thomas dipping his hands into the mud puddle located just in front of where they were standing. When he placed mud on her eyes, it felt cold and sticky and smelled slightly stinky. "Oh!" escaped.

"Jesus asked the man to go wash the mud from his eyes." Thomas placed the bucket in front of Lottie. She bent down and carefully washed away the mire.

She then demonstrated the keenness of her sight by shooting various objects off Pastor Thomas' head.

The children cheered and a crowd soon gathered. Lottie saw Pastor Rex looking out the train window. His smile of encouragement said it all.

Ernest was excited to the point of earning himself a nervous stomach about the big day. Lottie was finally coming home! But, first things first, Ernest had a busy day planned for his students.

The summer learners would arrive at the schoolhouse in no time, and the lesson he planned required unique preparations. A cooking fire was already lit and the ingredients for making stone soup gathered.

Upon arrival, each student would receive a small poke with an item for the soup. As he shared the fable about a hungry traveler needing help, he would call upon the learners to add their own contributions to the stone and water mixture.

Adam, Beau, Claude, and Dean were the first to arrive. The boys, as unusual, grumbled among themselves but were willing to help their teacher carry the benches from inside the schoolhouse to the fireside.

As the other children appeared, Adam took charge and directed his peers to sit. Beau, Claude, and Dean distributed the small sacks containing soup ingredients. The children showed their curiosity. Ernest believed inquisitiveness to be the perfect platform for learning.

"I once heard a story about a hungry man traveling through Big Creek," the teacher started.

"Folklore was an important part of Appalachian culture. Stories passed down from generation to generation carried facts, truth, and other tidbits about the life. The art of storytelling was considered a gift, and those with the gift were often called upon at mountain gatherings to share superstitions, accounts, and yarns.

"The traveler stopped at several houses in Big Creek askin' for food," Ernest continued. "But it was winter, and food was done scarce. The clever man built a cook fire just outside the church house and begged of the pastor a big soup pot to be borrowin'. He then put a goodly sized flat stone in the bottom of the pot and added water."

With exaggerated movements, Ernest placed his fire pot on the heat and added a stone and water. "The man told the pastor that he was makin' a family dish called stone soup and to gather the town folk."

While Ernest gave account after account of the Big Creek community adding their own ingredients to the soup, the students contributed their part and parcel. Ernest also supplemented the soup with rabbit meat. He knew that the additional protein would benefit his students. When the teacher added spices to the gently cooking mixture, Dean stepped forward with his own herbs.

"Whoa, young man, what are you addin' to our pot?" Ernest asked with a chuckle and smile.

"Teacher, I done gathered this in the woods for my mama. I'm thinkin' they is special plants for addin' goodness."

"Let me be takin' a look-see."

The pokeweeds that Dean placed in Ernest's hands were considered a mountain delicacy. The weeds in raw form, however, were poisonous and needed to be washed and soaked repeatedly before eating. Ernest set the plant aside and took a moment to explain the required preparations for making the plant to be edible.

While the stone soup simmered, the learners told their own tales of sharing with others. Ernest also taught a lesson on the consonant digraph "sh" and included a memory verse from Hebrews 13:16.

And do not forget to do good and to share with others, for with such sacrifices God is pleased.

When the school day ended, Ernest breathed a sigh of relief. He always enjoyed working with the learners but was more than ready to head down the mountain and fetch his girl. He doused the fire with water and put the benches back in place. A couple bowls of soup remained in the pot. Looking forward to sharing the savory dish with Lottie, he set the extra fixings aside for later. He had so much to tell his beloved: stories of humor and humbleness, tales of discouragement and destiny, reports of tenaciousness and tenderness. Mostly, however, he wanted to communicate to Lottie how that during their time apart the faithfulness of God was evident time and time again.

A female rabbit hopped by, Ernest couldn't help but notice her dewlap. The heavy fold of skin on the front of the neck appears when females can reproduce. The bunny can pull out her own fur from the dewlap and use it to build a nest for her babies.

Ernest closed his eyes, softly smiled, and gently shook his head in amazement.

God faithfully provides for his creatures from the giant blue whale to the pygmy shrew.

With the schoolroom back in order, Ernest turned his attention to Bullseye. The bird was sitting on the teacher's desk surrounded by a mess of seeds, hulls, and berries. The learners knew not to give the parrot food without permission but sometimes their youthful zealousness got the better of them.

Bullseye greeted him in Lottie's voice, "God bless you." It seemed to Ernest that the peculiar bird had a knack for knowing what voice to use at what time. The parrot often flapped his wings when happy, and would even wag his tail if entertained, although the tail wagging could also mean that the bird was ready to relieve himself.

With Bullseye perched on his shoulder, Ernest headed to the private room at the back of the schoolhouse. He picked up the tan-colored canvas satchel that was sitting on the worn chair. The parcel contained a few gifts for Lottie: notes from the learners welcoming her home, a light blue feather shed by Bullseye, homemade biscuits and jam prepared by Cece, and a pressed flower and poem penned by Ernest. The bird flew to the chair and turned his head upside down.

As Ernest exited the building through the back door, he heard someone yelling from the front of the schoolhouse. He hurriedly rounded the structure running into Adam.

"Mr. Ernest, my daddy's needin' you. Come quick! Dean's got the fever..."

Ernest's heart sank like an anchor heading to the bottom of the sea. The weight of what Adam said stopped the teacher in his tracks. If Dean had influenza, then all the learners had been exposed. He didn't want to think of the possible deadly consequences.

Ernest took Adam by the arm and started running toward Justice and Cece's home.

"Teacher, you is hurtin' me," Adam spoke. "I can't keep up."

Without uttering a word, Ernest released Adam's arm and ran ahead. When he arrived at the family home, he jumped the low gate to the yard, missed one of the two porch steps, and entered the house without knocking. Mercy was sitting in the everything room nursing Eli. He barely nodded in her direction and headed to the back of the small clapboard home.

Dean was lying on a rumpled bed. He skin was pale, and his eyes were glazed over. His forehead was covered in sweat, and he was shivering under the multiple blankets that covered him. Beau and Claude sat quietly on the floor in the corner of the room. Justice stood on one side of the bed and Cece on the other side. Worry was etched on all the faces present.

"The boy is chilled clear to the bone. We can't get 'um warm." Justice said.

Ernest stepped forward and placed the back of his hand on Dean's face. The lad was burning up with fever.

"Beau and Claude go and check on your sister and the baby," Ernest instructed. After the brothers left the room, Ernest spoke quietly to Justice and Cece. "If it's the Spanish Flu, we're needin' to get Dean quarantined."

The vigil began. Justice prayed, Ernest sang to the boy, and Cece wiped her son's face with a cold cloth every few minutes. The fever wouldn't break. Dean moaned and bent his legs toward the middle of his body trying to relieve the pain.

Just as Ernest made the decision to call for Samuel and begin the heart-wrenching process of notifying parents about the dreaded virus, Dean started to vomit which was puzzling. Generally, with Spanish Influenza, fever and congestion were the initial symptoms.

Bits of red could be seen at the corners of Dean's mouth. Ernest thought it might be blood, but when Cece wiped her son's face, the discharge appeared to be small pieces of berry.

Ernest sighed with relief. "Dean doesn't have influenza. He ate pokeberries."

Justice lifted the blankets from one of his son's hands and saw the purplish-red stains. He then called for the other boys. They confessed to seeing Dean pick the pokeweeds. They didn't initially realize that the plant was poisonous. After learning about the harm the plant could cause, the brothers witnessed Dean throwing away the leaves and stems. Claude also saw Dean feed a few berries to Bullseye. When the bird didn't become sick, Dean must have deducted that the berries were fine for human consumption.

Cece roused Dean from his semi-delirium. He had only eaten a few berries. The lad would be sick for several hours but hopefully fine once his body eliminated the poison.

Frustrated, Ernest realized that he had missed Lottie's homecoming. Fear for Dean and the other learners had consumed him. It would have been irresponsible to leave his students and their families without warning them of a possible epidemic.

Her train had arrived, and he had missed the fanfare. Though he knew that Lottie was safe, Pastor Rex and Rudy's parents would provide, yet he wanted to be the one to greet her, to be her provider and hero. It was too late now to trek down the mountain and rouse the residents of Big Creek looking for his love.

They arrived in Big Creek later than expected. Train schedules were published and studied by travelers and their families but, like most things in the hills, delays were part of everyday living. Meeting folks, sharing conversations, and enjoying a bite of food took priority over schedule keeping.

Rudy's parents were waiting at the train station. Pastor Rex embraced his daughter and shook hands with his son-in-law. He also introduced Pastor Thomas. Lottie stood back looking for Ernest. She had sincerely hoped that he would come to the station to greet her.

Pastor Rex was eager to return to the parsonage. He wanted to sleep in his own bed and start the following day by enjoying a cup of coffee on the front porch of his home. His daughter had left a food parcel for him at the church house. Her fried chicken was renowned, and her berry cobbler had won awards at the local fair. Pastor Thomas, who had agreed to help the elderly reverend minister to the community, would stay with Pastor Rex at the small home behind the church.

Lottie wasn't quite sure what to do. It was too late to walk the mountain trail. She knew that Emie and Rudy would welcome her, but their home was some distance away. When Rudy's mama linked arms with her, she knew all would be well. Plans were made for Lottie to spend the night in Big Creek and journey up the hillside in the morning. Thomas expressed interest in joining her on her journey to the upper holler.

The two pastors set off in one direction, and Lottie and Rudy's parents in the other direction.

"I'm knowin' that Rudy's friends simply call me Rudy's mama, and I'm honored by such. That boy and Emie and Jewel light my life."

When Rudy's daddy pretended to clear his throat, Lottie couldn't help but smile and giggle.

"My husband is also a light, my brightest light," Rudy's mama added. "But if you would be so inclined to call me Leigh, my given name, that would be fine, too. My husband's name is Hart."

"Well, Aunt Leigh and Uncle Hart, thank you kindly for openin' your home. I'm hopin' for a good rest and lookin' forward to travelin' the hill tomorrow."

"Now, I am knowin' a little about you and Ernest. Emie shared some bits. I'm thinkin' that he wanted to meet your train but couldn't. Influenza hit the upper holler."

Lottie caught her breath and placed her hand over her mouth.

Leigh put her arm around Lottie's shoulder. "Don't be worryin'. Ernest is fine. Accordin' to Doctor Bright, the infection was contained. Granny Laurel passed. We're all grievin' her loss but thankin' the good

Lord it didn't take more of the holler folk."

Hart opened the door to the couple's living quarters behind the store. "Leigh, let's be feedin' her dinner and then the talkin' can resume."

As Lottie ate the blackberry cobbler for dessert, she wondered if her dreams about marrying Ernest were merely pie in the sky.

A basket of dewberries sat on the counter. Some of the grannies in the holler said dewberries were blackberries, but blackberries weren't dewberries. Ernest had once explained that dewberries came from blackberries. Dewberries were a little sweeter and their vines not as sturdy. She wasn't sure how it all worked but knew both tasted delicious.

Leigh caught her looking at the berries and promised to make dewberry flapjacks for breakfast. Like a young calf that had over-indulged in sweet grain, Lottie's tummy felt full to the brim. Yet, thoughts of fresh berries in flapjack batter made her anxious for breakfast.

Leigh and Hart shared recent news about Big Creek and her residents. Lottie was initially stunned to hear about Ernest's plan to find Mercy a husband. Then shock gave way to laughter as Leigh described the succession of potential suitors.

The couple knew very little about the happenings in the upper holler. Though the two regions were connected by a mountain trail, residents from Big Creek had little reason to travel up the hillside.

When Lottie turned the covers down on her bed, her thoughts were of Ernest. Anxious to see him, she needed assurance that he was healthy and thriving not only in his life, but also in his interest toward her. She also looked forward to joining his work with the learners. She had so much to tell him.

Charlotte knew Ernest wouldn't be happy about Coral remaining in Charleston. She reminded herself that her responsibility was only to share the news. It was Ernest's responsibility to receive the report and work through his own thoughts and feelings. She loved Ernest to the degree that separating their emotions was sometimes difficult.

She looked forward to introducing Pastor Thomas. She hoped

Ernest would invite the pastor to share his life story with the students. Children in the holler often led such sheltered lives. Their encounters with hardship were broad, but their experiences outside the hill community were limited.

Charlotte was growing sleepy. All the blood from her head had rushed to her stomach. She yawned a few times, said her nighttime prayers, closed her eyes, and entered dreamland.

Just before daybreak, Charlotte quietly knocked on the parsonage door. There was a chill in the air. She was thankful she had decided against wearing her best dress. The satin frock was fashionable but offered little warmth. In Charleston, she had purchased it out of vanity wanting to look beautiful for Ernest. She knew that her confidence in their relationship had waned. In a weak moment, she had somehow believed that buying a new dress could be the answer. Impractical for holler life, it was a pale pink–she chided herself, not even her best color, given her red hair. Still, the fine material with the white trim had been so lovely, she could not resist it.

To her, the dress represented a dream of she and Ernest living happily ever after. Dreams weren't fulfilled according to what she wore, however. Dreams came true when they were covered in prayer and aligned with God's will. Charlotte sighed at the vast unknown. Togetherness required hard work and patience, but grace was something added, like a body being covered in beautiful attire. With all these thoughts in mind, she chose a common, but clean dress for what might come today.

Pastor Thomas opened the door. He placed a finger to his lips and whispered, "Pastor Rex is still restin'."

Thankfully, Thomas had also chosen casual wear for their morning walk. The trail was rocky and overgrown in places.

The sun was just starting to rise with the promise of a new day. Charlotte linked arms with Thomas. Off they went. She didn't take the time to show him Big Creek proper. Of course, there wasn't a lot to see: several houses, Rudy's parents' store, the sheriff's office and jailhouse, and the local post office with intermittent mail service. She told Thomas about each of these places instead, providing an introduction.

Big Creek Church was on the outskirts of town, and not far from the path to the upper holler.

Chapter Twenty-Two

If your right ear itches, someone is speaking well
of you. If your left ear itches, someone is
speaking ill of you.

Appalachian Folk Belief

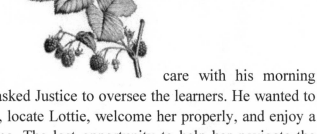

Ernest took extra care with his morning
ablutions. He had asked Justice to oversee the learners. He wanted to
head down the hill, locate Lottie, welcome her properly, and enjoy a
leisurely stroll home. The lost opportunity to help her navigate the
steps from the train, present her with wildflowers, and embrace her,
bothered him. He had missed out on memory making. He also never
wanted his gal to think she came second to his duties as a teacher.

He wanted to be Lottie's hero. Ernest's favorite frontiersman was
Daniel Boone. He was a legend among Appalachian residents. Boone
was a trapper, soldier, militia officer, politician, surveyor, merchant,
sheriff, tavern keeper, horse trader, and land speculator. Ernest
thought, however, that the trail blazer Boone's greatest
accomplishments were loving one woman, having ten children, and
building a road through the wilderness that others followed.

Ernest knew that he was acting like a silly schoolboy. He cupped
his hand to his mouth, breathed out, and smelled his breath. He also
sniffed beneath his arms. Body odor was a problem in the holler.
Bathing wasn't a priority. Some of the stink was due to a lack of water,

lack of soap, and scarcity of toothpowder. Though the holler folk appeared immune to smelly bodies, each school year Ernest spent special time with the boys while Lottie provided special time with the girls discussing hygiene.

The teachers also incorporated the help of some of the older holler women who were skilled at making soap and toothpowder. The soap was made from boiled fats and ashes. Toothpowder was made from orris roots. Both could be perfumed with lavender and rose petals.

Some of the older girls struggled with hygiene during their menses. It wasn't proper yet for him to discuss the situation with Lottie, but he knew that she gave the girls rags to help.

He stared at himself in a small looking glass. *I'm presentable,* he thought. *Smellin' good and lookin' good.*

As Ernest grabbed his boots from his bedside, he was startled by a noise in the schoolhouse. Even Bullseye quieted. Before he could investigate, the door to his private quarters flew open. Samuel and two other holler men stood before him. Samuel held a shotgun.

"It's time for a weddin', Ernest," Samuel practically shouted.

The two men behind Samuel looked sheepish. They appeared to be fearful, skittish, and easily led.

"Ain't you heard of knockin'?" Ernest asked. "I was in my drawers just a minute ago."

"I didn't wanna give you time to run," Samuel said.

"If I was gonna run, I would have already headed out when this weddin' nonsense done started." Ernest closed his eyes momentarily and shook his head unbelievingly. "Samuel, there ain't no need to be pointin' the gun. It's not safe."

Ernest was relieved when Samuel lowered his shotgun.

"At least let me get my boots on."

Samuel took hold of Ernest's arm. "No need for your boots. We're hostin' the weddin' just outside the school."

He forcibly removed Samuel's hand and proceeded to put his shoes on. Ernest took his time. He felt surprisingly calm.

Samuel and his companions stepped aside allowing Ernest to exit the room first. Justice was waiting in the schoolhouse. "I tried to stop 'um. You ain't wantin' this and neither is Mercy."

It was early morning. The front portion of the schoolyard was crowded with folks: naysayers, yeasayers, doomsayers, gainsayers, and soothsayers. However, as far as Ernest could tell, the bride was missing.

Samuel directed him to the front of the crowd. Some of the husband candidates were even present, including Homer and Orville.

Mercy was indeed missing, but Samuel wasn't persuaded. "The lass will soon be found," he declared.

In the meantime, there was a celebratory atmosphere. The Hollering Fiddle Boys band was present, fiddler and all. Ernest spied his students running and playing. The community women held hankies. A back-hill wedding always involved a good amount of crying. A group of men sat on the infamous bear log passing a flask back and forth. The holler folk weren't known for secret keeping. Ernest was amazed that Samuel had been able to organize things, more than likely, at the last minute.

Ernest wasn't convinced that Samuel would shoot him but felt his best option was to simply sit and wait. Maybe the bride would show up, maybe she wouldn't.

When Claude asked if he could fetch Bullseye, Ernest thought, *What the heck. Why not add a little more confusion to this chaotic caucus?*

Claude also quietly shared that Adam and Beau had headed down the hillside to retrieve Doc Bright and Sheriff Robbins. "Daddy told 'um to take the shortcut through the creek."

Ernest hoped the two boys didn't get distracted playing in the water. Of course, the water would be a mite chilly since it's swelling banks were still fueled by snowmelt from the higher hills.

The band played a melody of dancing ditties, traditional songs, and hymns. Bullseye loudly sang along. Ernest chuckled. The absurdity astounded him. He had lived in the Big Creek area all his life and had never experienced such foolhardiness. Auntie Ada and Uncle Christian's wedding had been a little off-kilter but nothing like the current happenings.

None of his family were present. This didn't surprise Ernest. They obviously hadn't been invited to the shindig, though it would have been mighty entertaining to see Emie raise a ruckus and to watch Rudy try to contain her. He was certain that they didn't even know about the ceremony, or they would have stopped the event.

When Samuel first charged into his personal quarters this morning, Ernest realized that he didn't really have a choice but to go along with the craziness. He knew this was a fight he couldn't win. God would have to deliver him from this absurd battle.

Ernest was presented with a variety of brooms and told to pick out the one he liked. He didn't really care for any of them, but it seemed important to some of the older ladies in attendance that he choose one. He assumed they had laboriously made the brooms. There was a witch broom made of birch twigs, a cattail broom, a cornhusk broom, a dried reed broom, and even a double broom made especially for weddings. He decided on the cattail broom. He knew the plant got its name from the fuzzy seed heads that resembled cat tails. The seeds easily blew in the wind. Ernest hoped the situation and its ridiculousness would blow away as well.

As time passed, he thought the celebratory spirit would wane. It didn't partially because the moonshine had taken effect among some of the men, who were foot stomping and swinging their gals.

In the distance, he saw Samuel's two friends ushering Mercy toward the schoolhouse. She held Eli protectively. Ernest rose from his seat and headed toward the men, the mother, and the baby. He insisted the men release Mercy.

Eli was bawling. Mercy was crying softly. He asked to hold the baby, then gently rocked Eli in his arms. When Justice and Cece approached their daughter, she ran into her daddy's embrace. Cece took her hankie and wiped away Mercy's tears. Babies stayed babies in the eyes of their parents no matter their age. Cece used the same cloth to wipe the baby's face. He smiled and cooed at his grandmother.

As the ceremony started, everyone quieted except for Bullseye, who was still singing. When the musicians struck up a wedding song, Bullseye accompanied them.

Blue skies smiling at me. Nothing but blue skies do I see. Bluebirds singing a song. Nothing but bluebirds all day long. Never saw the sun shining so bright. Never saw things go oh so right. Noticing the days hurrying by. When you're in love, my my how they fly. Blue days, all of them gone. Nothing but blue skies from now on.

Samuel stood in front of Ernest and Mercy with his shotgun in hand. It appeared he was officiating the broom jumping.

"We all know why we're here. Because of the part seeing and baby birthing, Ernest and Mercy will be jumping the broom. Slaves weren't permitted to marry so they united by jumping. It marks the beginnin' of a new life together. They'll be starting their new life with a clean sweep."

Samuel struggled to hold the shotgun with one hand and to make a sweeping motion with the other hand.

"It's mighty fine that we're all here to celebrate," Samuel added.

One of Samuel's comrades handed Ernest the selected broom and instructed him to make a sweeping gesture. Ernest complied.

Samuel appeared to have put some thought into the ceremony, surprising Ernest. "Would the groom please be handin' the broom to the bride?"

Ernest reluctantly gave the broom to Mercy who was instructed to place it on the ground.

Samuel continued. "I'm gonna count to three, and on three, the bride and groom will jump."

Ermest, who wanted to delay the jumping if possible, interrupted Samuel. "Before Mercy and I commence with jumping, we would like to sing a traditional song in honor of those who had no choice but to marry in such a manner."

He felt guilty for using the hardships of others as part of his delaying tactics. He quickly asked God for forgiveness. *Lord, you know the difficulties that slaves were facing. Let this song do right in honoring them.*

Samuel looked stunned but nodded for Ernest to continue. Mercy looked confused. Ernest smiled at her reassuringly. He thought that a song of deliverance was appropriate.

He delivered Daniel from the lion's den. And Jonah from the belly of the whale. And the Hebrew children from the fiery furnace. Why not every man? Didn't my Lord deliver Daniel? Deliver Daniel, deliver Daniel. Didn't my Lord deliver Daniel? And why not every man? The moon runs down in a purple stream. And the sun refused to shine. And every star did disappear. Yes, freedom will be mine. Didn't my Lord deliver Daniel? Deliver Daniel, deliver Daniel. Didn't my Lord deliver Daniel? And why not every man?

Ernest and Mercy sang the song a couple of times over. Ernest sang tenor, and Mercy sang alto. Samuel appeared frustrated by the impediment, but the folks present were swaying and singing along. Ernest was still holding Eli and jostling him to the beat of the music. He knew they could only sing the song for so long, and then it would be time to move on and jump over the broom.

"It's petered out," Samuel said. "You best get on with the jumpin'."

Petered is such a strange word, Ernest thought. He knew from Mrs. Randolph that the word originated from the California gold rush. Miners would use the phrase when a vein ran dry. *The song's petered out, and I'm petered out. There ain't nothin' left.*

Ernest took Mercy's hand.

"God bless you. God bless you," Bullseye spoke as clear as day in Lottie's voice.

Ernest looked up and saw Lottie standing with another man at the trailhead. His immediate jealousy gave way to wondering how he could be jealous of another man when he was holding Mercy's hand, holding her baby, and readying to get married; although he wasn't sure broom jumping was actually getting married.

Who am I kidding? Ernest thought. *I am makin' a public profession to another woman.*

Lottie leaned into the arms of the other man. Then, Ernest was beside himself. He released Mercy's hand, put the baby in her arms, and stormed toward the mysterious man. He tried to calm himself but couldn't seem to get a grip on his emotions. He grasped the man, and pushed him hard, away from Lottie. The man stumbled over a rock and fell to the ground.

The holler folk assumed that a fight was ensuing and began cheering for Ernest. He overheard one of his student's say, "It's just like them Hatfields and McCoys."

Lottie rushed to the man's side. "Pastor Thomas, Pastor Thomas, are you okay?"

Ernest had laid hold of a man of God and not like Elisha had laid hold of Elijah wanting more of the presence of the Lord. Anger and jealousy had gotten the best of Ernest. He wondered what Lottie was thinking.

Pastor Thomas stood up, brushed himself off, walked over to Ernest, and held out his hand. "Nice to meet you. I am assuming that you're Ernest, Lottie's beau. I'm Pastor Thomas from Charleston. I'm visiting Pastor Rex for a time."

Ernest was instantly intrigued by the man's features and skin color. He shook Pastor Thomas' hand and then spoke loudly above the shuffling and whispering of the crowd. He especially wanted his students to hear what he had to say. "Please forgive me. Anger is best expressed by usin' words not hands."

"I think I understand what was going through your mind," Thomas answered.

The young pastor motioned for Lottie to join them. "Let me talk to the good folk and see if I can help; that will give the two of you a moment alone."

Pastor Thomas began shaking hands and introducing himself to holler residents.

"You're in love with Mercy."

"I'm not, Lottie. I'm in love with you."

"You were holdin' her baby and holdin' her hand. It looked like you was ready to marry her."

"Please let me explain," Ernest pleaded.

Lottie wouldn't look at him, but he continued talking anyway. "I was with Mercy when she gave birth to Eli. Samuel and the town leaders are insistin' that Mercy and me marry. I ain't wantin' to marry her, and she ain't wantin' to marry me."

"I wouldn't bet on that," Lottie whispered under her breath.

"It's true, darlin'. Mercy even agreed for me to help find her a husband. Emie was tryin' to help, too. This mornin' as I was gettin' dressed and preparin' to find you, three men barged into my room. Samuel had a shotgun! Mercy was done hidin', but they found her. They was forcin' us to jump the broom."

"Broom jumpin'?"

"Yes, broom jumpin'! I was tryin' to delay things. Justice sent Adam and Beau to fetch Doc and the sheriff."

Much to Ernest's relief, Lottie reached for him.

"Why did you push Pastor Thomas?"

"I wasn't meanin' for him to fall, Lottie. I was jealous. I thought he'd stolen your heart."

"That ain't possible, my love."

Ernest got down on one knee. "Lottie, please be the legend in my life."

He took a scrap of paper out of his pocket. "Rudy's mama and daddy don't sell rings, so I ordered one from the Sears Roebuck and Company catalog. I am hoping you like it."

"It's beautiful, beautiful like the life we'll have together," Lottie waxed lyrical.

When Ernest and Lottie returned hand in hand to the schoolhouse, Pastor Thomas was sharing his life story with the crowd. He explained his unusual looks and his struggle to feel accepted. He talked about Lottie singing the praises of the holler folk and their willingness to embrace others who were different.

Mercy was still standing at the front holding Eli. Pastor Thomas motioned for her join him. The young pastor looked at the baby and smiled, then placed his arm around Mercy's shoulders.

Mercy told her heart-wrenching story. She began by talking about leaving the holler and her involvement with a married man who treated her harshly. She spoke about the evil game she played and renounced its wickedness. She even gave voice about attempting to trick and manipulate Ernest.

The holler ladies used their hankies. Men wiped their eyes on the backs of their hands.

"I've done wrong, but I ain't wantin' my baby to suffer..." Mercy sobbed.

A few of the single holler men, along with some of the men who Ernest had interviewed, stepped forward from the assembly.

"I'd done be honored to have you as my wife."

"We can build us a life together."

"I can take the baby and you as my own."

"Who wouldn't love a gal like you?"

Pastor Thomas gestured for the men to be silent. "Gentlemen, I can tell that your interests are honorable, but marriage is serious business. Mercy needs time to choose the man for her." The pastor then smiled and chuckled. "Plus, I am thinkin' that I would also like to throw my hat into the ring. It could be that Mercy's the right woman for me."

Ernest could see Pastor Thomas gently squeeze Mercy's shoulder. He also took the baby from Mercy's arms and held him high in the air. Ernest assumed the pastor was pointing Eli toward heaven and asking for a blessing.

Soon after, Uncle Christian and Sheriff Robbins arrived with Adam and Beau in tow. The boys were muddy and wet from their creek adventure.

When no one was looking, Ernest replaced the cattail broom with the special wedding broom. He took Lottie's hand and together they jumped the broom.

Chapter Twenty-Three

For good luck you must get out of the side of the
bed in which you got in.

Appalachian Folk Belief

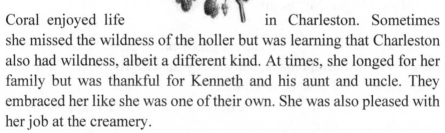

Coral enjoyed life in Charleston. Sometimes she missed the wildness of the holler but was learning that Charleston also had wildness, albeit a different kind. At times, she longed for her family but was thankful for Kenneth and his aunt and uncle. They embraced her like she was one of their own. She was also pleased with her job at the creamery.

Mr. Smith was a widower. He had two adult sons who assisted with the duties of bookkeeping, ordering supplies, receiving goods, and couriering items. Large wooden barrels were lined with ice so the store's confections could be delivered to local establishments. There were also three ice cream carts that Smith & Sons supplied. The vendors were assigned regions and sold ice cream along the busy streets of Charleston. No matter what shift she worked, Mr. Smith or one of his sons was always present. Coral knew at times they even worked late into the night.

It had been a long day. Her feet were tired. Her apron was askew, and the left cuff of her serving dress was stained with raspberry sauce which, to no avail, she had struggled to rub out. Ready to head home, Coral's stomach growled for supper. Kenneth's aunt made delicious food and would have it waiting.

"Coral, please put the Closed sign on the door," Mr. Smith requested.

As she posted the sign, she glanced out the window. There was a lamplighter across the street and a lone man standing on the corner. Coral couldn't help but smile. In Big Creek, the moon, stars, and the lightning bugs were the lamplighters.

She finished cleaning the table used by her last guest and pocketed the random change left as her gratuity. She was saving her money in a glass jar that she'd placed on the bottom shelf of the wardrobe in her room. She knew Ernest wouldn't be happy, but she wanted to cut her hair. Other than her mama or Auntie Ada occasionally giving her a trim, she had never had a true haircut and hoped to visit a salon. Her locks were long, and no matter how she tried, they couldn't be tamed to fit under the cap which was a required part of her uniform.

"Good night, Mr. Smith," Coral said. "Don't forget to lock the door."

"I won't, my dear," the elderly gentleman replied. "I know you're only walking several blocks, but watch yourself. In fact, if you'll wait a few moments, I'll walk you home."

When Mr. Smith grew tired, he used a cane. Coral knew he'd been on his feet most of the day.

"As much as I would enjoy your company, I'll be fine. I don't think I'm needin' an escort."

The proprietor smiled. "Enjoy your evening then, or what's left of it, and I'll see you tomorrow."

The night air was warm and humid. Coral took off her cap and used it to fan herself. She tied her hair in a quick knot to keep it off the back of her neck. As she rounded the corner, someone grabbed the knot on her head and half pushed, half pulled her into a dark alley. The force, together with the smell of liquor, startled and frightened her to her core.

Her defences permeated the air as did the whiskey fumes. She instinctively began kicking backwards, fighting the large man who now held her around the neck. The man was strong. He forced her flailing arms to her sides and lifted her off the ground. Her legs were still moving and kicking.

"Coral, stop it!"

It was James. She chided herself for not immediately recognizing him.

"What are you doin'?" she yelled.

He pushed her against a building wall and covered her mouth with one of his large hands.

With her freed arm, she immediately began to push, pinch, and punch.

"I ain't wantin' to hurt you, but if needed, I will."

Coral stopped. She knew that she could never win a physical fight with James. She was alone in the dark with an angry, inebriated man whose desire and wounded pride mounted a ladder of anger and bravado from being shunned by her.

James whispered softly yet harshly. "I'm removin' my hand from your mouth, but if you yell or scream, there are other ways for me to keep you quiet."

She didn't say a word. James' hands were against the wall on either side of her shoulders. She felt trapped. Ernest used traps to catch mink and muskrats. He sold the pelts to Rudy's mama and daddy. She would never look at his side business the same again.

"I came callin', Coral. I don't know why, but you get me riled—twisting your hair and swaying your hips does something to a man. Tell me that you love me."

Coral didn't say a word.

"I said, 'Tell me that you love me.' I know you do. Why else would you visit me at the jailhouse?"

"I wasn't visitin' you, James."

He grabbed her throat and applied pressure. "Say the words, Coral."

"I love you," she coughed and stammered.

"Take off that apron. Let me see you."

She untied the outer garment, lifted it over her head, and held it in her right hand. It was hard not to gag when James moved in for a kiss.

She tasted bile in her mouth but forced herself to playfully put the apron around James' shoulders.

"I knew you would like this, Girlie."

Repulsed, she made her move quickly pulling the apron tight around James' neck. The wall against her back acted as a brace and gave her additional strength. James was fighting her but also fighting for his breath. She held onto the cotton strands and prayed they wouldn't tear. When he collapsed, the apron was ripped from her hands. She stood in shock and wondered if he was dead. When she heard him groan, she sidestepped his body and started to run.

She escaped the dark alley only to run into Mr. Smith as she stumbled onto the main street. Her chest was heaving from exertion and fear. She pointed toward the backstreet. "James," she said between breaths. "He works at the prison." She could hear some rustling and assumed her assailant was getting up.

"I know the man," Mr. Smith said. He turned toward the dark chamber.

"No, don't go," she whispered. She grasped his arm. With surprising strength, he shrugged off her grip. She wanted to run away but knew she couldn't. Mr. Smith wouldn't stand a chance against James. Her heart was beating out of her chest. She turned and followed her protector into the dark.

She heard Mr. Smith address James, but she couldn't decipher the words. Her assailant was on his feet, his hands raised slightly in surrender. Mr. Smith's right hand had a glinting dagger close to his body, flashing and ready to lunge. In his left hand was the cane, also ready to be wielded.

Coral was shaking but moved closer still. She expected that James at any moment would turn the tables and spew his anger and violence against the older man. James, however, didn't move. His hanging head reminded her of a defeated rooster in a cock fight, with its red comb tipped toward the ground and its wattle obscured from view.

Mr. Smith drew a handkerchief from his pocket, wiped the dagger blade, and inserted it into the top of his cane. The ornate dagger handle doubled as the cane handle. Coral remembered Ernest once telling her about swordsticks.

"Coral, it's time to go." Mr. Smith took her arm and ushered her out of the alley. "Did he hurt you?"

"I'll have some bruisin', but fought best I could. He grabbed me by my hair, and my head is throbbin'. Nothin' is broken. I'm sure I'll be fine." She didn't want to cry, but the tears came anyway.

Mr. Smith put his arm around her shoulders. His act of comfort reminded her of Uncle Christian and Pastor Rex.

"Did he hurt you?" Coral asked in return.

"All is well. I'm sorry I didn't arrive sooner. I was tidying up a few things and then decided to check on you."

Coral kissed the older gentleman's cheek and whispered, "Thank you." She was curious about what exactly took place on the dark street between James and Mr. Smith. What she had observed wasn't the whole story. Observations often offered a limited perspective.

"I'm sure you've got questions, Coral. My sons have had dealin's with James. He didn't like my double-edged blade, but his true fear was directed toward my boys, not me. Hopefully, James will leave you be from now on."

Mr. Smith supported her arm and back as they walked up the front porch steps of the boarding house. Coral felt not only his physical support but his emotional support as well.

"Coral, I would appreciate it if you left my sons out of any conversations about what happened this evenin'."

She nodded her head in agreement as the kind man knocked on the front door.

"Mr. Smith, I'm thinkin' that I'm needin' a swordcane."

She was only home a short while when Kenneth arrived. He insisted on examining her. She drew the line, however, when he requested that she remove her chemise.

"Coral, I am a doctor."

"Kenneth, I am knowin' you're a doctor, I just ain't comfortable with you seeing me almost naked."

"I took care of you when you had the Spanish Influenza."

"Yes, but I'm only recollectin' some of what took place."

"I examine bodies for a living."

"Prison MEN, Kenneth."

She knew her friend was getting frustrated, but she couldn't help herself.

"Coral, I have also worked in hospitals and in medical offices. I have examined women."

"I am sure you have, but you ain't examinin' this woman this evenin'."

In the end, they compromised. Kenneth's aunt helped Coral remove her ivory-colored chemise. Aunt Ada had embroidered three pink roses on the bottom hem of the unmentionable. She appreciated Kenneth's aunt's help but wished it was her love aunt's ministrations. Her friend's kind aunt took her time examining Coral's back, upper arms, and thighs. Doctor Daniels asked needed questions through the door.

Coral's scalp felt tender enough to raise a yelp. "Small patches of hair are missing," the aunt reported. "There is a cut on the back of her head that is bleeding, but only slightly. . .There are bruises on her arms, legs, and around her neck."

Coral's hands and arms were sore from pulling so tightly on the apron strings. "You might experience cramping tomorrow," said the doctor.

Kenneth's aunt found a number of other grazes and scrapes, and some minor abrasions on her back from being pushed roughly against the building exterior. Each of these, she expertly reported to the doctor.

Kenneth also contacted the police. As a physician, he requested that Coral get a good night's rest and visit with the officers in the morning.

Coral tried her best to relax but couldn't stop shaking. The ordeal played over and over in her mind. Jewel liked to hear the same story repeated. Ernest said children learn by repetition. Coral just wanted to forget.

She had already reviewed some of the evening's lessons in her mind. She should pay attention to a person's character before physical attraction takes hold. Mr. Cupid with his curved upper lip was not who he initially appeared to be. When a kind gentleman asks to escort her home, she should reply "yes" even if the walk is slow going. No more knobs or buns on top of her head. She would visit a hair salon and find a store that sold swordsticks.

She heard a tap on her bedroom door. "Yes."

"I am ready for bed and wanted to check on you," Kenneth's aunt answered. "May I come in?"

"Please. I was just thinkin' about my mistakes. Things I should've done different so this wouldn't have happened."

"Women get trapped in their thinkin', Coral. Sometimes men do cruel things and women want to blame themselves. You did nothing wrong this evening. You were walking home from work, is all. A man attacked you."

Tears rolled down Coral's cheeks. When they landed on her bruised lips, she could taste them.

Under Kenneth's watchful eye, Coral slowly recovered. Mr. Smith sent a note to the boarding house requesting she take several days off from work. He also sent Coral a special gift. The swordstick was wonderfully feminine. The cane was capped at the bottom with dark mahogany wood. The slender stick was white ash with a prominent blond grain. The handle was a combination of mahogany and pearl. The pale and dark color combination was stunning. The cane looked like a piece of artwork. The stiletto knife was both beastly and beautiful.

Mr. Smith also had included in his note that the knife shouldn't be drawn as a weapon. "Coral, my dear, the knife could be taken from you and bring you harm. The cane should be used as a walking stick and aid in your recovery."

She stashed the swordstick in her room, not mentioning the hidden blade to Kenneth. Although Doctor Daniels was a marvelous man, she wasn't ready to invite him into every area of her life. Her choice of personal protection was her own.

Kenneth was a mystery to Coral. A practical man, occasionally his reserve would diminish, and his fun-loving side would appear.

He had taken her to see Charlie Chaplain's latest movie, *The Circus*. She was enthralled watching Tramp, the lead character in the silent picture, try to win the heart of a lovely woman. Kenneth belly laughed at his antics. The scene where Tramp walked the tight rope with an obnoxious monkey as his companion put both Coral and Kenneth in stitches.

At the movie house, Coral noticed Kenneth casually rested his arm along her shoulders. During the walk home, his hand had cupped her elbow.

She admitted that she had never been to the cinema, confessing it was an adventure all its own. Bolstered, Kenneth promised that they would return to view the next picture playing. He was anxious to see a talkie. Coral dissented saying she had enjoyed the silent picture so much, that it was hard to imagine hearing a talking film on the big screen.

Her dream of going to a beauty salon turned into a visit to a local barbershop. It seemed salons were located in Paris, London, and New York, but not in Charleston, West Virginia. Thankfully, the local barber was familiar with trending ladies' styles and converted her long tresses into a chin length bob with bangs. Kenneth's aunt said the hair cut made Coral look older. Kenneth said he missed her long hair but certainly understood the sensibility of her new city style.

She was ready to return to work. Mr. Smith offered to have one of the delivery men walk her to and from the boarding house, but Coral declined. Her childhood had taught her to face her fears head-on. Growing up, she didn't have a choice. Anger, accusations, and aggravation were part of everyday life. Ernest had taught her that the term, "violence" could also refer to heat, sunlight, and smoke—really anything that can produce a powerful effect. He had guided her spiritually and had reminded her frequently that God was more powerful than their daddy or the results of their daddy's actions.

James had been violent with her. Mr. Smith had also been violent but in a different way. Coral believed prayer could be violent. She was fervent in talking with God about James. At times, it felt like her conversations with the Lord were creating violence in the heavenlies.

Chapter Twenty-Four

An acorn should be carried to bring luck and
ensure a good life.

Appalachian Folk Belief

A banner hung outside Smith & Sons welcoming Coral back to the creamery. In honor of her return, Mr. Smith had procured mulberries. The first taste of the sweet concoction of cream, sugar, vanilla, and berries went to Coral. She closed her eyes, savored the taste, then loudly applauded in delight.

The day passed quickly. Coral was thrilled to be back at work. She had missed her ice cream comrades.

Toward the end of her shift, Mr. Smith asked to speak with her privately. "My dear, for the next couple of weeks, I want you safe and secure at home before dark."

Coral attempted to interrupt her employer, but he simply talked over her, forcing her to be quiet and listen. "My sons have looked into James' whereabouts. It appears he has left Charleston. He hasn't been to work at the prison, and mutual acquaintances say they haven't seen him."

Coral sighed with relief. "Mr. Smith, I ain't wantin' special treatment. Please, I can do my job."

"It's not a question of whether you can do your job or not. In fact, you do a fine job, a wonderful job. However, until we're sure James is out of the picture for good, I want you to leave in time to be home before dark. Coral, the days are getting longer. That's why we're staying open later. People are enjoying the summer night air. You won't have to leave much earlier than before."

She knew it was useless to argue. "Thank you, Mr. Smith. I appreciate all you're doin."

Mini was scared. She had never left the holler much less ridden on a train. Aunt Ada and Uncle Christian had been most welcoming. Emie and Rudy had also embraced her. It had taken sweet Jewel a bit of time to grow accustomed to Mini's marred lip. Emie had explained to her daughter that God was making a way for Auntie Mini to have her mouth fixed. At first, it felt awkward, but she had let Jewel touch her curled lip anyway. Somehow, the four-year-old's hands comforted Mini and gave her hope for the future.

Rudy's mama made her a special dress and matching hat for her trip. The dress was navy blue with white polka dots. It had a sailor collar in solid blue with matching sleeve cuffs and an embellished trim around the bottom. So the hat wouldn't take up too much space on the train, the woman selected one with a small brim. It was navy blue with a veil that covered her face. The veil was sheer by her eyes and nose and then slightly thicker by her mouth and chin. Mini felt for the first time that she wasn't an object of curiosity.

Uncle Christian and Rudy thought hiding Mini's lips with the hat was nonsense. People should simply understand that there were differences. Mini agreed, but the hat gave her a sense of confidence she had never before experienced.

Emie had gushed repeatedly about Mini's beauty. Riding the train, a man had even flirted with her by commenting on her unique attire and beautiful eyes. At least she thought it was flirting.

Ernest explained to her that the name Minerva came from the Roman goddess of music, poetry, and wisdom. According to mythology, Minerva had two pets, an owl and a snake. The teacher didn't believe in myths but in the power of God. He had prayed with

Mini and had encouraged her to pray during her travel to Charleston. He called her Mini Marvelous which made her smile and then conceal her lip with her hand.

He also told her the story of Minnie Buckingham Harper, a lady appointed by the West Virginia Governor to fill a vacant political position created by the death of Minnie's husband.

"Mini, you come from a long line of marvelous women. You will do the holler and yourself proud in Charleston."

As the train pulled into the Charleston depot, Mini's heart raced. She was thankful her window faced the train station. She looked up and down the platform and finally spotted a young couple holding a sign with her name.

Ernest had described Coral as looking somewhat like Emie. Their facial structure, mannerisms, and voice inflection were the same. Coral, however, was leaner in body, slightly shorter in stature, and had hair a couple of shades darker. He had entrusted a message with Mini to give his sister. "You had best be with Mini Marvelous on the train home."

She made her way through the train car. When she placed her foot on the first rung of stairs leading to the platform, she felt like she was entering a dream. The sights and smells tingled and tantalized her senses.

Kenneth and Coral rushed to her side.

Coral hugged her tightly. "Sister, I've been waitin' and waitin' to meet you. You're exactly why the good Lord had me stay in Charleston."

Kenneth raised his eyebrows at Coral. "I could not be more delighted for Mini to have arrived here safely, but I am hoping I'm part of the reason you chose to stay in Charleston."

Coral smiled and winked at Mini.

Arrangements had been made for Mini to stay with Coral at the boarding house. Coral was worried Mini might feel displaced. "Why, I had those same emotions myself when I first came to live at the boarding house," Coral told her.

Coral knew Mini was unaccustomed to place settings and special utensils at the dining room table and that linens and a soft bed not made of feather ticks were new. This was a time when Coral could show Mini the ropes, including teaching her the delights of an indoor toilet and the special paper, not newspaper or old rags, for hygienic purposes. Electricity was also new. Coral tried to explain not only how the switches worked, and plugs, but how it worked theoretically, the science of electrical currents, but its operation mystified Mini.

Mini understood numbers and measurements but had limited reading skills. Kenneth brought some simple books for Coral and Mini to read together. Though it muffled her speech, the young woman wore her hat and scarf during the day and only removed it at night after the lights in the bedroom were turned off.

Finally, Coral asked Mini if she could see her face.

"Sister," Mini replied. "I'm a fright. Granny said that I was cursed by God."

"God hasn't cursed you. In fact, He loves you."

"Ernest told me the same. I'm wantin' us to be friends, but I'm worried that if you see me, you'll turn away."

"I won't turn away."

Mini removed the veil.

Coral enfolded Mini in her arms. "Thank you for trustin' me."

"Tomorrow Kenneth is takin' me to my first doctorin' time. Do you think I'm so ugly that the doc will be turnin' me away?"

"Mini, there is nothin' ugly about you. The doctor will be helpin'. He ain't gonna turn you away."

Mini and Kenneth stopped by the ice cream parlor the next day. Mini was sporting a new hat and veil made by Kenneth's aunt. Though the veil hid her mouth, Coral could tell by Mini's raised cheeks that she was smiling. The doctor's appointment was a huge success. With surgery being scheduled, they knew Mini was on the road to recovery.

In the meantime, Kenneth insisted he and Mini enjoy some ice cream. Coral could tell that her friend was hesitant to eat in public. After one bite, however, Mini continued to spoon the deliciousness under her veil and into her mouth. Since Kenneth was needed at the prison, Mini decided to wait the afternoon out and walk home with Coral.

When Mr. Smith grew hurried at the counter, Mini offered to help. She was a natural at math and quickly learned the workings of the old-time incorruptible cash register. The owner of Smith & Sons and Mini quickly developed a system that readily made change for the servers and walk-in patrons. By the end of the day, Mini had gainful employment.

"Coral, I am thinkin' that the curse has lifted."

"There was never a curse, Sister. I believe the Lord is answerin' your prayers. Sometimes He does things in the beginnin' so that the latter things show off His goodness and love for us in ways we might never know otherwise."

Mini's eyes lit up. "I have been prayin' like Ernest told me to do."

As the young women rounded the corner by the boarding house, Mini slowed down and took Coral's hand. "Why are you carryin' a cane when you're walkin' fine?"

Coral related the story about James and showed Mini discretely how the cane was really a knife. "Mr. Smith told me the knife was more for showin' than doin'. He's worried I could be hurt."

"Granny used knives for cuttin' plants and spillin' innards. I'm agreein' with Mr. Smith. Since we'll be workin' side-by-side, we can walk home together."

"Thank you, Mini. Thank you for comin' to Charleston. I'm a bit afeared since what happened with James. I keep thinkin' now, that someone is watchin' me." Coral tightened her shoulders and shivered.

Over the next couple of weeks, Mini adjusted to living at the boarding house and working at the confectionary.

Coral was extremely patient with her. She was learning to read simple words and looked forward to having her lip repaired. Kenneth's aunt had made her several new hats with matching scarves. Mini was anxious to be freed from the burden of hiding herself. Coral had repeatedly asked her to remove the head and face covering, but Mini didn't like people staring at her. She realized that others didn't mean to be rude or to make her uncomfortable, and yet, it happened. People would try to look away, but curiosity generally brought them back for second attempts at hidden glances. Often, whispers came after with their companions.

Mini was concerned Coral might be correct about being followed. She didn't want to alarm her friend, but she also felt like someone was watching them on their journey to and from the creamery. She hadn't seen anyone outright, but there was a sense of someone being present. Once or twice, she thought she had seen a fleeting shadow. What if it were true?

While Mini was anxious for her facial reconstruction, she was also worried about Coral's well-being. Mini even questioned Mr. Smith about James. He assured her that his sons had heard nothing about James returning to Charleston. Mini wondered, however, if the villain had ever left. Maybe he had simply gone underground like the mole and vole.

Granny had taught her about potions and seeking help from the spirits of the dead, and Ernest had taught her that it was fine to use natural things for doctoring, but now she knew that it wasn't fine to call on spirits. Ernest had prayed with her for all forms of evil to depart and for her to be led only by the Holy Ghost.

Although Mini knew about the Ten Commandments, and understood that murder was wrong, she wasn't sure if it was wrong to poison a known villain. She didn't want to kill James but wanted him to suffer enough that he would leave Coral alone.

Poison hemlock grew along the back fence of the boarding house. Except for its pointed leaves, the plant looked like wild carrots or parsnips. The plant was also identifiable by its musty odor. Even in small doses, hemlock was deadly. Granny, however, had taught her how to use the plant to bring about only suffering, not death.

First, she needed to lure James from the shadows.

Mini began by eating her lunch at a nearby park. The area wasn't very large. To any passerby, she would be visible. Her hat and veil also distinguished her. After a couple of days, she saw someone staring from the other side of the grassy area. Coral had described James as a large man. The man in question had very broad shoulders. His attire was a clear giveaway. Unless people were trying to disguise themselves, they didn't wear wool toboggans and long sleeve heavy shirts in the summer.

It didn't take long until the man approached Mini and introduced himself as James. He was extremely polite and talked about his love for Coral.

"I don't mean her any harm. I just want to talk with her. I know you're her friend. Could you please tell her that I'm sorry about what happened? I just want to see her," James pleaded.

Mini did nothing to discourage James. Instead, she assured him she would invite Coral to join her for lunch the next day.

Mini arrived at the park at the designated time the following day. She brought with her a bowl of chocolate ice cream. The serving contained an extremely small amount of hemlock. She had thoroughly mixed the poison into the sweet cream so the claggy smell would not be detectable.

She motioned for James to join her and explained that Coral was on her way.

"I brought you ice cream," Mini said sweetly. "It's delicious." She handed the poison-laced confection to James.

When he hesitated, Mini told him that Coral had prepared the mixture herself.

He took a bite. Mini knew one bite wouldn't be enough. He needed to finish the bowl.

She began talking about her life in the holler. When James didn't appear interested, she switched the conversation to Coral. She talked about Coral enjoying her job, Coral going to the silent movies, and Coral living at the boarding house.

James finished and gave his spoon a final lick. Mini knew it would take approximately twenty minutes for the hemlock to work.

"Why don't I see what's keeping Coral?" Mini suggested. "I'll be right back."

James agreed to stay put but firmly insisted, "Please, hurry."

She left the park and appeared to be heading back to the ice cream parlor. Instead, she ducked into a woman's fashion store and began admiring the window displays. When the shop owner asked if she needed assistance, Mini mentioned wanting a handbag to match her hat. While the store purveyor looked for the perfect purse, Mini looked out the window.

When James tried to stand and fell to the ground, Mini knew the poison was taking effect. She quickly exited the store. The poison symptoms would include shortness of breath, loss of speech, digestive pain, and muscle weakness.

Mini wanted to distance herself from the park as quickly as possible. She hurried back to the ice cream parlor and took her place behind the counter.

"Did you enjoy your lunch?" Mr. Smith asked.

"Yes, it's a mite nice outside."

"Please excuse me, Mini. My sons are needing me in the back to oversee some business with the barrel loads and street vendors."

Mini nodded in response.

When the counter grew busy, and Mr. Smith didn't return, Mini grew concerned. It wasn't like her boss to leave the store during the afternoon rush. She was also out of change. Mini motioned to Coral that she would be right back.

Mini had learned early in life to be as quiet as possible. When she didn't make noise, others tended not to notice her —which suited her just fine. There were times when she longed to disappear, but God was helping her gain confidence. She hoped the surgery would enable her to be present, really present, to talk and interact with others.

The door to the back room was shut. Mini tapped lightly. When no one answered she tried to open the door, but it was locked. She used a side door that was reserved for employees and walked around to the back of the building.

The barrels were being loaded, not with ice and confection, but with moonshine. The street vendors were arguing among themselves. Mr. Smith's sons appeared to be overseeing the venture. Mr. Smith was standing off to the side, encouraging everyone to move quickly.

Mini stepped into the building shadows and quietly watched.

This is bad, real bad, she thought.

Coral had told her about James' drinking. Now it made sense why James and Mr. Smith's sons were acquainted.

Mr. Smith appeared to be a bystander, but Mini was disappointed in her friendly employer. People often made excuses for those they loved and even stood aside and allowed bad behavior to reign over right living and common sense.

Then, like a hammer hitting Mini on her head, she thought, *what right do I have being disappointed with Mr. Smith? I have poisoned James!* Ernest believed moonshine was poison; so was hemlock.

Mini knew that a judge could bring down his gavel when rendering a verdict. She also knew that to "drop the hammer" meant to finish something. There was a lot of hammering going on in her soul.

Chapter Twenty-Five

A pregnant woman should never look at a snake,
it will "mark" the baby.

Appalachian Folk Belief

"Somethin' is going on with Mini," Coral told Kenneth. "She ain't actin' herself."

"She's had a lot of adjustments to make or possibly she's anxious about her upcoming surgery."

"I'm sure you're right as a line." Coral answered.

Kenneth smiled. "There's somethin' I want to talk with you about, though, Coral."

"Ernest says that when someone wants to talk, it usually means bad news is comin'."

"Not in this case, Coral." He directed her to sit beside him on the veranda swing. "I have never said this before, so I'm a little nervous."

"I am doubtin' that," Coral giggled. "You ain't never been shy."

Kenneth took her hand. "I'm falling in love with you."

Coral drew on her reserves. "Fallin' don't seem like the right word when talkin' of love."

"I don't think it means falling down or falling over, more like unexpected and not planned. I didn't expect to meet someone like you, but now that I know you, I don't ever want to let you go."

When she didn't answer, Kenneth let go of her hand and sighed deeply.

"I've embarrassed myself and you, Coral. Your cheeks are crimson."

"I can feel the blush," She admitted. "But I ain't turnin' red for the reasons you think. I'm turnin' red because I ain't never told you yet that I have my own unexplained feelin's."

It was her turn to take Kenneth's hand. "My dear man, I ain't quite ready to declare myself like I think you're wantin'. With what happened with James, my feelings are out of sorts. I ain't in my usual state of mind."

"Coral, my job includes giving people peace of mind. I promise not to rush you. I want us to spend time together. I want us to pray and see where the future takes us."

Coral was worried. Mini was too quiet. No matter what Coral did to draw her friend into conversation, Mini responded with a nod of her head or a simple "yes" or "no."

"Minerva, you know you can be speakin' your mind with me."

"You ain't never called me "Minerva" before."

"I'm plain worried about you and tryin' to get your attention."

"Coral, I did somethin' bad. Ernest told me to tell my sins to God and that He would be forgivin' me because of His son dyin'. I told the Lord I was sorry, but I ain't feelin' forgiven and loved."

"When we share our sins with God, He forgives us. It says so in His book. I'm thinkin' you're havin' trouble forgivin' yourself."

"I poisoned James," Mini blurted.

Like a train broken down on the railway, Coral stopped dead in her tracks. "You what?!"

"I done gave him hemlock. I ain't thinkin' he died, but he was rollin' on the ground."

Mini recounted the story to Coral who now felt panicked. Mini, on the other hand, due to bearing her soul, looked somewhat relieved. Coral kept shakin' her head and sayin', "My, oh my, my, my, my…"

"We best get movin', Coral, so we ain't late for work."

Coral walked on, but her mind was in a fog. A cat had crossed the young women's path one evening, and she had been reminded of Carl Sandberg's poem. The poem had no regular rhyme or set meter and was written through the eyes of a cat.

The fog comes on little cat feet. It sits looking over harbor and city on silent haunches and then moves on.

Clouds are sitting on the earth, Coral thought. *More precisely in Charleston on the road I'm walkin', and I ain't seeing a way out of this mess.*

"Mini, for now, don't be sayin' nothin' about this. We need to be thinkin' 'bout what to do," Coral instructed as the two friends approached their place of employment.

Mini nodded her head toward the black Model T with the word "Police" written in white on the side panel. Coral turned her head and saw the bell ringer.

It was too late to run. Mr. Smith had already spotted the two and motioned them to hurry in. Besides, if they did run, where would they go?

"Ladies, James is dead. The officers are here investigatin'."

Mini looked like she was ready to faint. Even with her veil on, Coral could see a slight green pall cover her skin. Coral steadied Mini physically and tried to steady herself emotionally. When Mini started to speak, Coral pinched her.

"It ain't no good, Coral. I done kilt him and need to be tellin'."

Coral hushed Mini, but she pressed on, addressin' their employer. "He was hurtin' my friend, my sister. I didn't have no choice. I was just tryin' to scare him a bit. I know the commands say 'not to be murderin'...'"

Mr. Smith stared at Mini. Coral didn't know what to do. The two officers laughed uproariously.

"Miss," the older officer addressed Mini. "We've already made an arrest. An associate of this establishment was seen fleeing the crime scene. The 1908 Savage was still in his waistband when we caught up with him."

Coral quickly ushered Mini to a chair. "She's beside herself. Ain't talkin' with rhyme nor reason. I knew James and me had a run-in. Mini and me, we was frightened some after."

Coral sat down next to Mini.

"I kilt him, Coral." Mini softly spoke.

"Shhhh. You are needin' to be still," Coral answered. "You didn't kill him, Sister. A bullet took his life. There's mischief goin' on, and we ain't got no part in it."

When the officers left, Mr. Smith sat down at the table with Coral and Mini. He was upset. "Mini, I saw you that day in the shadows. You know what's been goin' on in the back. Did you tell Coral?"

Mini shook her head no.

"My boys have been runnin' bootleg. I didn't take part in it, but I didn't stop it either. James was workin' with them some but threatened to go to the police. He wanted a pay-off. My sons knew that he would only come back for more. A man workin' with them has shot James."

"No, I done took him with poison," Mini sobbed.

"She mixed hemlock in some ice cream and tricked him," Coral added.

"Mini, please take advice from an old man, advice I should have given my boys. 'Trouble finds trouble.' No more of this poison nonsense. When James was shot, he was standin' on his feet with a gun in his hand. Your poison didn't kill him. He was born for trouble and never turned away."

Mr. Smith ran his hands through his hair. His eyes swelled with tears. "It is only a matter of time before the police put two and two together…"

"Maybe they will put two and two together and make five," Coral interrupted.

"It's not likely. The back has been cleared out," He paused with the heaviness. "And my boys have left town." He looked at his hands, pulled at his fingers, and said finally, "I own this building and the creamery outright. I never gave any money for bootlegging and never took any money. The record-keeping is clear as can be. Moonshine selling took place in the back, and a legitimate business was run in the front. I'm an old man, ladies, and I'm tired. I'm wanting to rest. Coral, I am signing Smith & Sons Creamery over to you. It's yours for the taking."

"Coral, Mini is out of surgery and doing fine." Kenneth announced.

"I'm done relieved. Did you see her? How is she lookin'?"

"More beautiful than ever."

"She is beautiful, ain't she? Thank you for working with the other doctors to make her more lovely." Coral sighed with contentment. "Kenneth, I've been thinkin' some about me and you."

"That pleases me," Kenneth answered. "What have you been thinking?"

"Mrs. Randolph taught us in school about the adventures of Lewis and Clark. They explored regions with sights and sounds like no other. Their tales included strange wildlife with odd-lookin' horns, boiling pots of water in the ground, and steam and water spewing from the earth into the air…"

"What are you saying, Coral?" Kenneth inquired with slight impatience.

"No one would believe 'um, Kenneth. The newspapers wouldn't even tell their tales. I'm thinkin', my dear Kenneth, that you and me have some explorin' to do, and I'm hoping, in the end, we have our own unbelievable tales that need tellin'."

The End

Acknowledgements

The editors for my book were each outstanding in their own ways. Marilyn Bay Drake, who is a Colorado western author was the first to deal with the southern voicings of my characters, and the first to help me explain the backstory. Then, my cousin, Drema Shamblin, tackled the setting and characteristics of Appalachian ways having lived and taught school there. She and author, editor Beatrice Bruno further sifted through the dropped letters, the typos, the missing this-n-thats with my managing editor at Capture Books, Laura Bartnick, until they managed to polish the song and poetry of this story. I'm indebted to Beatrice for her advice on cultural sensitivities. Thanks to my many readers, especially Charmayne Hafen, and Linda Nobis who contributed to the proof edits.

If my husband was not so competent and generous to make me set aside writing time, staying home from our joint work in managing our ministry, Strong Cross, in southern Africa, I would not have been able to write this sequel in a whirlwind of weeks. I also appreciate the Strong Cross ministry team who rose to the occasion and helped with my ministry workload.

The Lord has been generous with me in my life experiences in West Virginia with my Appalachian family. I truly enjoy writing and dreaming up new stories! I am grateful to Him for His open hand in helping me.

I am very thankful to the gals at Honeyball Coffee Shop in Mokopane for giving me a table in the sunshine to write. I appreciate Marlize Photography for capturing my author headshot.

Finally, I want to acknowledge and thank my readers. A writer can be a writer without readers, but a writer cannot become an author of any success without the devotion of readers. I am grateful to each of you.

Endnotes:

I obtained the folk beliefs at the beginning of each chapter from the following resource: www.angelfire.com/tn2/ScottCoTnMemories/superstitions.html

Throughout the book, I cited typical community hymns, folksongs, and popular songs from the late 1920s. The names of the songs in each chapter are noted here with the author's name and date of publication. There are also several quotes and poems cited as well.

In chapter 24, I used the known sledding term, "toboggan" which is also an old-fashioned word for a cap on one's head–my parents used this word when I was growing up.

Chapter One
> *My Heart and I,* Elizabeth Barrett Browning. Edmund Clarence Stedman, 1895. A Victorian Anthology.

Chapter Two
> *Wonderful Peace,* Warren D. Cornell and William G. Cooper, 1889.
> (Special note: The words, "under God" were not added to the Pledge of Allegiance until 1954)

Chapter Three
> *Tis so Sweet to Trust in Jesus,* Louisa M.R. Stead, 1882.

Chapter Four
> *Pledge of Allegiance,* George Thatcher Balch, 1892.

Chapter Five
> Charlie Chaplain. charliechaplin.com/en/quotes
> *Ain't We Got Fun,* Raymond B. Egan, Gus Kahn & Richard A. Whiting, 1921.
> *Button Up Your Overcoat,* B.G. Sylva, Lew Brown & Ray Henderson, 1928.

Chapter Six
> *Dear Jesus, I Long to be Perfectly Whole.* James Nicholson & Fischer, 1872.

Chapter Seven
> *The Practical Garden Book,* L.H. Bailey & Charles Elias Hunn, 1900. Macmillan.

Chapter Eight
> *Battle Hymn of the Republic,* Julia Ward Howe, 1861.
> *The Love of God is Greater Far.* Frederick M. Lehman, 1917.

Chapter Nine
> *When You're Smilin'*, Larry Shay, Mark Fisher & Joe Goodwin, 1928.

Chapter 10
> *All Night All Day*, Otis Leon McCoy, year unknown.
> *The Bear Went Over the Mountain*, Anonymous, year unknown.

Chapter 11
> *Thinking of You*, Anonymous, year unknown.

Chapter 12
> *The Bear Went Over the Mountain*, Anonymous, year unknown.
> *His Eye Is on the Sparrow*, Civilla D. Martin, 1905.

Chapter 14
> *What Friend We Have in Jesus*, Joseph Scriven, 1855 & Charles Crozat Converse, 1868.
> *Yes! We Have No Bananas*, Frank Silver & Irving Cohn, 1923.

Chapter 17
> *I Surrender All*, Judson W. Van de Venter & Winfield Scott Weeden, 1896.
> *Breath on Me*, Edwin Hatch, 1878.

Chapter 18
> Rumi. Goodreads/Quotes/ …patience-is-not-sitting

Chapter 19
> *In the Sweet By and By*, S. Fillmore Bennett & Joseph P. Webster, 1867.

Chapter 20
> *Lost Thought*, Emily Dickinson.

Chapter 22
> *Blue Skies*, Irving Berlin, 1926.
> *Didn't My Lord Deliver Daniel*, Anonymous, year unknown.

Chapter 25
> *Fog*. Carl Sandburg.

About Tonya Jewel Blessing

Growing up, Tonya spent numerous vacations and holidays in the Appalachian Mountains of West Virginia. Most of her adult life has been spent in full time ministry with a focus on helping women. She has traveled nationally and internationally as a conference speaker. For a number of years, Tonya and her husband operated a retreat facility in Colorado for pastors and missionaries.

She and her husband currently live in South Africa. They are the founders and directors of Strong Cross Ministries, a non-profit organization that assists local churches, pastors, cross-cultural workers, and others in Christian leadership in providing spiritual reconciliation and humanitarian relief to the poorest in the world. Tonya writes monthly devotionals for women in ministry. She is the award-winning novelist of *The Whispering of the Willows,* which is Book 1 of the Big Creek Series. She is the co-author of Soothing Rain, a discussion starter handbook/devotional that provides women with important tools for sharing biblical truth.

Get Tonya's other books. Find out more about her:

Facebook Page:	Tonya Jewel Carter Blessing
Twitter :	@Tonya_Jewel
Author Web Site:	TonyaJewelBlessing.com
Ministry Web Site:	StrongCrossMinistries.org
E-mail Address:	Christonyablessing @ gmail.com
Bookstore:	CaptureMeBooks.com

Book Club Questions
can be found online:
http://www.TonyaJewelBlessing.com

Have you read Book 1 of the Big Creek Series?

The Whispering of the Willows

Go to: https://www.CaptureMeBooks.com
for other book selections

A Personal Note from Tonya:
Readers buy books based on other readers' endorsements.
I would appreciate yours!

Please rate my book at one of these places if you enjoyed it.
Facebook/Litsy/Barnes & Noble/ChristianBook.com/GoodReads

Reviews on Amazon & Twitter #BuyIt

I LOVE IT!

CPSIA information can be obtained
at www.ICGtesting.com
Printed in the USA
BVHW040158180323
660664BV00009B/715